Amber

Amber

Heather BURNSIDE

HEAD
of ZEUS

An Aria Book

This edition first published in the United Kingdom in 2021 by Aria,
an imprint of Head of Zeus Ltd

9 7 5 3 1 2 4 6 8

A CIP catalogue record for this book is available from the
British Library.

ISBN (PB): 9781800246072
ISBN (E): 9781838939618

Cover design © Debbie Clement

Typeset by Siliconchips Services Ltd UK

Printed and bound in Great Britain by
CPI Group (UK) Ltd, Croydon CR0 4YY

Aria
c/o Head of Zeus
5–8 Hardwick Street
London EC1R 4RG

WWW.ARIAFICTION.COM

For Kerry and Pascoe

Dear Reader,

This has been the most difficult one of my novels to write because of the sensitive subject matter of sexual abuse, particularly relating to a minor. When I thought of the idea for the book, I underestimated just how much it would affect me.

I am sending this novel out into the world with a great deal of trepidation in case its intentions are misinterpreted. I don't want readers to think that I am making light of the subject or treating is as merely a means of entertainment. For these reasons I have taken great care to show the pain and suffering caused by sexual abuse rather than portraying these scenes in a tantalising or titillating way. Therefore, this novel is dark and gloomy in parts.

Despite my reservations, I have gone ahead with this book because I feel that it is a story that needs to be told. Sexual abuse takes place every day and is often swept under the carpet. I hope that by highlighting this issue through this novel I am playing my part in addressing it and showing the lifelong damaging effects that sexual abuse has on the survivors.

This form of abuse should not be regarded merely as a sexual act but as a distressing emotional incident that causes feelings of shame, inadequacy, low self-esteem, lack of confidence, and vulnerability etc. It can also affect the survivor's ability to form stable relationships in later life.

This book is not just a story from an author's imagination; it is a story that affects countless survivors of sexual abuse in our society today.

If you have been affected by childhood sexual abuse or childhood abuse of any type, you can get support from the National Association for People Abused in Childhood (NAPAC). You can find more information on their website at: https://napac.org.uk/.

I apologise in advance if you find the subject matter distressing.

Yours sincerely,
Heather Burnside

I

September 2015

Amber stared at the grossly obese man in front of her called Bill as he held out the garments for her to wear. She shuddered when she realised what they were. This had been bound to happen sooner or later but the fact that Amber had been expecting it didn't lessen its dire impact.

'Well, aren't you gonna take them then?' he asked.

She stepped forward, cautiously, noticing the whiff of BO that emanated from him. Then she held out her hand while he passed her the clothing.

'I guessed your size from when we met last time,' he said, leering at her.

Amber knew that the client had probably chosen her because of her petite frame as she was only five foot two and a size eight.

They were in a hotel room, but it wasn't a plush hotel like the ones in Manchester city centre that a lot of her punters used. It was a bit neglected and situated in the inner-city suburbs; probably a three star, if that, she guessed.

During the time she'd been on the game, she had learnt that the choice of hotel said a lot about the punter. This particular hotel suggested that Bill either didn't have money to splash around, he was stingy, or he just wanted a quickie with a street girl who he thought didn't deserve any better.

Punters who opted for swanky city centre hotels generally had money to spare and they enjoyed the luxury and privacy that the more upmarket hotels afforded them. But when a punter chose this type of hotel it always made her more wary than usual. Why opt for a cheap hotel rather than visiting a whorehouse? Was it because there would be no one there to offer protection if things turned nasty?

If it hadn't been for the fact that she'd done business with Bill previously she would have declined but he'd treated her OK last time even though he was repulsive to look at. And, if she'd have known beforehand what type of job it was, she would also have turned him down, aware of the implications. But it was too late now. She was here and she had the outfit in her hand ready to put on.

Amber tried to block the doubts from her mind, telling herself that it was just like any other job. Sex with him was straightforward and she wouldn't be expected to do anything extreme. But as she looked at the clothing she was clutching, Amber couldn't avoid the tremor of fear and repulsion that ran through her body.

She separated the items: an extremely short grey skirt, a white blouse with the top two buttons missing, a striped tie and two bright turquoise hair bands.

'I hope you're wearing a push-up bra,' said Bill. 'I want to see your tits spilling out of that blouse.' He leered. 'Oh, and I want you to put your hair in pigtails.'

4

Amber tried to dismiss his comments as she took off her skirt and top. Whilst she did so, she could see Bill was also undressing, casting off his shoddy underwear and exposing the voluminous folds of fat that hung loosely around his body, his flesh slick with sweat. She averted her eyes and concentrated on what she was doing instead.

She put on the school uniform then tied up her long blonde hair into two pigtails. As soon as she had finished transforming herself into a schoolgirl, she could see that the punter was becoming very excited. His complexion was even more ruddy than usual, his eyes were almost bulging from their sockets and a quick look at his groin told her they weren't the only things that were bulging. She stifled the urge to retch as she waited to see what he would do next.

'Nice,' he said. 'You remind me of all those girls I see walking to school every day. Silly little bitches don't know what it does to a man. Or perhaps they do. Maybe that's why they wear their skirts so short.'

Amber ignored him, battling with her urge to flee from the room. But, before she could do anything, he was in front of her and running his large calloused hands down her back, over her bottom and along the backs of her thighs. Then he lifted the skirt, his palms seeking her flesh once again, then slipping beneath the thin material of her briefs and clenching her buttocks. She let out a gasp of alarm and pulled away from him, but he held her firm.

Seeming to sense her reluctance, he quickly said, 'I want the same as last time.'

Amber felt a tiny surge of relief and focused on that as she undressed and lay on the bed. But the feelings of relief came too late to dispel the anxiety that was already streaming through her body. Like last time, he wanted straightforward sex and Amber kept telling herself that it was no different than most punters and would soon be over.

But no matter how much she tried to convince herself, her mind was too preoccupied with the blatant meaning behind the choice of outfit. The man was a fuckin' paedophile! She dwelled again on the reason he had picked her out after their first meeting. Even though she was twenty-seven, the fact that she was only slight made her a suitable alternative to somebody far younger. Somebody who he would prefer to have been abusing if he'd had the chance.

Amber was so worked up that her body remained tense, making sex uncomfortable. The punter carried on even though she was unreceptive. As he thrust away inside her she became sore and found herself fighting back tears as the pain provoked a distressing memory from her childhood.

She had been twelve then; just a girl called Amy who later changed her name to Amber to satisfy the perverse ideals of her evil pimp. Apart from being painful, that experience had been a total shock and something that she would never forget.

2

Amy wanted to run through the rooms just one more time. She loved their home in Cheadle. It was big and cosy with a garden that went all the way round. Her grandparents said that was because it was detached, and it was in a good area too. She'd spent many happy hours in the playroom with her friends or in the sprawling back garden on the swing, slide and climbing frame.

She was going to miss it, but her mother had promised her that the house they were moving to was also very nice. It wasn't as big as this one and they would only have room for the swing in the garden but nevertheless her mother was going to make sure that it was just as cosy.

She had also told Amy and Nathan that their friends could come and visit them in the new house, and that they'd probably make new friends too. Amy enjoyed playing with her friends and knew that she was going to miss them, but she felt better knowing that they would be welcome anytime.

At the top of the stairs she turned and walked into her old bedroom, clutching her favourite teddy bear, Barney. Her bedroom was at the back of the house and overlooked the garden with its neat lawns and pretty flowers. Amy caught a glimpse of the slide and the climbing frame that would be left behind, and she felt sad. But she tried not to cry, knowing she had promised her mother she would be a brave girl when they had to leave their nice home.

'Come on, Barney,' she said, addressing her teddy bear. 'Don't cry. We've got to be brave for Mummy. The men have put my bed in the van, and I'll tuck you up nice and warm in it when we get to the new house.'

The garden was now devoid of the picturesque planters that her mother had lovingly nurtured. They were inside the big van that was parked outside the front of their house. Many of their belongings were also inside and as Amy walked through the empty bedrooms, she could hear the echo of her footsteps.

Next, she walked into her mother's bedroom and looked out of the window at the men who were busy carrying boxes from the kitchen. She spotted her friend, Maisie, with her mother, hovering at the edge of the garden, and Amy let out an excited squeal. She ran down the stairs, eager to see Maisie one last time before she had to leave.

'Maisie,' she shouted enthusiastically as she sped out of the front door, dodging one of the men who was carrying a box full of kitchen utensils. 'We're going to our new house today.'

Maisie smiled. 'I know. My mummy told me. She said we can come to see you off.'

'Barney's coming too. He's really happy.' Amy held up her teddy bear and addressed him. 'Aren't you, Barney?' She moved his head to indicate a nod.

'What other toys are you taking?' asked Maisie and for a few minutes they chatted animatedly until Amy's mother, Loretta, drew their attention. 'Come on, Amy. It's time to go.'

'Aw, Mummy,' complained Amy. 'Can I stay for a bit longer? Can Maisie come and play in the garden for a bit? The slide and climbing frame are still there.'

'No, Amy,' said her mother. 'The men are finished now. We need to go.'

Loretta was showing the strain of the day in her clenched facial muscles, which altered her normally pleasant features. But she was adopting a calm façade in front of her children, five-year-old Amy and her brother, Nathan, who was two years younger. Holding Nathan's hand, she walked over to where Amy was standing with her friend Maisie and Maisie's mother. Amy turned to say goodbye to her friend but the tears that had threatened earlier now fully erupted and were accompanied by a loud wailing sound.

Loretta put her arm around Amy. 'Now come on, love. Didn't you promise you'd be a brave girl?'

Amy tried her best to stop crying but the thought of leaving her friends, her lovely home and her garden toys was too much. Three-year-old Nathan, picking up on Amy's upset, began to bawl loudly too without realising why he was doing it.

Loretta turned to Maisie's mum. 'I'm afraid we'll have to get going before these two get any worse. The removal company are charging by the hour, so I need to dash. But don't forget, you and Maisie are welcome to visit anytime.'

'That's great. Thank you,' said Maisie's mum who gave Loretta and both of the children a hug before saying goodbye.

Amy looked at her mother, who seemed sad. She'd thought her mother was going to cry too when Maisie's mum had hugged her, but she hadn't. Instead she turned to her and Nathan, smiled and said, 'OK, kids. Let's go and start our new adventure.'

Amy was confused. Her mother had looked like she was going to cry so why was she smiling? Taking her cue from her mother, Amy dried her tears on her sleeve and tried to be brave as they got inside her car and set off down the road, following the removal van to their new home on a housing estate in Withington.

It was later that evening and Loretta had finally managed to put the kids to bed. It hadn't been easy as they were both overexcited for the first few hours after arriving at the new house. Then the enthusiasm wore off and Amy seemed to realise that this new house wasn't such an adventure after all.

As day turned into evening the children became tired and all the upheaval of the move finally caught up with them. They had been reluctant to go to bed, Amy because she was scared of the strange new house, and Nathan because he didn't like his bedroom.

It had been one of the most trying days of Loretta's life and one that she had been putting off for the last three years. After her husband Greg had died when Amy was only two and Loretta was pregnant with Nathan, she had fought to keep the house on, not wishing to deny her children or herself the lifestyle that they had become accustomed to.

Unfortunately, Greg had died leaving no life insurance. He was only thirty-five when he had an unexpected and fatal heart attack, leaving Loretta heartbroken, out of work and struggling to manage the finances. Because she hadn't worked since before having the children, the only work she was able to find was poorly paid and, once she'd paid for childcare, she would have been worse off.

Loretta had therefore managed as best she could, trying to live frugally and borrowing from friends and relatives. In the end, the debts had become too much and, with relatives no longer willing to bail Loretta out, she'd had no choice but to sell up, clear the debts and move.

She considered the place they had moved to. It was on a housing estate in Withington, which was noisy and run-down. Outside she could hear shouting in the street, dogs barking and a child screaming. The neighbours had seemed friendly enough when they were moving in but then she had noticed two women whispering to each other as they eyed the high-end furniture that the removal men were carrying inside the house.

She looked at it as she entered the living room. Her quality items seemed so out of place in the shabby surroundings, even though they were now several years old. The whole place looked as though it could do with a damn good clean, and the smell was just as bad, a sure sign that the previous occupants had neglected their pets when it came to hygiene.

Aside from that, the rooms were poky, the kitchen was dilapidated, and the bathroom needed updating.

Despite how she felt about the new house, she had done her best to put on a brave face for the children, emphasising the house's few good points and encouraging them to look forward to this new adventure. But she sensed that she had fallen short. Amy was five now. It was an age when memories were formed and Loretta feared that one of her daughter's earliest recollections would be the day that they had had to leave their beloved home and all their friends behind to come and live on a vulgar housing estate.

Loretta had been holding back her own tears all day but now, as she thought about her reduced circumstances and how she still missed Greg every day, the tears gushed. Never would she have envisioned that by thirty years of age she would be living on a rough council estate bringing up two children alone. Her instinct was to pour herself a nice soothing cup of tea but that was impossible. She hadn't yet found where she'd put the bloody kettle!

But she'd managed to find the few bottles of wine that she had packed so she sat down and poured herself a large glass of red. She knew she shouldn't really seek solace by drinking alone but these were exceptional circumstances. Anyway, she told herself after a couple of glasses, the situation was only temporary. Somehow, eventually, she would find a way to get back what they had once had. But without a job and no skills she wasn't yet sure how she was going to achieve it.

3

September 1993

Maisie was due to visit with her mother, Yvette, and Amy was excited. As she waited by the living room window for them to appear, she asked, 'How long will they be, Mum?'

Loretta smiled. 'I've told you, darling, they'll be here as soon as they can. Why don't you go and play in your room to help pass the time?'

'No, I want to wait here. I won't be able to see them from my room.'

It was only the third time Yvette had arranged a visit in the few months since Amy and her family had moved house. Amy had been to visit Maisie just once and when she'd asked her mother why they couldn't go more often, she had told her that they had to wait to be invited.

'What if I ask Maisie's mum if we can visit?' she had asked.

But Loretta hadn't been very receptive to her suggestion.

'No, Amy. You mustn't do that; it's bad manners to ask. You have to wait to be invited.'

Although Amy would have loved to visit Maisie's nice big house again, in some ways she had found that one visit strange. She had seen her own old house, which had looked different somehow. The front garden had different plants in pots on gravel with tiny stepping stones and, although it looked good, it didn't look like their garden anymore.

Somebody had also painted the front door green. Amy didn't like green but when she'd complained to her mother, Loretta had told her there was nothing they could do about it as they didn't live there anymore. Her mother had looked sad when she said that, so Amy hadn't pressed her any further.

Amy loved it when Maisie came to visit. She was her best friend in the whole world, and she didn't like anybody else as much. Amy's mother had encouraged her to make other friends at her new school and she had made a few but they weren't as nice as Maisie.

When Yvette pulled up in her car, Amy was elated. She raced across the room, shouting as she did so, 'They're here, Mummy. They're here.'

She was already at the front door by the time her mother came through to the hall from the kitchen. 'Quick, Mummy. Open the door,' she said.

Her mother chuckled as she grabbed her keys from the hook on the wall. 'Be patient, Amy. They haven't even knocked at the door yet.'

Once Maisie and Yvette had parked the car, they walked up the garden path to find Amy and Loretta standing outside the front door. Amy dashed down the path as soon as she saw her friend. 'Maisie, let's go to my room and play!'

Amy took Maisie's hand and led her towards the front door. Loretta laughed again. 'Hang on, give her a chance. Would any of you girls like a drink and a biscuit first?'

'Yes please,' the girls sang in unison.

They ate the biscuits straightaway then took their drinks with them up to Amy's room where they played for a while. The time seemed to fly by, and it wasn't long before Loretta was shouting up to let them know it was time for Maisie to go home.

Amy appeared at the top of the stairs. 'Aw, Mum. Can't Maisie stay a bit longer?'

'I'm sorry, love, but Maisie's mum is a very busy lady and she's got other things to do.'

Amy returned reluctantly to her bedroom where Maisie was still playing. She looked at her friend, 'My mum says you've got to go.'

Maisie put down the doll she had been playing with. 'OK,' she said.

'Will you be able to come again soon?'

Maisie shrugged but she looked upset. 'I don't know. Mummy didn't want to bring me today, but I kept asking her till she let me come. She says it's too far away and that I've got plenty of friends nearer to where I live.'

Amy didn't say anything. She could feel herself getting upset but was trying to be brave. She followed Maisie down the stairs and watched while she and her mother got inside the car and drove away. Once they were gone Amy gave in to her tears and cried freely.

'Amy, whatever's the matter?' asked Loretta when she noticed her daughter had burst into tears. 'Maisie hasn't done something to upset you, has she?' Amy shook her head but seemed too upset to speak. 'Come on, let's go and sit down. Then you can tell me all about it.'

Loretta took Amy through to the living room, sat her on her knee and cuddled her while she waited for her to calm down. Nathan looked up from the puzzle he was doing. 'Amy cry,' he stated before returning to the puzzle, his three-year-old brain more interested in slotting the wooden animals into the relevant gaps.

Eventually Amy calmed down and told Loretta what Maisie had said. Loretta wasn't surprised really; she'd had the feeling for a while that Yvette visited them reluctantly. She knew Yvette's excuses about being busy were lies as she was a full-time mum who employed a cleaner and spent her days looking after Maisie or socialising with friends when Maisie was at school.

Yvette had seemed such a decent woman when they had lived near to her and when Loretta had enjoyed a similar standard of living. But now Loretta could sense the change in her one-time friend.

She noticed the way Yvette eyed the place warily each time she came to the house. She would also perch herself awkwardly on the edge of the sofa as though it was contaminated. Then there were the discussions about mutual acquaintances and activities when Yvette would suddenly become uncomfortable once she remembered that Loretta wasn't a part of that world anymore.

But the thing that had got to Loretta more than anything had been the way Yvette had patronised her. 'It's such a shame you had to come to an area like this. I really feel for you, Loretta. It can't be much fun having to mix with these people.' Then, before Loretta had had chance to respond, she had said, 'Never mind, you'll meet a nice man one day from the same background as you and remarry. Then you'll be able to get out of this place.'

The fact was, now that they had come down in the world, they were no longer good enough for the likes of Yvette and her precious daughter Maisie, and today that had become startlingly apparent. Despite how upset she had been at Yvette's comments, Loretta knew she had to make the best of the situation for the sake of her children. And sometimes, if you wanted to make your children feel good, you had to indulge in a few white lies, so she thought carefully before addressing her next comments to Amy.

'When I was a little girl, I had a best friend too but then she went to live somewhere far away. I was upset at first but then I made lots of new friends and I got a best friend who I liked even better. You've already made lots of new friends at school, haven't you?'

Amy stared up at her mother and nodded while Loretta took out a tissue and wiped away her tears. 'So, you see, Amy, it might seem bad now, but it won't always feel like that, I promise.'

'Honest?' asked Amy, her little lip trembling.

'Honest,' said Loretta, hoping she would somehow find a way to live up to her promise to improve their circumstances.

4

October 1993

Loretta was standing in the schoolyard waiting for the bell to ring so she could collect Amy. In her hand she was clutching a bag of groceries. She'd been shopping beforehand, taking care to arrive at school early enough that she wouldn't keep Amy waiting but not so early that she would have to stand about in the yard for too long.

She always had mixed feelings about this part of her day. Amy was more settled now and as much as she enjoyed seeing her rushing out of school eager to tell her all about her day, it was the waiting that got to her. All of the other parents would stand about in groups chatting, but she just didn't seem to fit in with any of their cliques. She knew she should heed her own advice to Amy and make new friends, but she found it difficult when the other parents all seemed so detached from her.

While she waited, Nathan dashed about the yard with the other toddlers. Loretta tried to keep an eye on him as he weaved in and out of the groups of parents that were dotted around. When the bell sounded and the yard became more crowded with children emerging from the building, she lost sight of Nathan.

Loretta panicked and rushed to where she had last seen him playing. Fortunately, she found him chatting away in toddler speak to another young child who was snuggled up close to his mother. Loretta took hold of Nathan's hand, her movement more rash than she had intended as she was preoccupied with keeping an eye out for Amy too.

'Come along, Nathan. Amy will be out any minute.'

Then, aware of the other child's mother surveying her, Loretta smiled. 'You can't afford to take your eyes off them for a minute, can you?' she said but the other woman didn't return her smile. Instead she just nodded and turned back to her friends.

As Loretta walked away, she heard one of the group imitating her in an exaggerated posh voice. '*Come along, Nathan.* Did you hear her? Who the fuck does she think she is with her bloody Marks and Sparks shopping bag and her posh clothes?'

'Yeah,' agreed another parent. 'She thinks her kids are too good for ours. Snobby cow!'

The words stung but Loretta tried to ignore them and focus instead on her children. 'Look, here's Amy now,' she said to Nathan, feigning excitement despite the downbeat change of mood that had now taken over her.

Amy was clutching a picture she had done that day and was gushing about a birthday party she had been invited to. Loretta became enveloped by her daughter's enthusiasm and for the next few hours she was fully occupied with the children.

After Loretta had taken them home, encouraged them to play with their toys while she made tea then bathed them and put them to bed, it was time for herself. She switched on the TV and tried to focus on the episode of *The Bill* that was being shown but she couldn't concentrate. Now she was no longer busy with the children, the words of the other mums invaded her mind.

They were so hurtful! How could they judge her like that just because of how she spoke, what she wore and where she shopped for food? But Loretta realised that, sadly, they did. Prejudice didn't just occur amongst the middle classes; it was rife among the working classes too. Her old world had abandoned her and the new one wouldn't accept her. Loretta was stuck in the middle, in some kind of societal limbo where she no longer fitted into either group.

But maybe she could change. She thought about the clothes she had been wearing, a smartly tailored skirt and a formal three-quarter-length coat. Maybe they were a bit inappropriate for the schoolyard. When she tried to recall what the other parents were wearing, she realised that most of them had been wearing jeans or tracksuit bottoms with casual coats. Maybe it wouldn't be a bad idea to raid her wardrobe and drag out the couple of pairs of jeans she still possessed. It wasn't her usual style, but she knew that if she wanted to make her life easier in this neighbourhood then she needed to fit in.

*

A few days later, Loretta needed to buy some more groceries. Her instinct was to get on the bus and go to her nearest Marks and Spencer. It was a habit of hers as she'd always shopped there. But then she remembered how the other mothers in the schoolyard had criticised her for her choice of shop.

She'd passed a discount supermarket along with a discount frozen food retailer in the local shopping precinct but had avoided going inside, assuming that the food would be of a lower standard. But now she thought that maybe she should give them a whirl. Why not? She had nothing to lose.

She felt uncomfortable at first, especially when she heard the bad language that a couple of the other shoppers were using. Loretta had rarely heard those sorts of words being spoken by young women and she was shocked. For a moment she was tempted to ask them not to use such language in front of Nathan, but she didn't want to make any more enemies.

Ignoring the two foul-mouthed women, she looked at the products lining the shelves. She hadn't heard of any of the brand names on the tins but what she did notice were the prices. They were unbelievably cheap! The fresh food was cheap too and surely that couldn't be much different to what she normally bought. Figuring that it couldn't hurt to try them, especially at those prices, she loaded her shopping trolley with meat, fruit and veg, and threw in a couple of tins of beans and soup. If the food tasted a bit bland then she could get creative with herbs and spices, which were also inexpensive.

Emerging from the supermarket, Loretta was delighted to find that she had saved herself a small fortune. And with her finances in their current dire state, she couldn't really afford to be too choosy. Looking down at what she was wearing, a pair of jeans and the only anorak she possessed, Loretta felt a sense of achievement. She had taken the first step in adapting to her new surroundings.

5

September 2015

It was several days since the session with Bill. Amber had been glad to get it over with, subsequently deciding that she would never again offer her services to him and she'd probably run a mile if anyone else suggested she should dress up as a schoolgirl.

Since then she'd tried to put the experience out of her mind and carry on as normal, or what passed for normal in her life. She was taking a day off work and had decided to go shopping before having a few drinks with some of the girls in the Rose and Crown, a run-down city centre pub frequented by prostitutes and the criminal fraternity.

She had just come out of one of the major stores and was turning into Market Street when she spotted a woman she thought she knew. Could it be Crystal? But it was hard to tell as she was a few metres away and surrounded by hordes of people who crowded Manchester's shopping areas.

Amber thought fondly of her old friend. They'd shared

such good times together. She was a bit older than Amber and had acted like a big sister, always making sure she was looked after. Delighted at the prospect of chatting to Crystal, Amber stopped and watched as she approached.

As she drew nearer, Amber knew for certain that she hadn't been mistaken; it was definitely her old friend. She looked different though; smarter and more groomed. She was wearing a pair of skinny jeans, low-heeled expensive-looking shoes and a smart jacket, and she had changed her hairstyle again. It was still that nice mid-brown colour that she had swapped to from the fiery red she'd sported during her days on the game, but instead of the straight bob she'd previously opted for, it was now shoulder length and wavy.

Remembering how harsh and chaotic Crystal's hair used to be, Amber was amazed to see the wonderful condition of it now. She watched, mesmerised, as it swayed lightly in the breeze and bounced about Crystal's shoulders as she walked towards her. It seemed to underline the newfound confidence that Crystal displayed, her head held high and a smile painted on her flawless face as she chatted to the young girl who walked alongside her.

Amber hadn't seen Crystal for over a year and, although Crystal had changed her image a while before that, it still took Amber by surprise. She somehow seemed even more attractive than the last time she'd seen her. Maybe it was the wavy hair that did it or perhaps she used expensive products or treatments to give her such a radiant glow.

It seemed that with the new image and lifestyle came progressively less frequent visits to the Rose and Crown. So, whenever Amber thought fondly of Crystal, her mental image was of the woman she knew when she had been on the game. The woman who was a real character with wanton red hair, skimpy clothing, a coarse complexion and language to match.

Amber realised that the girl with Crystal must have been her daughter, Candice. She would have been about fifteen by now, but Amber had never seen her. It was surprising really considering how long they had been friends and how much Crystal used to talk about her daughter.

Candice was really pretty and resembled Crystal. Her clothes were trendy but had an edge to them, her skirt short and flowy and teamed with opaque tights, utilitarian boots, a smart denim jacket and an oversized scarf. She was slightly taller than Crystal although slim like her mother. The two of them painted a picture of familial bliss as they strolled along together.

When they had drawn almost even with Amber, she realised that she had been staring open-mouthed in awe at the two of them and she quickly checked herself. She stepped forward, grinning at her one-time friend.

'Long time, no see,' she announced. 'How are *you*?'

Crystal's eyes flitted across to where Amber stood, and a look of recognition flashed across her face. Straightaway her expression changed, the smile now replaced by a worried frown, and she turned her head away and kept walking.

Amber remained rooted to the same spot, staring in astonishment after her one-time friend and calling out to her, 'Crystal, it's me, Amber.'

Her words drowned out the comment that Candice made to her mum but Amber clearly heard Crystal's response.

'I don't know, love. I think she must have mistaken me for somebody else.'

For a moment Amber was tempted to run after Crystal to make sure she knew who she was. But then she thought about the look on Crystal's face and realised that Crystal had recognised her. She just hadn't wanted to acknowledge her.

Of course, Amber realised, Candice would have known Crystal by her real name of Laura so she could have passed it off as a case of mistaken identity. But no matter what name she chose to use and how she presented herself, there was no doubt that it was her old friend. And Amber was devastated to think that she had just snubbed her.

Crystal had been so busy chatting to Candice that she hadn't noticed Amber till she'd stepped out and spoken to her. The sight of her one-time friend threw Crystal into turmoil. Candice had no idea about her old life, and she couldn't risk her finding out!

She was finally living the life she had dreamt of for so long; a life where she could afford shopping expeditions like this one when she could treat her daughter without having to think about the cost. It was also a life where she wasn't hooked on drugs and having to sleep with seedy men to feed her habit.

Just a wrong word from Amber and it could all come crashing down around her. Thank God Candice hadn't made the connection with the name Crystal, which was also the name she had given to her high-end fashion shops. How on earth would she explain to her daughter what she used to do for a living? She couldn't. Candice would probably disown her and then everything she'd been through would have been for nothing. She'd worked so hard to make a better life for herself and her daughter, and she couldn't risk being exposed.

So, she'd decided not to acknowledge Amber. It was a spur-of-the-moment decision fuelled by panic. Crystal didn't like having to lie to Candice by telling her it must have been mistaken identity but what else could she do?

As she continued walking past Amber, she could hear her calling after her. Crystal's heart was beating frantically at the thought of her catching up with them and telling Candice who she really was.

Thankfully, Amber must have thought better of it and as they drew further away, Crystal felt relief wash over her. But it was quickly replaced by another feeling: guilt. How could she have abandoned her old friend? She might have needed her help. Crystal knew only too well how desperate that lifestyle could make you.

She thought about turning back and acknowledging Amber. But how could she do that while she had Candice with her? And she couldn't think of any excuse to break away from her daughter. She wouldn't have done that anyway, not when Candice was enjoying their day out so much.

So, she focused on her daughter instead and tried to put Amber and her past life out of her mind.

6

When Amber arrived at the Rose and Crown two of the girls were already there. Seated around their usual table were Sapphire and Cora. With her jet-black straight hair, heavy eye makeup and abundance of piercings, Sapphire was almost gothic in appearance, but the overall image was contested by an affable nature and her overuse of fake tan.

Cora presented a different picture altogether. Unlike a lot of the girls who were skinny because of drug abuse, Cora was slightly overweight. She was an attractive girl, but she had a hard edge to her.

After she'd got the drinks in, Amber slid into a seat next to her two friends.

'You alright?' asked Cora, who had picked up on Amber's sombre mood.

'Not bad. I've just bumped into Crystal on Market Street.'

'Oh yeah,' said Sapphire who had also been a friend of Crystal's. 'How is she?'

'I don't know. I didn't get the chance to ask.'

'What do you mean?'

'She blanked me.'

'Really?' asked Sapphire.

'Yeah, I shouted after her, but she just ignored me and walked on. She was with her daughter and I heard her say to her that I must have mistaken her for somebody else.'

'You're fuckin' joking!' said Sapphire. 'I didn't think Crystal would be like that.'

'Doesn't surprise me,' Cora chipped in. 'She doesn't want to fuckin' know us lot now she's made a better life for herself. And there's no way she'd want her daughter to find out what she used to do for a living.'

'Do you think Candice doesn't know then?' asked Amber.

'Does she fuck! Would you tell your kid you used to be on the beat if you'd got this new cushy life?'

'OK. But I wouldn't have given the game away to Candice anyway.'

'I fuckin' would have done and it would have served Crystal right for trying to be something she's not.'

'She's worked for what she's got, and good luck to her,' said Sapphire.

'Hmm. Well, I'd love to know who put the money up for her business. I heard a rumour she'd fuckin' blackmailed someone then checked into rehab.'

Sapphire was quick to counter Cora's speculation. 'No, that's not true. I mean, she did check into rehab, yeah, but Ruby gave her a loan for the business.'

'Wish someone would give me a fuckin' loan,' grumbled Cora. 'And that Ruby's another one who doesn't want to know us now she's doing alright. I wouldn't mind but she's only running a fuckin' brothel. She's hardly Mother Teresa, is she?'

'Bet you wouldn't be fuckin' saying that if she were here now,' said Sapphire.

Amber knew she had a point. Ruby had a fierce temper and the other girls had always been wary of her, but she'd always been good to them and Amber was quick to defend her. 'Ruby's alright if you stay on the right side of her. Anyway, you didn't know her and Crystal as well as me and Sapphire did. They were both sound.'

'Well Crystal doesn't seem so fuckin' sound now if she's snubbing you, does she?'

'She had her reasons. Like you say, it must have been because of her daughter. She probably didn't want her to know she used to be on the game.'

Further retaliation from Cora was halted by the appearance of Angie who came back from the bar carrying a drink for herself and pulling up a seat.

'Look what the fuckin' cat's dragged in,' said Cora as Angie approached.

Angie put her drink down on the table and was seized by a coughing fit. It took her several seconds to get her breath back. She then sat down with the other girls, seemingly oblivious to Cora's barbed comment. She was an ageing, skinny prostitute whose complexion bore all the evidence of alcohol abuse with her flushed cheeks, dry skin and abundance of wrinkles. Many of the girls pitied her.

It was well known that Cora didn't have much time for Angie who was viewed as a sad figure by many of the girls. As time had passed and her looks had faded, Angie had become increasingly desperate to obtain cash with which to feed her alcoholism. This meant she was willing to sink to depths that the other girls regarded as off limits, taking the worst punters and performing the most degrading services at the lowest prices. This was frowned on by girls such as Cora, who thought it was putting pressure on them to reduce their prices accordingly.

'Don't fuckin' bother asking us if we want a drink, will you?' snapped Cora.

Angie sniffed. 'I could see your glasses were full.'

'A likely story. Anyway, I've got a fuckin' bone to pick with you. I was a tenner short in my purse last night and I've been told you took it when I went to the loo.'

'I never did. Who told you that?'

'Never you fuckin' mind who told me. You know you've got it and I want it back, now!' Cora held out her hand while glaring at Angie.

'Hang on,' said Amber. 'We were with Angie last night and we didn't see fuck all, did we, Sapphire?'

'No, we didn't.'

'You two were so fuckin' busy gassing that you wouldn't have noticed if a bomb went off, but I know she took it because I was told.'

'Who by?' asked Sapphire.

'Never you fuckin' mind! I'm not grassing them up.'

Amber had a feeling Cora was making it up. There was no way she and Sapphire wouldn't have noticed Angie dipping into Cora's purse. The mystery witness probably didn't even exist. It was more likely that Cora had just miscalculated how much money she had in her purse or perhaps somebody else she hung about with had taken the tenner. And sad old Angie was an easy target for someone to blame. But there was no point arguing with her, knowing that Cora would always defend her other friends over Angie.

'I haven't got your poxy money,' slurred Angie.

'Oh yes you fuckin' have!' yelled Cora, getting out of her chair and standing menacingly over Angie who seemed to cower.

Then she grabbed hold of the shoulder of Angie's top, the sudden movement shocking her into another bout of coughing. 'Give me my fuckin' money or you'll get a smack in the mouth.'

Amber jumped up out of her seat. 'Alright, alright, calm down, Cora. I'll give you the fuckin' tenner if it means that much to you.'

Straightaway Amber regretted her decision, but she'd done it on the spur of the moment knowing she had to do something to stop Cora attacking Angie. She'd been hoping to buy some coke with her money but now wouldn't have enough so she'd have to do without unless Sapphire had any to spare.

She withdrew a tenner and held it out to Cora who let go of Angie while she snatched it out of her hand. Then Cora grabbed her drink and stormed away to another area of the pub, leaving a parting shot: 'I don't know why you fuckin' defend her all the time, Amber. She's nowt but a fuckin' old alcy and she doesn't deserve anyone's sympathy.'

By this time Angie was breathless once more, her head bowed low, while she tried to get some air into her lungs. She was so focused on her breathing that she seemed oblivious to what was taking place around her. This surprised Amber as she knew how wary Angie was of Cora.

'Are you OK, Angie?' asked Sapphire, slapping her on the back.

Angie nodded but the cough persisted.

Once Cora had gone, Amber sat back down. As she picked up her glass to take a calming gulp of her drink, she could see her hands were trembling. The confrontation with Cora had shaken her. Amber knew Cora could be nasty, but she was usually alright with her. It was Angie who she had it in for.

'You OK?' Sapphire asked Amber while Angie remained silent.

'Yeah, I'm glad she's gone though.'

Sapphire grinned. 'I know what you mean. Cora can be a right twat at times.'

They remained at the table for a few minutes, Amber and Sapphire discussing what had just happened then making small talk to try to take their minds off it. Angie didn't join in the conversation, but Amber noticed how quickly she was downing the glass of whisky she'd just bought. It was a large measure, possibly a double, and by the time she had drunk most of it her cough seemed to have eased. But Amber knew it was only a temporary reprieve.

Eventually Angie spoke but not before she had finished the last dregs of her drink. 'Well, that's me done. I'm off now.'

'Where to?' asked Amber.

'Work. Where d'you think?'

'It's raining. Surely, you're not going out in that weather with a cough like that, are you?'

'Course I am. I've got no choice. Anyway, it's not stopped me yet.' Angie grinned back at her, but it looked forced.

When she walked away Amber flashed a look of concern at Sapphire who shrugged then resumed their conversation. But while Amber chatted, she couldn't help but think about Angie. Her appearance. Her state of health. Her total disregard for life. She suffered from COPD, yet she still drank excessively and would probably light up a cigarette the minute she was outside. Amber knew that Angie was a sad warning to them all of how they could end up in the future.

Maybe ten years. Maybe twenty. Who knew when the drink or drugs would finally grip them in a stranglehold and the downward spiral that their lives had taken would quickly shift into high speed?

7

July 1995

Loretta heaved a sigh of relief and walked down the stairs into the living room. Thank God the kids were in bed! Having a seven-year-old and a five-year-old could be challenging and it was always good to finally unwind at the end of the day. Unfortunately, however, the evenings were also the time when she felt most lonely.

When she reached the living room, she was already reflecting on how much her life had changed during the past two years. She plonked herself down on the armchair and felt it sag beneath her. Loretta's once immaculate and tasteful furniture was now becoming as jaded as she felt.

A look around the room confirmed to her that the furniture wasn't the only problem. It was badly in need of an update. The wallpaper, apart from being old-fashioned, was also torn in parts. But Loretta couldn't afford to have it redecorated and she didn't have a clue how to go about it herself. The carpet was stained and was becoming threadbare.

Apart from the living room, all the other rooms demanded serious refurbishment. The kitchen still had the same worn-out cupboards that had wanted replacing when she moved into the house. And the bathroom was also outdated and grimy with mildew. She'd tried her best to make the home look presentable but no matter how much she scrubbed and cleaned, she couldn't disguise the fact that the whole place needed some money spent. Neither could she get rid of the musty smell that seemed to permeate the rooms.

The house wasn't her only concern. Loretta had never liked the area and, when she had first moved in, she had felt like an outsider. For one thing, she spoke differently to all the other people on the estate and they were quick to spot her cultured tones. She was grateful for the fact that the children had been only young when they moved. They had therefore slotted in better than they would have done if they had been at an age when children became more judgemental about different classes of people.

It would have been nice to have someone to talk to at the end of the day about how she felt but a lot of her old friends and relatives had now distanced themselves. The children had often asked why they didn't have visits from their aunts and uncles anymore and it had been heart-breaking having to come up with convincing excuses. She still saw her parents from time to time, but they were becoming increasingly disapproving of her lifestyle.

Loretta would never have expected her life to come to this: stuck in a place she didn't want to be and scraping an existence on benefits. She went through to the kitchen and grabbed a bottle of wine and a glass. She'd told herself she would resist the temptation tonight, but it was difficult when the warmth of a glass of wine helped her to deal with the lack of other comforts in her life.

It would have been so easy for Loretta to have sunk into a pit of despair. But she was determined to make the best of things, for her children as well as herself. At first it had been a painful experience each time she had waited in the schoolyard for the children to come out of school while the other parents snubbed her. But eventually, with perseverance, she had made a few friends.

The woman she had connected with most was called Debbie and she was also a single mum. She wasn't the sort of person Loretta would have chosen to befriend in her previous life. Debbie had a vulgar sense of humour and could be foul-mouthed. But she was also kind-hearted and very accepting of Loretta despite her background.

Loretta had nurtured the friendship, desperate for someone in whom she could confide and maybe find an alternative solace to her frequent glasses of wine. Their playground chats had developed to the stage where they were now popping round to each other's homes for coffee and Loretta found herself looking forward to their get-togethers.

As she got to know Debbie, she was surprised to find out that they had more in common than she would have imagined. As well as both being full-time single mothers with young children to raise, and they were both lonely and looking for company.

Eventually, the friendship had progressed to the stage where Debbie had suggested a night out together and Loretta had welcomed it. Unfortunately, their first night out wasn't a success. Loretta had felt ill at ease in the pubs that

Debbie took her to. They were full of dubious characters and, at first, she found she couldn't settle, expecting trouble at any minute. It was only when she had drunk a great deal that she finally relaxed.

Despite the experience, Loretta wanted to go out with Debbie again; she'd just make sure that they avoided the haunts Debbie had taken her to last time. As she sat there, guzzling wine, she reflected on their last conversation.

'Do you fancy another night out?' asked Debbie. 'I'm hoping that guy called Andy will be in the pub again. He was gorgeous and I wouldn't mind hooking up with him.'

Loretta recalled the man and how loud and foul-mouthed he had been, and she suppressed a shudder. 'I wouldn't trust him if I were you. According to his friend he's already seeing someone and they're quite serious.' She noticed Debbie's glum expression and quickly added, 'Actually, I was thinking, Debbie, I know somewhere I could take you where there are loads of lovely men, and they've all got plenty of money too.'

'Oh yeah, where's that?'

'It's near to where I used to live.'

'What, in bloody Cheadle? That'll cost us a fortune.'

'Not necessarily. We can have a few drinks before we go out, use public transport to get there and then hopefully find some nice men who will buy a few rounds for us.'

'Ooh, you're not daft, are yer?' said Debbie. 'Count me in.'

Loretta smiled to herself as she thought about their forthcoming night out. Not only would it give her a break from her daily routine, but it would also serve another purpose. When she'd mentioned the rich men, it wasn't just because she wanted to tempt Debbie, it was because she wanted that for herself too. Loretta was still relatively young and with her shiny blonde hair and slim figure she knew men found her attractive.

After two years living here, Loretta had had moments when she began to despair of ever escaping. But then she thought about her former friend Yvette's words two years ago, "You'll meet a nice man one day from the same background as you and remarry. Then you'll be able to get out of this place."

The more Loretta thought about it, the more it made sense. After all, she couldn't think of a better way. She didn't have any skills with which she could get a job and she wouldn't have wanted to leave her children while she went out to work anyway. Meeting a rich man was the only way she would be able to raise her children to a better way of life.

And now, Loretta was going to make it her mission.

8

Loretta was at Longsight Market with Debbie. It had been a trek getting there as they'd had to get two buses, but Debbie had raved about it for so long that she'd finally given in to her. Besides, Loretta and the children needed some new clothes and she could no longer afford to shop at the upmarket stores and boutiques where she used to shop.

'I can't spend too much on myself,' she said as soon as they got off the bus. 'The kids need new pyjamas and underwear.'

'What's wrong with the ones they've got?'

'Well, some of their pyjamas are ripped, their socks have got holes in them and a lot of their underwear got dyed in the wash.'

'Oh, you mean when they go a bit grey?'

'Yeah, that's right.'

'Well, it's no biggie,' said Debbie. 'It's not like your kids

40

are old enough to worry about what colour their underwear is. And who else sees it anyway?'

'Yeah but, what about the other stuff with holes in it?'

Debbie tutted. 'Have you never heard of a needle and thread? Bloody sew them. For fuck's sake, Loz, you don't have to rush out buying them new gear every time they get a little rip in summat. D'you really think your kids will notice the difference?'

Loretta shrugged.

'There you go then. Save your fuckin' money. You'll have more to spend on yourself, and you do want some new gear, don't you?'

'Yeah, but…'

'But, nowt. Haven't you sewn anything before?'

'Not recently, no.'

'OK, well if you want a needle, I've got plenty. I can lend you some cotton too. Right, now let's have a look what they've got here,' said Debbie, approaching a stall with women's garments hung on display.

Loretta went over to the stall with Debbie and, following Debbie's lead, she started rummaging along the rails while the stallholder hovered in the background. She pulled out a nice top and held it against her but as she touched it, she noticed that it was damp from when it had rained earlier.

'Actually, I think I'll give it a miss,' she said, walking away.

Debbie put down a dress she had been admiring then rushed to catch up with her. 'What the bloody hell's wrong? I thought you liked that top.'

'I did but it was wet.'

'So?'

'Well, it'll probably smell of damp.'

'Will it, buggery. Just sling it in the wash when you get home. It'll be fine. Right, watch this.'

Debbie went back to the stall leaving Loretta no choice but to join her as she wasn't familiar enough with the area to wander round on her own. She watched as Debbie picked up the same dress she had been admiring earlier then spoke to the stallholder.

'Can I try this on?'

The stallholder nodded to a makeshift changing room at the back of the stall, which was really no more than a curtain used to partition off a small area.

'You stand guard,' said Debbie.

Loretta did as she asked but she didn't like the fact that she could see Debbie in her underwear through a gap in the sides of the curtain. She had no doubt that if she could see her then so could the stallholder who was hovering even closer and leering at her.

After a few minutes of fumbling around in the tiny curtained-off area, Debbie emerged wearing the dress. 'Well, what d'you think?' she asked, twirling around.

Loretta had to admit to herself that, although it wasn't something she would have chosen, the dress showed off Debbie's figure well. 'Lovely,' she said.

When Debbie emerged from the tiny cubicle again later, she held up the dress to the stallholder, asking, 'How much d'you want for this?'

When the stallholder asked for twenty pounds, Loretta was amazed at how cheap it was, but Debbie had other ideas. 'I'll give you fifteen. It's wet from the rain.'

The stallholder rushed over and felt the garment. 'It's only a bit damp, that's all. It's a bargain at twenty quid.'

'Look, I don't wanna go out wearing a dress that stinks like an old umbrella. I'm gonna have to use half a bottle of bloody perfume on it to get rid of the smell.' She then sniffed at the dress dramatically. 'I'll give you fifteen quid and that's that.'

When the stallholder shook his head, Debbie stomped towards the rail, ready to put the dress back.

The stallholder quickly spoke up. 'I'll go down to eighteen and no less.'

'Sixteen.'

He sighed. 'Look, I'll meet you halfway at seventeen, but I can't go any lower.'

'Done,' said Debbie, a triumphant smile lighting up her face.

As the stallholder wrapped the dress, Debbie turned to Loretta. 'Why don't you get one too if you like it so much?'

Loretta was stuck for what to say at first, not wanting to offend Debbie. 'I- I'm not sure it's really me.'

'Give over, with the cracking figure you've got? You'll have the fuckin' blokes fighting over you. And you do want a bloke, don't you? Anyway, we don't have to wear them on the same night if you're worried about that. Go on, see if they've got your size and try it on.'

Picking up on Debbie's encouragement, the stallholder joined in. 'Oh yeah, we've got a nice blue one. It'll look stunning on you, love.'

With pressure from both of them, Loretta felt as though she had no choice but to look at the dress, but she refused to try it on in the makeshift changing room. She held it up and had to admit to herself that the colour suited her. 'Why not?' she said. 'As long as you let me have it for the same price as my friend.'

'Go on then,' said the stallholder, wearily, 'but I hope you know I'm shooting myself in the foot here.'

They walked away from the stall, laughing together. 'See, you're learning,' said Debbie. 'Now, why don't we treat ourselves to some dinner?' she asked, leading Loretta towards a dingy-looking café at the side of the market.

'Ooh, I'm not sure,' said Loretta.

'Listen, don't worry about the fuckin' furniture and décor. That's how they keep the prices so low. Take it from me, the food's great, so who gives a shit what the place looks like?'

'I don't know. I don't want to stop out too long. I need to tidy up before I collect the children from school.'

'Eeh, Loz, you've got a long way to go yet, y'know. It's time you stopped putting them first all the time. Today is our day to enjoy ourselves. You should be making the most of it now they're both in school. You deserve it after what you've been through and it's not as if the kids are gonna notice whether you've tidied the place up, is it? Knowing what kids are like, it'll probably look like a bomb's hit it within five minutes of them being home anyway.'

Loretta couldn't resist laughing at the accuracy of her friend's words. She knew she had a point and she couldn't help but give in to persuasion once again.

At the end of the day, Loretta went home a much happier woman. After feeling miserable with her life for so long, it was great to finally be having some fun. Debbie had a way about her that lifted your spirits and Loretta couldn't wait for their next outing. In fact, she was even looking forward to wearing the dress to see how much male attention she could attract.

9

September 2015

Crystal was standing outside her own high-class fashion store in Altrincham's main shopping centre with her best friend, Ruby, and Ruby's partner, Tiffany. It was early evening and a group of onlookers had gathered around the store. As she peered through the crowd Crystal could see her parents arrive with her daughter, Candice, and Candice's friend, Emily.

'Here they are now,' she said to Ruby and she watched as Candice rushed eagerly over to them.

'Is he here yet?' asked Candice, her voice full of excitement. She turned to Emily and they shared a nervous giggle.

Candice didn't need to say who she was referring to; Crystal had heard about nothing else all week. Brad Swain, reality TV star, local celeb and schoolgirl heartthrob. At Candice's insistence Crystal had chosen him to declare her new store officially open, and now they were just awaiting his arrival.

'Not yet,' said Crystal. 'But he has been in touch to say he's been held up in traffic and shouldn't be long.'

'Wow! You mean he rang you?' asked Emily.

'Texted.'

'Oh wow!' the girls both said in unison.

Crystal laughed. 'How else did you expect him to contact me? Morse code?'

Ruby, Tiffany and Crystal's parents joined in with her laughter, but the girls were too consumed with thoughts of Brad Swain to see the funny side of things.

For a few minutes they waited impatiently. 'Aw, Mum; he's taking ages,' grumbled Candice.

'You've only just got here. How do you think me, Rubes and Tiffany feel, and my new manager, Deanna? We've been here all day getting the new store ready. All you've had to do is turn up and wait a few minutes. Then she noticed a stirring in the crowd, and she nodded in the direction of a good-looking young man who was walking towards them, flanked by two well-built men. 'He's here.'

'Brilliant!' gushed Candice and she and Emily chatted exuberantly.

'Bodyguards for a bleedin' reality TV star!' muttered Ruby who was shushed by Tiffany.

The crowd parted to let Brad through, except the young girls who thronged around him eager for selfies. Crystal could see how animated Candice and Emily were becoming and she smiled at them. Once Brad had worked his way through the crowd, Crystal stepped forward and shook his hand.

'Deanna!' she called, and her manager came over to join them.

'This is Brad. Brad, this is Deanna. She's going to take care of the lights once I give her the OK.'

Out of the corner of her eye she could see Candice and Emily staring open-mouthed at Brad, both suddenly silent in the presence of their idol.

'Oh, and this is Candice, my daughter,' she added. 'And Emily, her friend.'

Brad turned and shook the hands of each of the girls who blushed furiously, then he spoke to Candice. 'Lucky you, having a mother with such a fabulous fashion brand.'

Crystal could see that Candice felt a bit awkward and didn't know what to say so she quickly stepped in. 'And we're very lucky to have you here today, Brad. Thanks for coming. Oh, by the way, would you mind posing for a quick piccie with the girls?'

He beamed a captivating smile. 'Sure. No problem.'

Once the photo had been taken, Crystal asked, 'OK, should we get started then?'

She spent a few moments giving out instructions then Deanna ducked underneath the red ribbon that was draped across the shop doorway and went inside. Crystal pulled her mobile out of her handbag and opened the texting function.

'OK, when I say ready,' she said to Brad, passing him a pair of scissors.

She brought up Deanna's details on the phone screen and typed *now* into her phone. 'OK, Brad, ready.'

Crystal quickly hit the send button as Brad cut the ribbon. The shop lights lit up showing a fabulous window display of all the latest fashions in coordinating colours. The backboard was covered in a glittery paper so that it sparkled under the lights that surrounded it on all sides.

Above the shop doorway, the signage was also lit up, showing the business name, *Crystals of Altrincham*. The letters were large and formed from glass in a 3D effect. Inside them numerous tiny bulbs glowed like crystals in sunlight. The effect was dazzling.

Just as Crystal was about to tell Ruby that she was going to change the signage in her other two shops to match this one, a loud cheer went up from the crowd. She looked around at all the happy faces and couldn't help but feel emotional. For Crystal it was a big day. She had just opened her third store and this one was bigger and better than either of the other two. It felt so good to be going from strength to strength.

10

September 2015

Amber was surprised as well as wary when Cora joined her and Sapphire at their table in the Rose and Crown the evening after their disagreement. As Cora pulled up a chair, Amber began to subconsciously chew her bottom lip, a nervous habit that had persisted since childhood.

But Amber wasn't going to hold a grudge and it seemed that Cora wasn't either because the three of them chatted amicably for half an hour.

It was while Sapphire was at the bar that Cora struck. 'How long is it since you've seen Crystal? I mean, before yesterday?'

Amber shrugged. 'I dunno. A year, maybe more.'

'And what about Ruby?'

'I dunno, even longer I suppose.'

'Then why the fuck are you still defending them? They don't give a shit about you anymore.'

'Because they were friends. And I was close to Crystal. She helped me a lot.'

'Yeah, only 'cos it suited her own purposes to get you working for that fuckin' seedy pimp, Gilly.'

'Crystal didn't get anything out of it.'

'Course she did. He was her fuckin' fella, wasn't he? He was always giving her money. Money that you and the other mugs fuckin' earnt for him.'

Cora was starting to wind Amber up and she retaliated aggressively. 'You don't know fuck all, Cora! Crystal hardly got anything out of him.'

'You believe that if you want, Amber.'

'I believe it 'cos I know it's true.'

'You're such a fuckin' mug, Amber, defending people who don't give a toss about you, like that Angie. She's such a fuckin' loser. Everybody gives her a wide berth but not you and Sapphire.'

'Shut the fuck up!' yelled Amber. 'It's nowt to do with you.'

In a repeat of last night's performance, Cora got up from her seat. 'Who the fuck are you telling to shut up?'

She was about to thump Amber when Sapphire returned from the bar. 'What the hell's going on?' she shouted, drawing not only their attention but that of the landlord too.

'Turn it in!' he shouted, rushing towards the table to find out what all the commotion was about.

Cora's eyes shot momentarily to Sapphire then she lashed out at Amber. Before anybody had a chance to stop her, she landed a punch on Amber's nose. By that time, the landlord had reached the table and he jumped in front of Cora to stop her doing any further damage.

'Right, you're barred!' he yelled, grabbing hold of Cora's arm and dragging her towards the door.

'Get your fuckin' hands off me!' shouted Cora. 'I can walk on my own.'

The landlord let go for a moment and Cora grabbed her jacket from the back of her chair and put it on, glaring menacingly at Amber as she did so. 'You've not fuckin' heard the last of this,' she yelled as she turned to go.

'You alright?' Sapphire asked Amber once Cora had gone and the landlord had resumed his duties behind the bar.

Amber rubbed her nose, which was throbbing. 'Yeah, think so. I'm glad you and the landlord stepped in though. She's a fuckin' lunatic.'

'What caused it?'

'Oh, she was just going on about me sticking up for people like Crystal, Ruby and Angie, and I lost it. She was really pissing me off and, when I had a go back, she went and fuckin' smacked me one. Anyway, I'm glad the landlord's barred her. We won't have to put up with her crap anymore.'

'Don't count your chickens,' said Sapphire.

'What do you mean?'

'Well, Cora's a nasty piece of stuff and I'd be surprised if she let this go without a fight. She'll be raging that she's been barred, and she won't like you standing up to her either.'

'Jesus, Sapphire, cheer me up why don't you?'

'Sorry but I'm just warning you for your own good, Amber. From now on you need to watch your back.'

11

September 2015

When Amber returned home from work in the early hours of the morning, she was sore from overly ardent punters and her nose was throbbing where Cora had hit her. The drink and drugs she had taken earlier were now wearing off and she was starting to feel melancholy.

She checked around the house and found that both her mother and brother were out. It didn't surprise her; Loretta was rarely in and Nathan was probably staying out with his fancy friends again. He hardly ever came home these days, not that she blamed him. He was probably too ashamed to let his friends see where he lived. A quick look around the house told her that her assumption was most likely correct; the place was a tip.

All the carpets were threadbare, and the furniture was worn and mismatched where the worst of the items had been replaced by cheap, second-hand alternatives. There was also a dirty smell that hit you as soon as you walked through the door. Amber had tried cleaning it up occasionally but most of the time she was tired from working all night. Besides, it didn't seem to make any difference. A bit of cleaning wouldn't erase the offensive smell and layers of filth from years of abandonment.

It was in everything: the rarely washed curtains, the carpets that held spillages from years gone by and the ancient sofa, greasy with the remnants of takeaway food and alcohol.

She went through to the kitchen in search of something to eat. It still had the same old grimy wooden cupboards and when she opened the fridge door it gave off a different stench of rotten food. But Amber was suddenly hungry, so she ignored the state of the fridge.

Its contents were sparse, just an opened can of beans, a packet of ham that was well past its sell-by date and a lump of cheese. She grabbed the can and peered inside but found that a layer of mould had formed on the top of it, so she opted for the cheese. It had become crusty but was still edible and would be fine on toast.

When she found the bread in the cupboard, it was also mouldy. But Amber was going to eat it anyway; it wouldn't be the first time. So, she picked the mouldy parts off the edges, sliced up some of the crusty cheese and put them together under the grill while making a mental note to buy some food the following day. She doubted whether her mother or Nathan would bother.

As she ate the cheese on toast Amber became pensive. Although she'd been angry with Cora, her words had hit home. If she was honest with herself, she felt abandoned by Crystal who had once been a good friend. With Ruby it was different as they had never been close. A lot of the girls were wary of Ruby including Amber, whose caution had prevented her from really getting to know her. One thing she did know, though, Cora would never have overstepped the mark if Ruby had been around. She would have put a stop to her straightaway.

But Ruby wasn't around anymore, and neither was Crystal. Amber's mother was a waste of space and she was beginning to feel that, apart from Sapphire, there was nobody who really gave a damn about her.

Her thoughts turned to her absent brother, Nathan, who was increasingly leading his own life separate from her and their mother. She knew he had lost respect for both of them a long time ago, but she had hoped that he would at least have shown some compassion. He could easily have afforded to stock the cupboards but, no, it seemed that the only person Nathan cared about was himself.

It was a week later, and Amber was with a new client, Derek. He was an average punter in every way: average looks, average height and average age of around forty something. There was nothing that set him apart from any other punter, no sparkling personality or wit. Even his requirements were standard, just an hour in a hotel room and straight sex. It wasn't until Amber was getting dressed ready to leave the hotel that the punter's preferences came to the surface.

'Do you want taking back to where I picked you up?' he asked.

'Yes,' said Amber.

Then he seemed to hesitate before asking his next question. 'Could I take your number so I can book you again?'

Amber smiled, thinking that perhaps he was a bit shy of asking. Maybe that was why he had booked a hotel room, because he preferred discretion.

'Course you can. Here's my mobile number.' She handed him a slip of paper with her number on it so he could decide whether to store it in his phone.

'Erm... will it be OK if it isn't just me next time?' he asked.

Amber looked at him, alarmed, her strained features mirroring her concern. 'I don't do gangbangs.'

'No, that wasn't what I meant.' The punter looked uncomfortable, his face slightly flushed. 'I mean, my wife. We're looking to spice up our sex life and I wondered... well... if you could help us out.'

He was blushing furiously by now and Amber couldn't resist an amused smile. 'Course I can – maybe teach you a few tricks too.'

The punter smiled back but his blush remained.

They left the hotel room and walked to the car in silence. On the journey back to Piccadilly, Amber reflected on her time spent with Derek. He was obviously very much in love with his wife otherwise why would he take the trouble to seek help with their sex life, especially when she considered how uncomfortable he had been about asking her to see them both together?

When she thought about the connection between the couple Amber couldn't help but feel a little envious. It was a while since she'd had a partner and she missed the intimacy of a relationship. Doing her job wasn't the same; it was all about satisfying the customer's needs, not about expressing love for each other.

By the time she reached the back of Piccadilly, she wasn't feeling quite as upbeat as she had been at the hotel. Clients like Derek were rare and, as she looked around the grim streets of the red-light area, she resigned herself to the fact that the rest of the night would be filled with seedy clients wanting instant gratification for the lowest possible price.

Amber gazed through the windscreen as they made their way to her spot near the arches. They were almost there when she noticed Cora deep in conversation with a man she vaguely recognised. She felt an involuntary shudder recalling the way Cora had assaulted her in the pub and Sapphire's warning that she needed to watch her back.

Her feeling of uneasiness was exacerbated because of the man Cora was talking to. Although Amber had never had any dealings with him, she knew who he was and had heard of his reputation. Kev Pike, known by many as Pikey, was bad news. Although not a major addict, he was a drug user who would obtain money by whichever means came easiest, including robbery and violence. For him street girls were a soft target and she presumed Cora had just become his latest victim.

Regardless of what she had heard about Kev Pike, Amber couldn't help but admit to herself that she found him attractive. Tall, good-looking and well-dressed, many of the girls aspired to be with him in spite of, or perhaps because of, his reputation. It gave them a buzz to be seen with somebody who instilled fear in so many people. But Amber was cautious and preferred to keep her distance.

Even though Cora had treated her badly, she pitied her. But she was also concerned. If he was targeting street girls near her spot, then she was worried he might seek her out too. She tried to put it out of her mind; his threat was one of the numerous risks that girls on the street had to face. But at least if she were aware of it, she could make sure she had her wits about her.

12

May 1997

Amy's mother had been with her current boyfriend for a few months. He was just one of many who her mother had dated over the last two years and Amy dared to hope that this time the relationship might last.

The man's name was Sean, but she had been told to call him uncle, just like the previous boyfriend. Amy recognised that he wasn't perfect; he and her mother rowed a lot, usually after they'd been drinking, but he often bought Amy gifts or gave her money, especially when he'd returned from the pub in one of his better moods.

This night Amy's mother, Loretta, had gone out with Sean leaving nine-year-old Amy in charge as the oldest child. Amy hadn't heard them return from the pub as she was asleep. But as she lay in her bed, a noise disturbed her. She listened keenly, trying to decipher what had woken her up.

It was distant and she couldn't quite fathom what it was or where it was coming from so she crept out of bed and onto the landing. She soon realised that the source of the noise was in her mother's room. Cautious about turning on the light and disturbing everybody, she tiptoed up to the bedroom door, feeling her way along the wall in the dark. Once she had reached the door, she listened carefully but she still couldn't recognise the sound.

As she stood there her heart was pounding. She was terrified of being discovered as her mother had told her many times that she must never go inside her bedroom under any circumstances. All seemed to go quiet for a few seconds so when she overheard a loud moaning Amy jumped back in shock.

She heard some shuffling and her mother asked, 'What was that?'

'What? I can't hear owt,' replied Sean.

'It might be one of the kids,' her mother said.

'I thought you said they're not allowed to come in here.'

'Well, they're not. But you never know.'

'Oh, for fuck's sake!' shouted Sean.

He sounded angry so Amy dashed back into her room as quietly as she could, diving under the quilt and pretending to be asleep. All seemed to go quiet again, but Amy couldn't sleep. She was troubled by the sounds she had heard, especially the loud moaning. It sounded like her mother, but Amy had never heard her moan like that before. What if Sean was hurting her? He did sound angry and Amy knew that he and her mother had had some ferocious rows over the past few weeks.

It was a while later and Amy was still awake. She was troubled, the thoughts going around in her head. She didn't like her mother bringing men home. The way they acted around her mother made Amy feel uncomfortable; the kisses and pats on the backside were too embarrassing.

And when they weren't doing that they were usually arguing, which Amy found upsetting. She wished life didn't have to be like this and that they could go back to the time before her mother had started bringing men into the house. It had been good then with just the three of them: her, her mother and Nathan.

When Amy had once asked her mother why it couldn't be just the three of them like it used to be, her mother had said that she couldn't manage on her own. Amy didn't know what she meant but she had a feeling it had something to do with money because the treats always stopped once the uncles were no longer around.

All of a sudden, she heard Sean yelling. He sounded even angrier now and she could also hear her mother pleading with him. But, instead of it calming him down, he seemed to grow even angrier. Her mother began arguing back as Amy lay in her bed with her heart thumping and her hands clenched.

Then she heard footsteps and she held her breath. She was frightened they might have heard her eavesdropping on the landing. What if they were going to punish her? As she heard her mother's bedroom door swing open her muscles tensed. But then she heard the heavy tread of footsteps on the stairs and let out the breath she'd been holding.

The footsteps were followed by the sound of a slamming door downstairs and then her mother sobbing. Amy sat up in bed wondering whether to go and see if her mother was alright. She crept out of her bed and onto the landing once more. To her surprise, her mother's bedroom door was ajar, but she didn't see Amy. She was lying on the bed, sobbing into her pillow, and Sean was no longer there.

Amy instinctively knew they'd had a big falling-out and she tentatively entered the room and walked over to her mother who looked up momentarily, her face blotchy and tear-stained. Amy took her mother's lack of words as a sign that she wasn't angry, and she sidled up to the bed and climbed in, flinging her tiny arms around her. Loretta turned and snuggled her sodden face into Amy's chest.

'You're such a good girl, Amy,' she said, her voice shaky.

They lay there for a few precious minutes, Amy feeling a bit awkward and not really knowing what to do or say to offer her mother comfort, other than to stay and hold her till they both drifted off to sleep.

Amy was late out of bed the following day, still tired from the events of the previous night. As she dragged her feet down the stairs, she could hear her mother's voice drifting up from the living room, and she guessed she was on the phone. Being a curious nine-year-old, Amy decided to eavesdrop, knowing her mother would probably be confiding in her best friend about what had happened.

She crept into the hall and stayed there, afraid to get too near to the living room in case her mother spotted her as the door wasn't fully shut.

'No, I'm not,' Amy overheard. 'He's not worth it. Anyway, it's been coming to a head for a few weeks. He's so bloody jealous of the kids and when he knew one of them was up and about, he went ballistic, frightened in case they came in the room while we were getting busy.'

Amy knew her mother was referring to her and what had happened the previous night. She felt a pang of fear, worried that her mother might blame her for the breakdown of the relationship and, as she listened to her mother's side of the conversation, she chewed her bottom lip nervously.

There was the sound of reluctant laughter before her mother spoke again. 'I know, I'm a fool to myself but I keep hoping this one will be different, that maybe one day I'll meet someone as good as Greg. They never bloody are though, are they? There's none of them can hold a candle to him. I just wish he'd had the sense to arrange some life insurance instead of leaving us in this mess.'

Then she paused a minute, as though listening to the person on the other end of the phone before she replied. 'I've got no bloody choice, have I? I can't manage on what the social security gives us. Anyway, it's nice to be taken out once in a while and treated.'

There was another pause then her mother said. 'Doing what? I'm not bloody trained for anything. I always thought Greg would be around to take care of everything. Well, who wouldn't? I certainly didn't expect him to die at that age. Anyway, even if I managed to find a job, I'd have to start on minimum pay so I'd probably be worse off than I am now.'

The conversation seemed to go on for a while, but Amy had heard enough so she went through to the kitchen and swung open one of the cupboard doors. While Amy helped herself to some cereal she thought about her mother's words. She didn't have any memories of her father, Greg, as he'd died from a heart attack when she was only two and her mother was heavily pregnant with Nathan. What Amy knew about him was mostly from what her mother had told her and a little from other people. She wished he had lived because, from what she had been told, he was a wonderful man and a highly successful bank manager.

Amy's mother said they hadn't wanted for anything when her dad was alive but after he'd died, they'd had to sell up and Amy had only scant memories of the house where they used to live in Cheadle. Then, as time went on, even renting a smaller house became a struggle and they were always short of money.

When Amy was settled at the dining table eating her breakfast her mother walked into the room.

'Oh, hello, love, how long have you been up?' she asked, sounding surprised.

'Not long,' said Amy, looking up and smiling tentatively at her mother who pulled up a chair next to her.

Loretta smiled back but Amy could tell she was doing it for her sake. She wished she could tell her that she didn't have to act happy and that it was OK to cry if she wanted but she knew it would sound stupid saying that to a grown-up. Her mother would probably tell her it was her job to look after her children and not the other way round, and Amy would feel silly.

Then her mother spoke, her voice sounding matter-of-fact but her face bearing an uncomfortable expression. 'Sean won't be coming here anymore.'

She smiled again and Amy, not quite knowing how she was expected to react, just muttered, 'Oh.'

'I'm afraid that means there'll be no treats for a while,' her mother continued.

Amy shrugged, knowing she'd miss them but glad there'd be an end to the arguments.

'Don't worry, I'll make it up to you once I can get some money together,' her mother added, ruffling her hair.

'It's OK,' said Amy, looking back down at her breakfast dish and loading up her spoon.

'Good girl,' said her mother, mussing her hair once more before getting up and walking away.

Amy had mixed feelings. On the one hand, she was glad to have Sean out of their lives; lately, he'd stopped treating them quite so much anyway, but the rows had become more frequent. On the other hand, though, she was afraid of what lay in store for them in the future. She knew it wouldn't be long before her mother brought another boyfriend home; she only hoped that the next one would be better.

13

September 2015

It was approaching the end of the night and Amber was in the shadows of the railway arches behind Piccadilly waiting for more business. Just one last punter should do it, she decided, then she would finish work and go back home. She was craving some coke and was deliberating whether to sneak into a nearby back alley and have a quick snort when a car pulled up.

Amber stepped forward but was too late. Another street girl had beaten her to it, and she watched, dismayed, as the girl stepped inside the car and the driver pulled away from the kerb. Knowing she couldn't wait until she was home, Amber made her way into the back alley.

She had only walked a few paces and was pulling the coke from her pocket when she heard footsteps behind her. She turned around to see a stranger heading her way. He was a youth – big, scruffy and wearing a hoody – but she didn't have chance to take in any other details before he made a grab for the small container of coke she was carrying.

Amber instinctively clung on tightly, her street girl resilience kicking in and her need of a fix overriding any common sense. But he was stronger than her and she felt the grasp of his huge hand, her fingers beginning to lose their grip as his nails dug into her flesh.

He yanked at the container, but she held on, sliding towards him with the force of his strength. She pulled back and for a fleeting moment their hands remained locked in the same position. She stared into the hard lines of his face, which displayed his steely determination.

He gave a huge tug on the container and her fingers slipped away. With nothing to drag against, her momentum sent her reeling backwards and she tumbled to the ground, her buttocks slamming hard against the flagstones. She was dazed and desperately trying to regain her senses. Anxious to get up. Wanting to run. But then he flicked out a knife and she drew back in shock.

'Give me your fuckin' cash!' he demanded.

'I haven't got any.'

'You fuckin' liar. I know you have. You've done at least four punters tonight.'

So, the bastard had been watching her! Waiting till she had earned enough money to make it worth his while. The shock realisation sent the adrenalin pumping around her body, priming her responses. She knew she'd lost. This was no chance mugging. The fuckin' scrote had planned it and there was no way she was getting away until she'd given him what he wanted.

'OK. OK!'

She held up a hand palm outwards, hoping he'd hold off till she got up off the ground. Once she was on her feet she reached into her pocket and pulled out the wad of cash she had earnt that night. She'd hardly brought it out into the open before he snatched it from her and sprinted back down the alleyway.

'Bastard!' she yelled, as she hobbled towards the street, bruised and utterly pissed off.

But the night wasn't over yet. As soon as she reached the mouth of the alleyway, she was greeted by the appearance of Kev Pike. 'Shit!' she cursed under her breath, dreading what he was about to do.

The incident had left her shaken and as she looked into Kev Pike's eyes, she anxiously worked the tender flesh of her bottom lip between her teeth. There was now a permanent cut there, in addition to her facial sores, which bore testimony to her life of drug abuse.

Kev, on the other hand, didn't have any facial sores although he did have the pale complexion common to drug users. Despite his good looks, he always wore a grave expression with his eyebrows scrunched and he seemed to stare down his nose at people as though he was analysing them.

'I saw him running off. Are you alright?' he asked.

His words took Amber completely by surprise. The last thing she had expected from Kev Pike was sympathy, and she relaxed slightly. Perhaps his grave expression was out of concern this time.

'Yeah, just a bit shaken up,' she said. 'But the bastard took all my cash.'

'I know. I saw it in his hands, but he was too far away for me to catch him.' There was a moment's hesitation before he spoke again. 'That's always a problem for you girls. You're vulnerable. These little twats know you've got cash on you, and you're an easy target for them.'

Amber shrugged.

'You don't need to put up with it, y'know,' he said. 'If you were my girl, I'd be able to protect you.'

His words drilled into her with the force of an impact driver. She was confused. Was he suggesting that she should have a relationship with him, or did he mean she'd be one of the girls he was protecting? Unsure, she decided to play safe. 'No, it's OK. I'm fine.'

He grinned disarmingly. 'Suit yourself. But don't say I didn't warn you.'

Amber stared at his retreating back, dazed for some moments. She didn't quite know what to make of it all. Was she putting herself at risk by refusing his protection? She wasn't sure. But then, on the other hand, by turning him down, she might be leaving herself more open to danger.

14

October 1997

Amy was perched on her mother's bed watching her applying makeup in preparation for a night out. Loretta was wearing a satin wrap and, as she got ready, she took regular sips from a glass of wine that was on the dressing table.

It was a rare privilege for Amy to be allowed inside her mother's bedroom and something that she could only do with her permission. She was fascinated at the way makeup transformed her mother's moderately attractive features into something that was captivating.

As Loretta swept the mascara along her lashes she chatted to Amy: 'I just hope this one's worth the effort. You can never tell with men.' Then she put the mascara brush back in its tube, turned around and smiled sardonically at Amy. 'You're too young to understand yet but you will in time.'

She turned back, took up a tube of bright red, glossy lipstick and applied it, pouting into the mirror to make sure she was happy with the results. For a few seconds Loretta admired her own reflection before standing up and flinging off her satin wrap.

Amy always felt a bit uncomfortable when her mother was in her underwear, but it didn't seem to bother Loretta at all. Despite her discomfort Amy couldn't help but look. Loretta was wearing a black lingerie set with accents of fiery red. The bra was plunging, the briefs satin with lace edging and the suspenders to match. She pulled a body con dress out of the wardrobe and slipped it over her head before smoothing it over her curves.

The dress sat just above the knee and was strappy and low-cut at the front. Loretta stood in front of the mirror and twisted and turned, admiring her slim but curvaceous figure from every angle as she pulled in her tummy then adjusted her cleavage.

'Well, what do you think?' she asked.

'You look lovely, Mummy.'

Her mother preened, grabbed a pair of high heels from the wardrobe then headed for the bedroom door. With the makeup and change of clothes came a total mood switch. Loretta had gone from moping around the house to a state of animation, full of anticipation for her forthcoming meeting with a new man.

Amy followed her mother downstairs where they found Nathan in the lounge watching a *Dexter's Laboratory* video. Amy was fed up of seeing the same programme, but she knew there was no point in arguing as Nathan nearly always got his own way.

'Aw, you watching *Dexter* again, love?' asked Loretta but Nathan ignored her, his eyes fixed on the screen in front of him.

Loretta stepped closer to him. 'It's your favourite programme, isn't it, love? Do you like him because he's clever like you?'

Then she patted his head affectionately. 'Take after your dad, don't you, love? You're going to do well when you grow up, just like him. And you'll earn lots of money so you can look after me in my old age.' She laughed as though it was meant as a joke, but Amy knew it wasn't.

Loretta was now near the door and putting on her coat, which she had grabbed from the hall. As she slipped her arms into the sleeves, she issued a set of instructions. 'Right, now I want you both in bed for nine. Are you listening, Nathan? Look at me.'

She stepped over to the clock on the mantelpiece, grabbing the attention of both of her children as she pointed to the clock face. 'When that little hand is on the nine and the big hand is on the twelve, I want you both in bed.'

'I know, Mum. You've told us before,' said Nathan, switching his attention back to the TV.

'Right, well make sure you do. I want you both asleep when I get home, and no answering the door to anybody, do you hear?'

When the children had agreed to her instructions, Loretta planted a quick peck on each of their faces and then she was gone.

Once her mother had left the house, Amy's first reaction was to walk over to the video player and flick out the *Dexter* video her brother had been watching.

'Hey, what are you doing? I was watching that.'

Amy smiled sarcastically. 'Not anymore, you're not. I'm having a turn.'

'But Mum said I could watch what I want. She didn't give you permission.'

'Well, she's not here now so I don't need permission, do I?'

Amy enjoyed seeing the petulant look on her brother's face. She knew she was being mean, but she was so fed up of seeing him get preferential treatment that she took the opportunity to get one up on him whenever she could. She knew he wouldn't fight back physically; he knew he'd come off worse as Amy was two years older and bigger than him.

Instead he jumped up off the sofa and stamped over to the door. 'Bitch! I'll tell Mum about this tomorrow and you'll be in trouble.'

'Do what you like,' said Amy.

'You're just jealous 'cos Mum likes me more than you 'cos I'm cleverer and I'm a boy.'

Amy took no notice. She'd heard it all before. She knew it was her mother's fault for letting him think he was something special and she wished there were a way she could stop it. But there wasn't. She was just a child and she had to take whatever was handed to her.

Amy switched from video mode to TV and watched a bit of *Brookside*, but she couldn't really concentrate on what was happening on screen. Her mind was too occupied with other things. She focused on her mother and her ever-changing love life.

Since Loretta had split up with Sean several months previously, she had gone through a series of different men. But none of them had lasted long. In fact, as time went on, they seemed to stay around even less. Some of them Amy didn't even get to meet but she knew they'd stayed the night as she would hear them leave early the following morning amidst hushed conversations with her mother.

Amy had grown used to her mother's mood swings: up one minute at the prospect of a new date but then down when the phone didn't ring. She had become programmed to it, recognising that her mother's future happiness and prosperity was dependant on finding the right man. So, as she sat there going over everything in her young mind, Amy desperately hoped that this one would be nice to them and that he would be the one who would make her mother happy forever.

15

October 1997

It was a few nights later and Loretta was out again. Amy didn't know if she was out with the same man as last time or with a different one, but she had learnt not to ask too many questions. Her mother only told her what she wanted Amy to know and if she didn't want her to know then she would tell Amy that she shouldn't be asking such questions at her age.

Amy had been curious for some time about her mother's bedroom. It seemed strange to her that she wasn't allowed in there. She had told her friends about it at school and they agreed that it wasn't right. Apparently, they were allowed in their parents' bedrooms any time provided they knocked on the door if it was shut while their parents were in there.

While Nathan was occupied watching one of his favourite shows on the downstairs TV, Amy thought she would take the opportunity to explore. Apart from being curious, she had often admired her mother's makeup and clothing and wanted to have a good look at them.

She started at the dressing table where the makeup products were scattered haphazardly with smudges of mascara and a faint dusting of blusher littering the tabletop. She took a lipstick and opened the container. Then she wound the bottom up like she had seen her mother do until the lipstick was poking out. It was a lovely bright red colour and Amy was drawn to it.

Giving in to temptation, she put some on her lips and glanced in the mirror, hoping for the transformation she had seen on her mother's face. But she had missed her lips' natural outline and the lipstick looked silly. Unperturbed, she opened the blusher next and used the brush to dab some on her cheeks. Again, it didn't look the same as is it did on her mother and as Amy stared in the mirror she decided she looked more like one of her dolls than a woman made up to go on a night out. Perhaps that was why makeup was really for grown-ups – because it only looked right on them.

Ignoring the failed attempt at making up her face, she went over to the wardrobe and riffled through her mother's outfits. She loved admiring the fashionable styles and bright colours, especially the glittery ones that her mother wore over Christmas. Her favourite was a short red dress that was all sparkly and made from swishy material with sequins sewn onto it. She remembered her mother wearing it last New Year.

She took the dress out of the wardrobe and held it up to herself, spinning around in a circle and taking delight in the way the material floated on the air. It must feel wonderful to dance in a dress like that, she thought, before placing it carefully back in the wardrobe and hoping her mother wouldn't notice that her clothes had been disturbed.

Next Amy went through the shoes that were lined up on a rack at the bottom of the wardrobe. She selected a black pair with a peep toe and high heels, and she put them on. Wondering what it was like to walk in shoes like that she took a few tentative steps across the bedroom floor.

She was disturbed by the sound of someone on the stairs and for a few nervous seconds she held her breath, desperately hoping that her mother hadn't come home early. As she heard the footsteps pass near to her mother's bedroom she felt as though her heart would explode in her chest. Expecting the door to open any moment she stood tense and rigid. But then the footsteps faded, and she figured it was her brother going into his bedroom. A few seconds later she heard him go back downstairs and, relieved, she carried on trying out her mother's shoes.

Once she had grown tired of that, Amy went over to the chest of drawers and had a rummage through them. She pulled one of her mother's bras out of the top drawer and put her arms through the straps, giggling when she looked at her reflection in the mirror.

There was nothing else of interest in the drawers – just pullovers, T-shirts and other everyday clothing – until she got to the bottom drawer. Surprised to see some sort of toys in her mother's bedroom along with other items, Amy knelt on the carpet and peered at them.

One was a black ring with little lumps on one side of it. She wasn't sure what it could be, so she pulled it out of the drawer to take a closer look. But she was confused so she put it on the bed and then pulled out the next item. This one was long and pink with a switch at one end of it. She pressed the switch and it juddered in her hand, making her jump in shock and drop it. She quickly switched it off and put that on the bed as well.

Amy was just about to take out another item when she heard voices coming from downstairs. She wondered who her brother could be talking to; perhaps he was on the phone. But then one of the voices drew closer and she recognised it instantly as her mother's.

As soon as Amy heard, 'I'll go and see what your sister's up to,' she panicked.

Her first thought was to put the shoes away and remove the makeup. She quickly shoved the high heels inside the wardrobe and shut the door. Then she thought about the makeup; her mother would be furious if she knew she'd been using it. Amy tried to wipe it off as quickly as she could using the back of her hand but when she looked in the mirror, she found that all she had managed to do was to smear it across her face.

Her clown-like reflection in the mirror almost reduced her to tears of desperation but then she spotted a box of cosmetic tissues on the dressing table and grabbed one. She was rubbing away at the makeup when the bedroom door opened and in walked her mother with an expression of fury emblazoned across her face.

'Just what the bloody hell do you think you're up to, young lady?' her mother raged.

Amy stared at her, open-mouthed in shock and with her bottom lip trembling, but she was unable to utter any words of defence. As well as guilt she was besieged by a feeling of shame, which was emphasised by her outlandish appearance.

'How dare you interfere with my things? How many

times have I told you not to go in my room without my permission? And do you realise how bloody ridiculous you look?'

Her mother was furious, and Amy felt afraid. She had rarely seen her mother this angry and it startled her; normally she was so nice to her. She opened her mouth to speak again. 'Sorry, Mummy,' she managed in a tiny voice.

'Don't you bloody *Mummy* me. You're nine years of age, not a baby. You should know better!'

Then Loretta's eyes shot to something on the bed and she glared at the items as though she couldn't quite believe what she was seeing. She marched across the room and grabbed hold of the weird toys, pushing them into the bottom drawer as she continued to remonstrate with Amy.

'You shouldn't be looking at things like this. For God's sake! These are private. They're not for little girls.'

Her voice was loud and whiny, and Amy picked up on her distress. As she drew nearer Amy could also smell the alcohol on her breath and could tell something about her was different. She had that strange face she got after drinking wine where her cheeks were flushed and puffy.

'I'm sorry, M-mum. I won't do it again. Honest.'

Loretta swung around, the look of anger on her face now suffused with something else. Guilt? Embarrassment? Amy couldn't put the right words to it. She didn't know what it meant but it was all a bit strange. She had never seen her mother like this before and it was scaring her.

'You bet you bloody won't because you're staying in your room for the rest of tonight and all of tomorrow, too. Now get out of my sight and get my bloody makeup off your face. You look pathetic!'

Amy shuffled out of the room, her eyes downcast and filled with tears. Once inside her own room she let the tears spill over and carried on crying for a while. It wasn't the fact that she had been caught out that had upset her; it was the way her mother had reacted. Amy was already aware that she was second best to Nathan, and she feared that this would only make matters worse.

Something major had just happened. Amy wasn't sure exactly what, but she did know that she had really upset her mother. Why? What had she done that was so bad? She had only wanted to have a look. She couldn't understand why her mother was so angry. If she hadn't come back early, she would never have even known that she had been trying her things on. Then she puzzled over why her mother had come back so early. Perhaps she had had a falling-out with her latest boyfriend. It wouldn't be the first time.

With that thought in mind Amy settled down to get some sleep. But she couldn't help but fret over what had just happened. She was convinced there was something not quite right. There was a whole secret side to her mother's life, and the world inhabited by adults seemed alien to her at times. Her mother's scolding had unsettled Amy so much that she wasn't sure she wanted to become a grown-up anymore. And she certainly didn't want to do the things that grown-ups did if that's how they made you feel.

16

September 2015

Amber was surprised to see an open bottle of pills on the coffee table when she walked into the living room the following afternoon. Before she had chance to check what they were, her brother, Nathan, walked in carrying a glass of water and snatched them away.

'Keep your fuckin' mitts off,' he hissed.

Amber looked at Nathan who was as dark as she was fair. He took after his father in appearance, which their mother was fond of reminding them. Nathan had classic good looks with strong, well-defined features and was just above average height. He was also better dressed than she was and kept himself well groomed.

She didn't want to get into a confrontation with him. Still tired and unsettled from the previous night, Amber just wanted to grab something to eat before she got ready for work again, so she tried to ignore his aggressive attitude as she said, 'Oh, it's you. Where's Mum?'

'Out shopping for food. I know, I couldn't fuckin' believe it either.'

Amber knew that meant there wouldn't be much food in the house again until her mother returned, and she resigned herself to grabbing something from a takeaway while she was out. Nathan swallowed down two pills with the glass of water.

'What the fuck did you want with headache tablets anyway?' he asked. 'I thought coke was more your style.' Amber's eyes shot up in surprise. 'Oh yeah, don't think I didn't fuckin' know. I've seen all that shit in your bedroom, and the lighter and spoon. I'm not stupid. But you are. Don't you know crack is the most potent form of cocaine?'

Amber knew full well the effects of crack. She had graduated to it after snorting coke for some time and now she took both. But she wasn't going to get into a conversation with Nathan about it.

'You shouldn't be in my fuckin' room! Keep out.'

'I'll do what the fuck I want seeing as how I'm the only person who works for a living in this shithole.'

Amber was sick to death of hearing about his job, which he'd started a couple of years ago after graduating from university. He had been bad enough to live with before but now that he was working as a trainee accountant, he had become unbearable. Every chance he got he was denigrating her lifestyle and lording it over her.

'I work too,' she snapped.

'If you can call that work! Up to date with your tax and national insurance, are you? No, I thought not because you don't fuckin' pay any, do you? What's your job description anyway? Tart? Slapper? Dirty fuckin' junkie who'll do anything to feed her habit.'

Nathan was really starting to annoy her. 'Shut the fuck up!' she yelled.

'No, I won't. You make me fuckin' sick. Do you realise what it's like to have a family like you two? Why do you think I never bring anyone back? Because I'm too ashamed, that's why. Look at the state of the place. I would have thought at least one of you could clean it up once in a while.'

'Why don't you fuckin' clean it up?'

'Because it isn't up to me. Like I said, I work for a living!'

Amber had had enough. 'Don't take it out on me just because you don't fuckin' feel well. It's alright to be given the chance of a fancy education so you can get a good job, isn't it? But I never had that fuckin' chance!'

She was screaming at him now and tears of fury were threatening to erupt. But she didn't get any sympathy from Nathan who had always refused to see things from her point of view.

He was just about to retaliate when their mother walked into the house. 'Oh, I can't be fuckin' doing with her as well,' he muttered before he stormed out.

'What's wrong with him?' asked Loretta as she passed the living room door laden with shopping. Then, before Amber had chance to answer, she carried on, 'Help me get this lot away will you, love?'

Amber followed her into the kitchen and began unpacking the bags. Her mother left her to it and went upstairs. Great, thought Amber who had been planning to get ready for work. But at least now she could have something to eat before she left the house.

A quick scan of the shopping bags left her disappointed. There were just a few essentials, but it was enough for her to make a sandwich and a cup of tea, so she quickly rustled them up then went through to the living room. Her mother hadn't come back downstairs yet so she sat alone for some minutes, still reeling from the argument she'd had with her brother.

She hated the way he acted towards her and for a few moments she sat thinking about the injustice of it all. How she wished she'd had the same opportunities as Nathan. She'd always known from a young age that her mother viewed them both differently and as time went on Amber had grown to resent it more and more. She wished she could break away from the drugs and not have to resort to prostitution. But she couldn't. She was stuck with it and there was no escape.

17

Amy had heard about nothing else but Dale from her mother for the past few weeks. Sean was now a distant memory as were the various other men who had filled Loretta's life since her split with him months ago. Dale was apparently an executive for a company that imported machinery and, although Amy wasn't exactly sure what that entailed, she could tell that her mother was very proud of that fact.

Her mother had been so much happier since she met Dale, and Amy loved it when her mother was happy and being nice to her and Nathan. She also knew that his presence in Loretta's life would mean better food, more gifts and other goodies. Amy cast her mind back to her tenth birthday several weeks prior, recalling her disappointment when she hadn't received the presents she really wanted, and she couldn't help but share her mother's enthusiasm for her potential new 'uncle'.

It was now the day on which Loretta had decided

her children should meet the new man in her life and, at her insistence, they were wearing their best clothes in readiness for his arrival. Loretta had made a special effort and cooked a three-course Italian meal, harking back to a more prosperous time of dinner parties with well-to-do professional types.

'Now don't forget, Amy,' said her mother, 'I don't want anything out of place. Dale is a really special man and we need to make sure that we create a good impression.'

As Amy set the table, Nathan sat watching, his irritation evident as Loretta straightened his hair, and he continuously tried to pull the collar of his too-tight shirt away from his throat.

'Aw, Mum,' he complained. 'Can't I undo the top button?'

'No, Nathan, I've told you before, you're to keep it fastened like a good boy. We don't want Dale thinking we're a scruffy lot, do we?'

'But it's too tight, Mum.'

'Well, you never know, you might get some new clothes soon enough, but only if you're on your best behaviour. I want Dale to see what lovely children you are.'

She planted a kiss on the top of his head, the action making him scowl rather than smile but, despite his discomfort and his annoying whining, Amy could tell that her brother was looking forward to meeting this new visitor too. If he was as wonderful as her mother claimed, then Amy felt confident that the fortunes of their family were about to improve.

Once Amy had done everything to her mother's satisfaction, Loretta suggested that she and Nathan should go through to the living room and watch some TV while she kept an eye on the food. 'And when you hear the doorbell, stay where you are and wait for me to answer it,' she insisted. 'I don't want you two getting overexcited.'

But it was obvious to Amy that, despite the impression her mother was trying to create of casual indifference, she was also excited. In fact, she seemed a bit on edge too as she continually fussed over their appearances and kept checking on the food that was cooking.

When the doorbell rang, Amy looked up from the programme she was only half watching on the TV to see her mother scurrying down the hallway. But she didn't answer the door straightaway. Instead she hovered close to the living room entrance holding her forefinger to her lips in a shushing motion. Amy had seen her mother keep men waiting like that before.

When she eventually answered the door, Amy could hear a man's voice followed by her mother's. 'Oh, Dale, you shouldn't have. That's really lovely of you.' Then, after a pause, she said, 'Come and meet the children. They're in here.'

Amy looked up from the TV again when her mother entered the living room with a tall, well-dressed man. She was clutching a bottle of wine in one hand and a bunch of flowers in the other. Dale was quite handsome and, although his looks were by no means outstanding, he had a kind face. He was wearing fitted jeans and a smart overcoat, which was unfastened revealing a lightweight pullover underneath, and he was holding a carrier bag with something inside.

'This is my daughter, Amy,' said Loretta, 'and that's my son, Nathan.'

A nod of Loretta's head told the children what was

required of them and Amy and Nathan approached Dale and took turns in shaking his hand. 'Pleased to meet you,' they choused.

'Oh, Loretta, what lovely polite children you have,' he said. Then he fished two bars of chocolate out of the carrier bag and passed Amy and Nathan one each.

'Yeah!' Nathan gushed as he tried to pull off the wrapper that covered the bar of chocolate.

'Erm, haven't you forgotten something?' prompted Loretta.

Nathan looked up at Dale, shamefaced. 'Thanks,' he said, which reminded Amy to do the same.

'I'll take them for now,' said Loretta. 'You need to eat your tea first.'

Amidst Nathan's half-hearted protests, Amy kept quiet. She knew it was a waste of time protesting. She'd get the chocolate in good time, but she knew she had to play along with her mother's wishes first.

Loretta held out her hand, pointing to an armchair, 'Take a seat, Dale. I'll just go and put the finishing touches to the dinner and make myself look ravishing.' As she spoke the last words, she tugged at the apron she was wearing.

'No need,' he replied, smiling. 'You already do.'

Then their mother disappeared into the kitchen leaving Amy and Nathan with Dale for the next few minutes.

'What's this you're watching?' he asked.

'*Dexter's*,' muttered Nathan, keeping his eyes fixed on the screen and leaving Amy to take up the conversation.

'It's his favourite. It's about a boy called Dexter who has a secret laboratory in his bedroom.' Then she sniggered. 'He has an older sister who always spoils things for him.'

'Interesting,' said Dale. 'And what do you like to watch?'

Amy smiled, flattered that he was showing an interest in her. He seemed a nice, friendly man who smiled a lot, and he spoke a bit posh like her mother. And he'd brought them chocolates, which was definitely helping to win her over. Amy didn't talk posh like her mother; she spoke more like the kids where she lived but he didn't seem to mind that she spoke different to him, unlike some of the local kids who often asked why her mother spoke that way.

For the next few minutes Amy chatted to him about school, her friends and her favourite foods while Nathan continued to stare fixedly at the TV screen. Dale took an avid interest in everything she had to say, and Amy couldn't help but feel a little smug that finally she was the special one rather than her brother.

In fact, Amy much preferred him to Sean, who had seemed to resent her and Nathan, or to any of the other men that Loretta had brought into their lives. It seemed that perhaps their mother had finally met the man she had been searching for all these years.

18

It was a Saturday morning and Loretta was waiting for Dale to arrive. They hadn't seen him for two weeks. From what Amy had been told he lived in Harrogate and regularly travelled to Manchester on business or sometimes just came for the weekend.

Because it was sometimes up to two weeks between visits, the house would always be filled with eager anticipation when he was due to arrive. But this time he was a day late and, as well as Loretta's usual enthusiasm, she was full of nervous energy. Amy watched as her mother continually tidied the house, plumping up cushions and wiping away tiny spots of dust in between gazing through the window.

But Amy wasn't worried. She knew Dale wouldn't let them down. He was the best 'uncle' she'd ever had. Gifts were never in short supply when Dale was around.

Dale had even won Nathan round and he was now much

more willing to chat with him instead of ignoring him while he watched the TV. But Amy knew she was his favourite. He always seemed to know just what sort of things she liked because he took the trouble to ask. He seemed to take an interest in everything she and Nathan did, and had endless patience.

When the doorbell rang, Amy and Nathan could hardly contain their exhilaration. Nathan even broke away from the TV screen while he raced Amy to the front door. But Loretta stopped them before they reached the hallway.

'No you don't! We don't want Dale thinking I've raised a couple of wild animals. Go and sit down quietly and give him a chance to get in the house. He's travelled a long way and will probably want to settle with a nice cup of tea rather than have you two pestering him.'

They did as they were told and Amy waited patiently with one eye on the living room door, watching for Dale. Her mother seemed to take an age to answer the door and Amy could picture her checking her appearance in the hallway mirror first.

Eventually Dale appeared at the living room door. 'Well, aren't I getting a hug from my best girl?' he asked.

Amy looked at her mother for approval and when she smiled half-heartedly Amy jumped up off her seat and ran across the room, flinging her arms around him.

'What about you, Nathan?' asked Dale and within seconds both children were hugging Dale tightly.

'OK,' said Loretta. 'Let Dale sit down now. I'll go and put the kettle on.'

'Not until I tell you all that I've got in store for you,'

said Dale. Amy and Nathan released their hold and looked up at him, waiting to hear what he had to say. 'Well, I know you were disappointed because I was a day late so, as a special treat, I've decided to take you all for a day out. We'll go to the science museum in Manchester. I believe it's very good.'

'Yay!' shouted Nathan and Dale ruffled his hair.

'Isn't that for boys?' asked Amy.

'Not at all. There's plenty of things there for us all to enjoy, apparently. And there's a restaurant there too so, as an even bigger treat, we'll have our lunch with cake afterwards. Oh, and here's something else you might like.'

He handed Amy and Nathan a carrier bag each and they both grasped excitedly at the gifts inside.

'Brilliant! Thanks,' yelled Nathan, examining the toy car that he was clutching.

But Amy was more interested in her own present. It was a set of hair accessories, all sparkly bows, hair slides and scrunchies, and she was overjoyed.

'Thank you, Uncle Dale,' she said, smiling at him.

Then she rushed to open the packaging and try out some of the hair slides in the hallway mirror. Yet again, Dale had walked into their home, bringing with him the joy that always accompanied his visits. Not only did he cheer her and Nathan up, but her mother was also happier when he was around. In fact, she behaved more like her old self instead of going out drinking and leaving them alone in the house.

*

January 1999

It was more than a year since Loretta had met Dale, and he was still a fixture in their lives and the whole family were much happier because of it. Loretta often went around the house singing, giving Amy and Nathan impromptu hugs and telling them how special they were.

Amy's eleventh birthday had come and gone several weeks prior complete with lavish presents and her own party at a local social club. Birthday parties were something her mother hadn't been able to afford for many years and Amy knew it made her mother happy now that she could.

This particular evening, Dale hadn't been to the house for three weeks, because, according to Amy's mother, he had been too busy with work. Loretta told Amy and Nathan that she was preparing a lovely meal for him and she served their dinner separately beforehand. Then she busied herself at the oven and, once Amy had helped her set the table, she adorned it with candles in fancy holders and bottled wine on trivets.

Amy sensed that he was late. She didn't like to ask her mother about it, but she noticed how long the table had been set as well as the number of times Loretta had checked her watch. She also knew there had been two opened bottles of wine on the table earlier but now there was only one, and her mother was slurring her words.

Loretta was becoming irritable with her as well. Where she had been happy for Amy to help in the kitchen earlier, now she just wanted her out of the way.

'For God's sake, Amy, why don't you go into the living

room and watch some TV with your brother?' she pleaded when Amy had tried to strike up conversation with her at the dining table.

She looked across at her mother who was sitting at the table with her chin cupped between her hands. Amy noticed the way this made the flesh scrunch up around Loretta's mouth and caused tiny lines to form at the sides of her eyes. This, together with Loretta's downturned eyebrows made her appear older and dowdy despite the abundance of makeup.

Amy did as she was told, and she hadn't been in the living room long when the phone rang. She got up to answer it but, as she did so, she heard her mother shout, 'Leave it, I'll get it.' Then she saw her dash past the living room entrance, making her way to the phone that sat on a small table in the hallway.

It was noticeable to Amy how quickly her mother had rushed to answer the phone. Amy strained to listen to the conversation, but she couldn't pick out any sentences, just the odd word and her mother's glum tone of voice.

Then Loretta slammed down the phone and dashed back to the kitchen, her head bent forward. Amy didn't know what to do at first. It seemed that her mother was upset over something and she wanted to find out what, but she was wary of being rebuked again. She looked across at her brother who was staring fixedly at the TV screen, oblivious to what was going on around him.

Amy knew there was no point in conferring with Nathan so after a while she decided to venture into the kitchen to find out what was wrong. There she found her mother sitting at the dining table. It was as though she had never moved except that this time her chin was nestled on only one of her hands. The other was clutching a tissue, which she was using to dab at her eyes.

Amy dashed towards her and placed her tiny arms around Loretta's shoulders. 'Mum, what's wrong?' she asked.

Loretta began to sob, and Amy could feel her shoulders juddering with the might of her sorrow as she clung on, not knowing what else to do. When it seemed that Loretta's sobbing would never subside, Amy became distressed. 'Mum?' she asked, pleadingly. 'Mum, what's wrong?'

She watched as Loretta raised her head, then she let go of her and stood back waiting for an explanation. Loretta dabbed at her eyes once more and blew her nose into the tissue before squaring her shoulders.

'I'll tell you what's wrong,' she said. 'That bastard Dale's gone back to his wife and kids. That's what's bloody wrong!'

Amy was shocked at her mother's bad language and didn't know what to say. For a few painful seconds she hovered close by, watching as her mother's head slumped forwards again and her sobbing resumed. Then the implications of their new reduced circumstances hit Amy and thoughts began to crowd her mind; it was goodbye to presents and abundance, and a return to making do and going without. She also feared that it was goodbye to her happy, affable mother.

Amy succumbed to the sheer despair of it all and her own tears surfaced. Her mother reached out and pulled her towards her again and for a few minutes they remained

HEATHER BURNSIDE

locked in a sorrowful embrace. Nobody spoke but Amy shared her mother's sadness. Dale had made such a positive impact on their lives and with him no longer around she dreaded to think what lay in store for the three of them now.

19

September 2015

Amber hadn't been at her usual spot long when Kev Pike pulled up in a black BMW. Despite herself, she couldn't help but be impressed. With his smart gear and good looks the flash car seemed the perfect fit. He wound down the window and called her over.

'You OK?' he asked when she approached the car.

'Yeah, why wouldn't I be?'

'Well, I know what you girls have to put up with. You seem a nice girl, Amber, and I wouldn't want anything bad to happen to you.'

Thinking he was offering protection, she responded sharply, 'I told you, I'm fine. I've been working the streets for years. I'm used to it. I can handle the punters.'

'OK, suit yourself,' he said. 'But the offer's still there if you want it.'

Then he drove off, leaving Amber wondering again about his motives. For somebody with such a hardman reputation, he seemed to be taking a soft approach with her. Was it because he genuinely liked her or was he just trying to lull her into a false sense of security?

Later that night she noticed Cora in the distance. She was heading towards her accompanied by a male. As they drew closer, Amber saw that the person with Cora was big, scruffy-looking and wearing a hoody. It was the youth who had robbed her. Her fight-or-flight response kicked in and Amber took to her heels. She could feel rapid footsteps coming from behind, and her heartbeat sped up as she was consumed by fear.

In her haste to get away, Amber turned off the main street and into another road where she dashed into a lengthy railway tunnel. It was dark and dreary, its grimy stone walls and moss-covered pavements exposing years of neglect, and the place was deserted. Amber cursed her choice of footwear, a pair of high heels, which slowed her progress. As she sped through the eerie tunnel, she could hear nothing but her own shallow breaths and the sound of running feet drawing closer.

Once through the tunnel Amber rounded the corner into the next street. It was one she recognised through her work. She was no sooner there than she felt someone grasp at the hair on the back of her head. Still she carried on running, shouting for help as loud as she could and hoping somebody would hear. But there was still no one around. This street was more deserted than the last, which was why Amber sometimes took clients there. But this time, its abandonment worked against her.

It wasn't long until her pursuer caught up with her again, grabbing at her shoulder until Amber was forced to a stop, sensing the pointlessness of carrying on. She swivelled around and looked into the scabby face of the youth who grinned in satisfaction as he gripped on tightly. Amber's lungs screamed in pain as she panted for breath. At the same time, she became aware of his offensive body odour and the sight of Cora a few steps away, running to catch up with them.

'Hold on to her, Jack!' she shouted breathlessly.

While Jack's attention switched to Cora, Amber made a last attempt at escape, tugging against his grip, which had now slackened. But she didn't get very far before Jack had her in his clutches again. He thrust her up against the wall and Amber felt the back of her head slam against the bricks, the impact making her dizzy.

Before Amber could recover, Cora had joined them. 'Give her a fuckin' good hiding, Jack! That'll teach her not to run off.'

Without pausing Jack continued to bash Amber's body repeatedly against the wall. At first all she felt was light-headedness, the solidness of the stone and her intense fear. But as Jack carried on, and Amber regained her balance, the agony took hold. She pushed her head forward, trying to avoid the wall, but was rewarded with a sharp slap across her face. For a moment she didn't know where it had come from. Then she spotted the smug grin on Cora's face and saw her hand snap back for a repeat.

The beating seemed to last forever and yet it was quick. Blasts of hard knuckles and fleshy hands bruised and ruptured the soft skin of Amber's face and body, and soon she sensed the metallic taste of blood on her lips.

Unable to break free, she begged, 'Please, no!' and sobbed.

But it wasn't over yet. The blows were so rapid that it

was difficult to tell who was doing what. She felt the force of sharp kicks to her shins and thighs along with rapid slaps to her face and upper body till she could take no more and her legs collapsed, sending her sliding down the wall while the attack persisted.

For a few moments longer she was on the ground, crouched forward now, and willing it to be over. The sight of her like this must have unnerved Cora who yelled an order at Jack.

'OK, that's enough!'

Amber could sense someone leaning over her then she felt her hair being tugged violently until her head was raised from the ground. Her eyes flickered open and she stared into the evil face of Cora whose own eyes burned with hatred.

'That'll teach you not to get cocky with me!' she hissed. Then she yelled instructions at Jack again. 'Get her up off the ground so we can search her.'

Amber felt herself being lifted and Jack's big, rough hands searching around her body until he found her wad of cash. He smirked at Cora who grinned back. Then they let go of her and walked away, jubilant.

October 2015

'Oh my God! What the hell happened to you?' asked Sapphire when Amber walked into the Rose and Crown a few days later and went straight across to the table where Sapphire was sitting.

Her shocked expression drew the attention of other customers who stared at Amber's bruised and swollen face.

'Shush!' said Amber, fearful of repercussions.

She waited until the customers had got over the initial shock and were no longer focused on her before she confided in Sapphire about the attack. Her friend's alarm was evident as her eyes grew wide and her jaw slackened.

'Oh my God!' Sapphire repeated. 'I knew she was a bit of a bitch, but I never thought she'd go that far. Are you OK?'

'Better than I was.'

'Your face looks really sore.'

'It's my fuckin' head that's the worst. That bastard who was with her kept slamming it against the wall. There's a big lump on the back of it. I thought I was gonna pass out the first time he did it. My legs are full of bruises too. They kept kicking them even when I was on the ground.'

'Shit! They've beat you up summat wicked, haven't they? Did they get what they wanted?'

'Oh yeah, the pair of twats took all my earnings for the night and I've missed out for the last few days too 'cos I felt too shitty to work. But I've had to come back. I've run out of gear.'

'Aw, mate. I can help you out with that.'

'Aw, can you?' asked Amber, desperately.

'Sure, let's nip to the loos,' Sapphire whispered.

Once she'd had her fix they went back into the bar, Amber eager to top it up with a few drinks before she spent her first night back at work. She couldn't help but feel worried considering what had happened the last time, and Sapphire seemed to pick up on her glum mood.

'You OK?' she asked.

'Yeah but... y'know.'

Sapphire nodded. 'I know; it can't be easy. I was just

thinking about what it used to be like before and what Crystal would have thought about what's happened to you. I miss her, y'know.'

'Me too. She was always good to talk to when you had problems. It doesn't feel the same without her still around and a lot of the old girls. Even Ruby was alright if you stayed on the right side of her. And she wouldn't stand any fuckin' nonsense. I bet Cora wouldn't have tried it on with her around.'

'No way!'

'I still remember when Crystal first recruited me for Gilly and got me to change my name to Amber. We all had to have the names of jewels 'cos she said Gilly liked his girls to sound exotic.'

Sapphire laughed. 'Me too. Funny how we've kept the names even though he's long gone, isn't it?'

'Yeah, but it's what the clients get used to, isn't it? I never saw any point in changing it.'

'Me neither. I tell you what, I wasn't that keen on Gilly and the way he used to take a big wedge of our money, but he wouldn't have stood for all this shit from Cora either.'

'Yeah,' said Amber. 'I definitely felt a sight fuckin' safer when he was around. At least he didn't just take the money; he did try to protect us as well.

'Anyway, it is what it is, and we're stuck with it. But I'd change your patch if I were you and watch your back. It wouldn't surprise me if that bitch Cora puts him onto you next.'

'Thanks for the tip,' said Sapphire before they continued the conversation, reminiscing about the old days.

Amber knew she was stalling for time. The truth was

that, despite the coke and alcohol she had consumed, she didn't want to leave the relative safety of the pub and go back on the streets again. She was terrified. But then the conversation gradually ran out and Sapphire announced that she was off to work.

Amber said her goodbyes then checked the time. It was already far later than the time she usually went to work. She needed to go. There was no point sitting around here on her own downing more drink while she tried to pluck up the courage.

And it didn't matter how much drugs and alcohol she'd consumed because Amber would still be frightened. So, in the end, she finished her drink and set off through the shady backstreets of Manchester, dreading encountering her attackers once more.

20

March 1999

It was midday on Saturday and Loretta still wasn't up. Amy knew it had been late when her mother had gone to bed the previous evening as she'd heard her come in. She'd made a lot of racket and had been mumbling to herself. Amy couldn't tell what she'd been saying but, once she'd heard her mother on the upstairs landing, she'd closed her eyes, pulled the duvet around her shoulders and pretended to be asleep. She hadn't wanted her mother coming into her room and waffling on drunkenly about nonsense, which she'd got into a habit of doing lately.

Amy had already pulled the washing out of the machine, which had been in there since the previous day, and she'd hung it outside. Then she'd tidied up the kitchen that her mother had left in a mess the previous night. She was putting the last of the plates away when she heard her mother stir.

It had been a few weeks since Dale had left them and, despite being upset, Amy had accepted his departure and adjusted to their reduced circumstances. It was the change in her mother that she was finding more difficult to cope with. Loretta's tears had lasted longer than with any other relationship break-up and when they had finally subsided, they were replaced by bitterness and apathy.

When Loretta appeared in the kitchen, she had bed hair, and her face was pale and smudged with remnants of last night's makeup. Amy always marvelled at how her mother could switch from glamorous to shoddy within the space of a night.

'Put the kettle on will you, Amy?' she muttered as she trudged across to the dining table and plonked herself on a chair. 'Jesus Christ! My bloody head's throbbing. Fetch me my tablets, will you?'

Amy flicked the kettle on and reached inside a drawer for her mother's prescription tablets as well as some paracetamol. She didn't know exactly what the prescription tablets were, but she knew that her mother's hands gradually stopped shaking once she had taken one. And her mother's hands were always shaking when she'd been drinking the night before.

Loretta grabbed the pills from Amy. 'Ooh, fetch us a glass of water as well will you, love?'

Amy did as she was told but, by now, she was becoming a little irritated by her mother's demands. Loretta slipped a tablet from the packet and swallowed it down with a gulp of water before draining the rest of the glass. 'That's better,' she said, letting out a heavy sigh. 'I was bloody parched.'

Amy continued tidying around the kitchen, deliberately slamming the cupboard doors as she put items inside them. Loretta looked across at her and seemed to pick up on her irritation. She glanced around the room. 'Ooh, you've got it nice and tidy, love. You are a good girl. Why don't you go and watch some TV or something as a treat?'

Despite her irritation, Amy was grateful for her mother's compliment and even though she was becoming increasingly difficult to live with, Amy still sought her approval. Now that Dale was no longer around there was nobody else to impress except the occasional male visitor who stayed around long enough for Amy to meet him. But most of them quickly disappeared once they had spent the night.

She left her mother at the kitchen table downing her tea and comforters while she went into the living room to watch TV, glad that her brother was out at a friend's house. She wasn't in the mood for him at the moment.

It wasn't long before she heard her mother on the phone in the hallway. The first call was to one of her friends Amy assumed. Loretta was giggling like a young girl. There was a reference to the previous night out then she whispered something down the phone that Amy didn't catch. The tone of the conversation changed, and Amy soon realised that her mother was complaining about Dale again.

'I can't believe he had a wife all along. What a complete bastard!'

Amy had heard similar countless times over the past few weeks and, deciding she didn't want to hear any more, she went up to her bedroom. Her mother went quiet as she passed her in the hallway but didn't speak to her.

Amy wished she could ignore what her mother was up to, but she couldn't help being curious. Listening on the upstairs landing, she heard Loretta round up the conversation. But then she seemed to be talking to someone else. Amy presumed it was a man because she was talking all nice like she did when her boyfriends came round.

Amy stayed in her room for a long while until she heard her mother go into the bathroom. Still feeling irritated with her, she decided to get out of the house and spent a couple of hours wandering aimlessly around the shops.

By the time Amy returned home, her mother was dressed up and she was sitting in the living room with a glass of wine in front of her.

'Where the bloody hell have you been?' she asked.

Amy noticed straightaway that her voice had changed like it did when she'd been drinking. It was a bit slurry, and she could tell the glass of wine wasn't her first.

'Just out,' she said.

'Well, now you're back you can help me with the tea. We'll have to get a move on. I'm off out soon.'

'What, again?'

'Eh, never mind "what again", lady. I've a right to go out as much as I bloody well want. Anyway, you never know, my luck might be in.'

She winked as she said the last words, but Amy ignored the comment and went through to the kitchen. They didn't speak much while they prepared the evening meal and, when Nathan returned home, they all sat together and ate in silence.

It wasn't long afterwards before Loretta was ready to go out again. Amy smiled at her mother, noticing the transformation as she seemed to have added more makeup since that afternoon. Loretta gave both her children a quick peck on the cheek, left them her usual instructions about not answering the door to anyone, and then she was gone.

Amy gazed across at her brother who was transfixed on the TV screen. She hated it when they were home alone. Nathan wasn't very good company; he had his own interests and rarely made conversation with her. But, aside from that, it was scary being home without their mother, especially at night.

She went up to her room but couldn't settle, worried about noises coming from outside. She gazed through her bedroom window into the overgrown back garden but wished she hadn't. It was dark and she thought she saw the shadow of a person on the garden path but as a bush swayed in the evening breeze the shadow moved and she realised that was what had caused it.

Apart from being scared, she was bored. She decided to go downstairs and watch TV. At least now that her mother was out, she wouldn't be bothered by her drunken ramblings for a while. So, although she worried about being at home without an adult, there were some consolations.

But there was another reason she didn't mind her mother going out so much. Because maybe, like she had said, her luck might be in, and, if it were, then perhaps she would meet another man like Dale and things could go back to the way they once were.

21

October 2015

Amber walked along the backstreets behind Piccadilly station figuring there was no point in changing her patch. It would mean starting all over again trying to find a good spot that wasn't occupied by any of the other girls. Besides, Cora had done her worst and hopefully that was an end to it. She knew it was a risk though and that Cora and Jack might return. Tonight seemed quieter than usual but maybe that was her imagination. As she walked, she could feel the rapid pounding of her heart and she continuously glanced around, dreading a repeat of the attack.

She reached her spot at the mouth of a railway arch and waited, afraid of venturing too deeply into the gloomy interior of the tunnel. Even where she stood the light was muted as the streetlamps were widely spaced. She felt the chill of the night air carried on a breeze and shivered.

Further up the street she could see another girl, but she was too far away to chat to or to summon for help if needed. Amber could vaguely pick out her short skirt and high-heeled boots and she surmised that she was also doing business. Occasionally a car passed by but none of them stopped for either Amber or the other girl. Was business slower tonight or was that just her imagination too?

Amber's ears were so attuned to what was happening around her that she picked up sounds she wouldn't normally notice. The trickle of running water coming from somewhere above. Traffic in the distance. Voices from a nearby street, which reached a crescendo then faded away.

It was a while before a car pulled up. But it didn't stop for Amber; it stopped for the other girl who got inside, making Amber feel even more alone and vulnerable when it drove off. But as she looked in the other direction, she could see another car approaching. She stepped forward and the car stopped. Still feeling cautious, Amber bent and peeped through the side window before going any further. Relieved that it wasn't one of her attackers, she walked over to the car, negotiated a price with the driver and jumped inside.

Two customers later and Amber was standing back at her spot when a black BMW pulled up. She recognised it as Kev's car and peeped through the passenger's side window, her heartbeat speeding up when she spotted Kev Pike at the wheel. Internally she cursed her own weakness; why did he have this effect on her?

'Come here,' he said, and Amber approached the BMW.

Kev Pike wound down the window. 'Fuckin' hell! Someone's done a good job on you, haven't they? Who was it?'

'Just some random mugger,' said Amber. She didn't want to give him any names in case it came back on her.

Kev got out of the car and reached up to touch her face, gently caressing her bruises with his fingers. 'Shit, what a mess!' he said.

'Thanks,' said Amber in an attempt at wit.

'No, I didn't mean that. You're a good-looking girl. I meant the bruises. I don't like violence against women.'

He observed her for a few minutes without speaking. Amber felt uncomfortable under his scrutiny, but his reaction had also surprised her. She had been given to believe that he traded in violence but maybe she had got it wrong.

While he watched her, Amber took in his appearance. He oozed masculinity and she couldn't help but feel drawn to him despite her previous mistrust.

Then he spoke. 'I can make sure they don't do it again, y'know. No one will bother you once you're under my protection.'

This time Amber didn't turn him down. Spurred on by fear and by what seemed to be his genuine concern for her safety, she asked, 'How much?'

'Hundred a week.'

Amber chewed on her bottom lip while she thought over her response. 'I haven't got it yet, but I should have by the end of the night.'

Kev grinned, and his normally hostile expression changed to one that was almost welcoming. Amber couldn't help but notice how he looked even better when he wasn't scowling.

'That's OK,' he said. 'I'll swing by later.'

Then he got back inside his car and set off, revving the engine noisily before he sped up the road.

★

Later that night Kev Pike found Cora who was also plying her trade on the mean streets of Manchester. She was exactly at the spot where he thought she would be, and he pulled up the car. He didn't have to beckon her over; Cora was at the window as soon as he'd stopped, and she had her hand outstretched.

'Have you got my share?' she asked.

'No.'

Cora scowled. 'Why not? Jack's already had his.'

''Cos you're not fuckin' getting any, that's why not.'

Cora's hands shot to her hips, the scowl still on her face. 'What the fuck d'you mean? I sorted her as well and it was me that fuckin' put you onto the bitch in the first place.'

Kev got out of the car. He didn't like the way Cora could sometimes be cocky and peevish. Taking in her attitude, he almost felt sorry for Amber, knowing that Cora and Jack had given her a good going-over. He didn't really like to see women being set about; he remembered only too well the hidings his mum had suffered at the hands of his dad. But, in this business, it was all about easy money and, as long as someone else was dishing out the beatings, he tended to turn a blind eye.

He went over to Cora, his height giving him a psychological advantage, as he wanted to unsettle her. It worked. Cora's head and shoulders drew back as he stepped up close to her.

'Don't get smart with me! You weren't supposed to fuckin' sort her,' he yelled. 'That was Jack's job. Your job was to put me onto her. And you don't get fuckin' paid for that. The only reason you're not paying *me* is 'cos you gave me her in your place. And I still want you to give me another girl by the end of the week so get onto it. In the meantime, unless you want me to start charging you, fuck off out of my face.'

He looked at Cora's startled expression and, satisfied that his message had got through, he walked back towards the driver's door. But then he remembered the message that he had come to deliver, and he turned back.

'By the way. It's all been sorted. She's paid up so leave off her from now on, eh? Jack's already been told.'

Cora didn't reply. She just nodded slightly and narrowed her lips.

Kev got back into the car. He was feeling angry. Cora sometimes had that effect on him. But she had her uses too and could really pile on the charm when it suited her. She was an attractive girl and knew how to keep the punters happy, especially those who preferred a curvier girl. He quickly drove off before he really lost it with her. He'd always made it a rule of his never to hit a woman but sometimes he was sorely tempted.

22

April 1999

As the weeks dragged by things were getting worse with Loretta, and Amy was becoming concerned. Her drinking had increased, and she now drank most nights rather than just at the weekends when she was going out.

There were more men coming round the house too and, as well as Loretta bringing them back after a night out, they would come round to the house when she was in. It was usually late when they did so, but they rarely hung around for long the following day. Amy was disappointed with that. She would have welcomed the chance to get to know them; perhaps then she would find someone else to spoil her like Dale had done.

Amy wished she could confide in someone about her mother's drinking as she didn't like the way she behaved when she drank. But they rarely saw any relatives nowadays. They'd drifted away from her father's family over the years and her mother had forbidden her to visit her maternal grandparents a while ago as she had fallen out with them. She wouldn't tell her why they had fallen out, but Amy overheard her telling someone on the phone that Grandma 'ought to learn to mind her own bloody business'.

Miss Smedley at school was a nice teacher and Amy had been tempted a few times to tell her about her worries. But she daren't. Loretta had often warned her that what happened in the home was their private business and not to be spoken about outside. Amy therefore knew that she would get in trouble if her mother found out that she had been speaking to her teacher about her problems.

It was now mid-week and they were all sat watching TV. Loretta had an open bottle of wine in front of her, which was now almost empty, as was the glass that she held in her hand. Next to the wine was a pill packet with the blister pack still sticking out from when Loretta had taken a tablet earlier then plonked it back down on the coffee table.

Amy was perturbed to witness her mother's character transformation as she worked her way through the bottle. She was now running a commentary about the action on screen, the characters and their personality traits.

'Look at that bloody wimp! He doesn't deserve to be on TV,' she said, and Amy noticed that not only were her comments becoming louder and more belligerent, but she was also slurring her words.

Loretta suddenly got up and went to the window, pulling one of the curtains back and peeping outside. Amy wasn't sure what she was looking for, but she had lost interest. She just wished they could watch TV in peace without her mother's drunken interruptions. While Loretta wasn't watching, Nathan quickly grabbed the remote control and switched the volume up.

Loretta sat back down again. She didn't notice the change in volume or, if she did, she chose to ignore it. But her chatter became louder as she battled to make herself heard over the sound of the TV. This time her focus wasn't on what was happening on screen but on her own life. She went quiet momentarily, seemingly pensive before she came out with her next statement.

'I could never understand it, y'know, when Dale said he wanted to go back to his family. Said he missed his sons too much. I don't know why. From what he told me the pair of them were all for their mother. Anyway, he told me he'd always wanted a daughter. So, you would have thought, y'know, that he'd have been happy here. A ready-made family for him, wasn't it?'

Amy spun around and stared into her mother's bloodshot, droopy eyes.

'What? What you lookin' at?' Loretta drawled. 'I thought you knew you were his favourite. Treated you like the daughter he never had, didn't he? Still didn't stop him from bloody leaving me, did it?'

Amy turned back towards the TV, trying to ignore her mother's ramblings. But her words had hit home. She had always wondered why Dale seemed to favour her over Nathan, and now she knew why. It was nothing to do with her being a good kid. In fact, it wasn't anything to do with her at all; it was purely because Dale didn't have a daughter of his own.

*

It was the following day and Amy was on her way home from school. She had just turned into her road, passing neighbouring houses with a mix of neatly compact front gardens and run-down, litter-strewn ones full of weeds, when her brother caught up with her. He had just said goodbye to one of his friends and now he seemed eager to chat, which wasn't like him.

He drew up alongside her and asked, 'Amy, what's a prostitute?'

Amy was shocked at his use of the word as she knew it was offensive. 'What do you want to know that for?'

He seemed to go coy, his eyes looking down at the ground briefly before he said, 'There's this lad in my class who's always being nasty to me and today he said our mum was a prostitute. Is she?'

Amy wasn't entirely sure what the word meant but she knew it was something to do with things women did with men, and she knew it had negative connotations. She was quick to defend her mother. 'Is she 'eck! She just has lots of boyfriends, that's all.'

'Well, what does it mean, anyway?'

'It's a bad woman who does things with men.'

'What sort of things?'

'I dunno. Like kissing and other stuff. Anyway, I know our mum isn't one because she's not a bad woman.'

'She does get drunk a lot though.'

'I know, but that doesn't mean she's bad. It's just that, well, she's missing Dale. So, next time he says that horrible word, you tell him she isn't one at all. And if he keeps doing it you need to tell the teacher about him. But don't tell Mum. I don't think she'd like it.'

Amy didn't know why she was defending her. She wasn't happy about her drinking either. But she couldn't have people saying bad things about her. She *was* her mother after all. And perhaps, in a way, she empathised with her. She remembered how devastated they had all been when Dale had left them, and she supposed that her mother was just taking a bit longer to get over it than they were.

Once Nathan seemed satisfied with her answer, he started dragging his feet and lagging behind. But Amy wasn't bothered by that; they never walked to and from school together anyway and the only reason he'd caught up with her was because he was bothered by the nasty comments from someone at school.

By the time she arrived home she was well in front of Nathan who seemed to be occupied with something he had picked up off the pavement. Amy unlocked the door and walked inside the hallway. She could hear the TV blaring, which wasn't unusual. Her mother often watched TV in the afternoons and had shunned housework in favour of drinking.

Amy walked through to the living room and wasn't surprised to find her mother sprawled out on the sofa. Drunk again, obviously.

She went through to the kitchen to grab something to eat, and heard the door being shut as she left the hall. That would be Nathan. He'd probably switch the TV over to something he wanted to watch while their mother was asleep and Amy was out of the room. She'd have to get back quick and kick up a fuss so she could get her own way for once.

She'd just buttered some bread and was quickly spreading jam on another slice when her brother ran into the kitchen, a look of terror on his face.

'Amy, Amy, there's something wrong with Mum. You need to come and have a look.'

He took hold of her arm and started dragging her towards the hall. 'Get off, I'm coming!' she yelled.

She wondered what the fuss was about. Their mother was just drunk, that was all. It wasn't the first time they'd seen her like that so she couldn't understand why he was carrying on so much. But something about his manner unsettled her and, even though she had already seen her mother when she came in from school, she dashed through to the living room after him.

Loretta was still sprawled along the sofa with a cushion under her head. Amy walked over and, on closer examination, saw that her mother's arm was draped over the side of the sofa, her hand empty but an upturned wine glass on the floor beside it with its contents pooled on the carpet. She shook her mother's shoulder. 'Mum, wake up.'

But Loretta didn't wake up. Instead her head lolled to the side then dropped back against the cushion. As it bounced back, she let out a murmur and claret-stained spittle trickled from the corner of her mouth. Amy took in her drooping mouth and sagging eyelids. Then she noticed something else. The pills!

An opened packet was on the coffee table next to an empty bottle of wine. The blister packs had all been emptied and a few of the pills were stacked next to the packet. But most of them had gone.

Amy couldn't put into words what had happened. She was only eleven. But she instinctively knew something was wrong and a feeling of dread clutched at her insides, making her feel as though she wanted to vomit. She swallowed down the bile that had risen to her throat and found her voice.

'Oh my God! Nathan! I think she's… I think she's… dead. Oh my God. What should we do?'

She stared at her brother who was just as alarmed as she was. 'I don't know,' he said, his lips trembling.

Then Amy seemed to snap to, and she rushed towards the phone, her hands shaking as she dialled 999 and waited for the line to connect.

'What service do you require?' asked the operator.

'I don't know. It's my mum. I think she's dead.'

The operator's tone switched from officious to coaxing and she talked Amy through procedure while Amy stood by the phone with trembling knees and hands, her shock now reducing her to tears. The operator tried to keep her on the line while she sent an ambulance, but Amy was desperate. Once she was assured that an ambulance was on its way her thoughts turned to what she could do in the meantime. With her mind in turmoil, she ran into the street screaming for help.

The next-door neighbour, Mrs Wiley, ran out of her house and Amy tried to tell her what was wrong. But she rushed her words and they came out fragmented. 'Mum. I think… she's… she's… come and look.' Then she grabbed Mrs Wiley's hand and led her to the house where Nathan was standing in the hallway. He was dumbstruck, with the colour drained from his face and his mouth hanging loose.

Mrs Wiley rushed inside ahead of her. 'Where is she?' she asked.

'Th-the living room,' said Amy.

'OK, you wait here,' she instructed, 'while I see what the problem is.'

Amy stood in the hallway with her brother, sobbing while he remained silent and numb with shock.

'Go and get Mrs Griffiths from over the road,' shouted Mrs Wiley. Amy could sense the panic in her voice even before she added, 'Tell her it's urgent. I think it's an overdose. And tell her to come straight through to the living room. You children can stay in the hall.'

Amy did as she was ordered, bringing back Mrs Griffiths who rushed into the living room. She wasn't in there long before Mrs Wiley dashed out following a harried conversation. 'Come on, come through to the kitchen,' she said, taking hold of each of the children in her big comforting arms. 'Mrs Griffiths is a nurse. She'll look after your mother while you wait with me for the ambulance.'

'Will she be alright?' sobbed Amy.

'Hopefully. Those ambulance people know what they're doing, love, so don't worry.'

Amy looked into Mrs Wiley's face, expectantly, but she could see that her expression belied her comforting words. And she knew that there was nothing they could do except wait for the ambulance and hope to God that everything would be alright.

23

October 2015

When Amber walked into the Rose and Crown for a pre-work drink, she noticed straightaway that it was a quiet night. She glanced around and could see that old Angie was the only one of the girls in, so she grabbed a drink and went over. Angie's eyes lit up as she joined her at the table then dulled again in disappointment.

'Have you not got me one then?'

'No. I thought you already had one.'

'It's finished.' Angie quickly lifted the glass and drained the remains. 'Pity,' she said. 'I'm a bit skint and I could do with another to ease my chest.' She put her hand up to cover her chest and coughed dramatically as she finished her words.

Amber obliged her with a concerned response. 'Yeah, I noticed it's bad again, isn't it?'

'It's always bloody bad lately.'

Amber was about to lecture her on how she could help herself by cutting down on the cigarettes and booze when a man called Tom joined them. He was well known in the Rose and Crown as a hardened boozer and most of the girls avoided him. Apart from being a heavy drinker, he was lecherous and prone to making inappropriate comments.

She noticed he was carrying a spirit of some sort in a glass as well as a pint. He passed the short to Angie. 'There you go. I noticed your cough was bad. That'll help your chest, girl. And if that doesn't work, I'll rub summat on it for you.'

He grinned lasciviously, displaying rotten teeth. Angie smiled back at him and Amber felt sickened. Angie had obviously sunk to a new low if she was now entertaining the likes of old Tom for the sake of a few drinks.

Once she had the drink in front of her, Angie continued speaking. 'I could do without going out tonight but what can you do? I need the money.'

Amber didn't respond and Tom seemed to be in a world of his own.

'I got a really bad one last night, y'know,' said Angie.

'We all get bad clients. It's just something we have to put up with,' said Amber.

'Not like this one though.'

Amber rolled her eyes in irritation. The last thing she needed now was to have to listen to Angie's self-pity. She knew Angie was wanting to sponge some money from her, but she wasn't in the mood for it tonight. She had enough problems of her own and couldn't spare the cash now that Kev Pike was taking a cut of her earnings.

Amber was saved from making a sharp retort when her phone rang. It was a client, called George, who wanted her to meet him in a hotel room. She was relieved; the client wanted to book her for the night, and it would save her having to stand out in the cold touting for customers. She had no doubt that Angie would get the money from elsewhere, probably from old Tom.

'Right, I'm off,' she said, downing her drink and dashing out of the door without even saying goodbye to either of them.

An hour later Amber was in a hotel room with George. They were both sitting on a double bed in their underwear getting high on cocaine. She welcomed nights like tonight when she could numb herself both to what she did for a living and to all her other troubles. A bonus was that she didn't have to buy the coke; the client supplied it as well as paying for her services.

George was OK as clients went, and he seemed in the mood to party. He was an older man, possibly in his early forties, above average height, medium build and balding. But what was most noticeable about him was that he had kind eyes and a friendly smile. To Amber those characteristics were more important than any other as they enabled her to relax a little while she was in his company.

'Come on, let's get started,' he said when he was ready to switch from polite chatter and drug taking to the real reason for the meet-up.

He twisted around and slipped his hand under the back of her bra, deftly unfastening it. 'Take your knickers off,' he ordered then he removed his own underwear, slid on a condom and climbed on top of her.

'Wait a minute,' said Amber, sensing that this was going to be quick and handing him a tube of lube.

He grabbed the tube and squirted it unceremoniously around her genitals. 'You're a good girl, aren't you?'

As soon as he said those words, Amber's memory went back to fifteen years ago. She was twelve and pinned to the bed by a brute of a man who couldn't wait to have his way with her.

'You're a good girl,' were the words he had chosen as he'd entered her, and the pain had shot through her insides.

She tensed, trying to blank out the ordeal that she had experienced as a twelve-year-old child. Feeling his presence. The rapid thrusting inside her. His hands grasping her breasts. And his lips slopping all over her face.

'Well, aren't you gonna give me something back, love? I feel like I'm flogging a dead horse,' said George.

Amber tried to focus, thrusting her loins in time with his and letting out tiny fake yelps of pleasure. She knew many clients laboured under the assumption that the girls enjoyed what they were doing to them and, like many of her friends, she was willing to satisfy their illusions.

Any minute now and it would be finished. Please, let it be over soon, her mind screamed while her mouth muttered, 'Ooh' and 'Aah'.

George let out a mighty groan and withdrew, flinging himself onto his back to the side of her and panting heavily. Amber tried not to wince as she felt his sweat on her stomach and the stickiness of the lube between her thighs.

'Good idea with the lube,' he commented while his eyes remained fixed on the ceiling. 'You *are* a good girl.'

Amber's control went. She could no longer pretend. That

childhood memory was still so vivid in her mind. And there was no way she could stand a repeat performance in the morning, not when her brain associated this man with what had happened to her back then. She shot up off the bed, grabbed her clothes and quickly dressed.

'What the bloody hell? Where d'you think you're going? I've booked you for the night,' said George. 'And don't forget, I haven't paid you yet.'

Amber eyed him cautiously while she finished dressing. Not until she was ready to go did she speak. 'Forget it. I'm done. And you can stick your money where the sun don't shine.'

She dashed through the door and down the hotel corridor, eager to distance herself from this man as much as she could. But no matter how hard she ran, she would never rid herself of the childhood memories that kept resurfacing when she least expected them.

24

It was Amy and Nathan's third day at their grandparents'. Amy didn't quite know how they'd ended up there seeing as how they and her mother didn't get along. She presumed Mrs Wiley or one of the other neighbours must have rung them because she and Nathan had spent some time with her after their mother had been taken away in the ambulance. Then, later, her grandparents had come to pick them up.

Amy and Nathan's grandparents had told them that their mother was out of hospital but that it would be a few days until she was feeling better. The children were therefore staying with them in the meantime.

Being with her grandparents had seemed weird at first. It had been so long since she'd seen them because of the falling-out with her mother. They were strict compared to her mother but not in a bad way. It was more in a caring way, like making sure they weren't left in the house alone and asking where they were going and what time they'd be back if they wanted to go outside.

Amy had been so used to her freedom that the change took some getting used to and, despite the drawbacks of her home life, she did miss the familiarity of it. Although she had a room to herself just like she did at home, it wasn't the same as her own bedroom, which was full of her personal possessions: presents from Dale and knick-knacks she'd collected over the years.

She also missed her mother. She wasn't perfect but Amy still felt more relaxed with her than she did with her grandparents who were more formal. But there were advantages to being with them. At least they weren't drunk all the time and she didn't have to help around the house as much.

The one thing she didn't like though was how they kept asking questions about her mother's behaviour and what life was like at home. She kept her answers vague as she didn't like to tell tales on her mother, and she warned Nathan to do the same.

At the moment, Amy was in the bedroom she was occupying, writing in a diary from her grandmother, when Nathan came to the door. She quickly shut the diary, not wanting anybody to be party to the troubled thoughts about her mother, which had spilt out onto its pages as soon as she was alone.

'What do you want?' she snapped, knowing it was unusual for Nathan to want to chat with her.

'I don't wanna look at that anyway,' he countered. 'I just wanted to talk to you about something.'

Amy sighed, locked the diary with the accompanying key and put it to one side, then said, 'OK, come in then.'

Nathan walked into the room, dragging his feet, and sat down on the bed beside her. 'I was just wondering why Grandma and Grandad keep asking things about Mum.'

'Because they don't get on with her. Don't tell them anything. They might use it in a row or something.'

'I didn't.'

'Why, what have they been asking you?'

'Just about what Mum makes us to eat and whether she goes out a lot.'

'You didn't tell them, did you?'

'No! I just said she made us the same sort of food as they did, and she didn't go out that much.'

'Good,' said Amy, but she could tell Nathan was troubled.

'Mum's food isn't as good as Grandma's though, is it? And we don't get as much.'

Amy shrugged but Nathan wasn't finished.

'I wish I'd have told them what she's really like, then we could live here instead. I don't like Mum anymore.'

'Why?'

'Because she does bad things. I wish she would have died.'

'Nathan! You can't say that,' said Amy, alarmed.

'Why not?'

'Because… well, because she's our mum. And you shouldn't say bad things about your mum. Anyway, she looks after us, and it's only because Dale left her that she does bad things so it's his fault really.'

'I don't care. I still don't like her,' said Nathan before jumping off the bed and dashing out of the room.

*

That afternoon, Loretta arrived to take Amy and Nathan back home. As soon as she heard her mother's voice, Amy ran down the stairs, flinging her arms around her in an emotional greeting.

'I've missed you, Mum.'

'I know, love; I've missed you too. I'm sorry.'

She didn't say what she was sorry about, but Amy didn't wait for her to elaborate. 'Are we going home today?'

'Yes, later. But I need to have a word with your grandparents first.'

'Oh, OK.'

'Where's Nathan?'

'Upstairs.'

'Can you go and get him for me please, love?' asked Loretta.

Amy dashed upstairs, noticing that her grandparents had appeared in the hallway. She found Nathan standing at the chest of drawers conducting some sort of experiment with his toy science lab.

'Nathan, Mum's here.'

'I know. I heard her.'

'She's come to take us home.'

Nathan looked as though he was about to say something but then changed his mind.

'Come on. She's waiting to see you,' said Amy. When he carried on playing with his science lab she added, 'You'll be in trouble if you don't.'

Nathan carefully put down the equipment he had been holding and followed Amy downstairs where his mother was waiting. Amy noticed that her grandparents were no longer in the hallway; they had retreated into the lounge.

'Come here. Let me have a look at you,' Loretta said to Nathan who slowly drew closer to her.

She flung her arms around him, but Nathan was unresponsive, his shoulders remaining slumped. Amy thought her mother either didn't notice his reaction or she chose to disregard it as she continued to hug him and said, 'I've missed you. I can't wait to take you both home.'

'Can I finish my experiment first?' asked Nathan.

Loretta made light of it. 'Trust you. Yeah, course you can. I've still got to have a word with your grandparents anyway before we go home.'

As soon as she released her grip, Nathan raced back up the stairs, but Amy hovered uncertainly.

'I need to talk to them in private,' said Loretta. 'I'll shout you when I'm ready to go.'

Then Loretta went through to the lounge and shut the door. But Amy didn't follow her brother back upstairs. She was curious about the forthcoming discussion, so she stayed at the foot of the stairs, ready to dash away if the lounge door opened.

She couldn't hear everything that was being said from where she was, but it was too risky going any nearer to the lounge door. At first, she just heard the muffled sounds of people speaking. She managed to pick out the various voices, but she couldn't tell what they were saying.

Then her grandad raised his voice. She still couldn't tell everything he was saying but she did identify the words 'bloody' and 'social services'.

Her mother shouted back, and this time Amy could hear every word. 'Don't you dare report me or you'll never bloody see them again.'

She didn't hear her grandad's response, but she heard her mother say something about the fact that things were going to be different. As she spoke her words became louder, but it was because she was getting nearer not because she was still shouting.

Amy fled up the stairs, afraid of being caught eavesdropping and she wasn't there long before her mother called for her and Nathan to come down again. Amy went into Nathan's room to make sure he had heard, and they went back down the stairs together.

'Come on, we're going. Say goodbye to your grandparents,' said Loretta, stony-faced. 'And don't forget to thank them,' she added as an afterthought.

Amy went over to say goodbye to her grandparents. She hugged her grandad who patted her awkwardly on the back. Her grandma's hug was slightly more relaxed although both of them weren't given to displays of emotion. Then Amy withdrew from her arms and looked up into her grandma's face.

'Thank you for looking after us,' she said.

Her grandma just nodded but Amy could have sworn she saw tears in her eyes. She didn't have time to say anything further though as her mother quickly ushered both her and Nathan out of the door ready to set off for their home in Withington.

25

April 1999

As they approached their home Amy was surprised to see that the small front garden had been weeded for the first time in ages. A quick look around the interior told her that it had been given a good cleaning too.

'Wow, Mum! The house looks nice and clean,' she said.

Loretta smiled. 'Well, I wanted it nice for when you and Nathan came home.'

Although Amy returned her smile, Nathan ignored her and was just about to run up the stairs when Loretta stopped him. 'Hang on a minute. I want to have a chat with you both. Go and sit down.'

The children did as Loretta requested and watched as she sat down too, ready to hear what she had to say.

'The reason I've made the house look nice is because I want things to be different for you from now on. I know it hasn't been easy since Dale went…' Her voice quivered and she paused for a moment, allowing herself to regain control. 'But I'm going to make it up to you.'

She leant over the side of the chair on which she was sitting and retrieved a carrier bag. Then she put her hand inside and withdrew first one box of chocolates and then another.

'This one's for you, Nathan,' she said, passing him one of the boxes. Then she gave Amy the other one saying, 'And this one's for you.'

'Thanks, Mum,' the children gushed.

'Can we eat them now?' asked Nathan.

'You can have a couple in a minute and the rest after tea, but I want you to listen to what I've got to say first.' The children looked up from their chocolates, paying ardent attention to her. 'I know you might have been upset by what happened, but I want you to promise me that you won't tell anybody else about it. None of your friends, none of the teachers, nobody. Do you understand? And if anybody asks you any questions, you're not to tell them anything.'

'OK,' said Amy.

'Nathan?'

'Alright,' Nathan muttered. 'Does that mean we can have some of our chocolates now?'

'In a minute. I haven't finished yet.'

Ensuring she had their rapt attention once more, Loretta added her killer line: 'If you tell anybody about it or about anything that's happened in this house then you know you could end up in a home, don't you?'

Amy gasped but Nathan remained impassive. Loretta looked directly at him for a reaction as she continued. 'Homes aren't very nice places, Nathan. They're full of really bad children who have done terrible things, and the staff beat you. And if you end up in one of those places, you'll never see me or your grandparents again. Do you understand, Nathan?'

This time Nathan's reply was more heartfelt, his eager words showing his obvious alarm. 'Yeah. Course I do. I won't tell anyone, honest.'

'OK, you can open your chocolates now. But don't have more than two. You're going to be having something else to eat soon.'

Their mother's efforts continued into evening. She made them a sumptuous roast dinner and Amy was pleased that the portions were akin to those at her grandparents' house. Loretta followed it with a treacle sponge pudding and custard and the children ate every bit.

Later, Amy helped her mother with the washing up, and then they went into the living room to watch TV. She was relieved when her mother didn't have a drink although she noticed that she seemed a bit on edge and snappy as the evening wore on. Then she saw her take one of her tablets, which soon calmed her down.

Amy wasn't bothered that they were watching one of Nathan's favourite videos yet again. She was just glad that they were all back home as a family and that things were much better. The way her mother was behaving was how she used to be before Dale went.

She recalled her words, 'I'm going to make it up to you,' and a feeling of contentment warmed her insides. It was so nice to have their mother back at home and back to her old self. She hoped that this was how things were going to be from now on.

26

October 2015

Crystal walked into her Altrincham store at midday. She'd left Candice there first thing and then dashed to Manchester and back so she could check on one of her other branches. Feeling the heat inside the shop, she quickly shrugged off her coat, revealing a pair of fitted trousers and a lace top, which was tantalising in a classic, understated way.

She smiled at her manager, Deanna, who was at the till and looked further down the store to see her daughter admiring high-end dresses as she carefully placed them on the rails. 'She looks happy enough,' said Crystal.

'Oh, she loves it,' Deanna replied. 'She's been a dream, good as gold.'

'Glad to hear it. Can you get someone to relieve you while we go through to the back for a chat?'

'Sure.' Deanna buzzed for one of the staff to manage the till and she joined Crystal as they made their way through the store to the back office, passing Candice on the way.

'You OK?' asked Crystal, patting her daughter on the shoulder.

'Sure, it's well cool.'

Crystal laughed. She'd had many positive comments about her shops since she'd started trading but never before had they been called 'cool'. Still, it was good to know that Candice was enjoying her Saturday job. It was still too early to decide whether it would be the career for her though as it was her first day.

Candice was still only fifteen and had talked about nothing else but working in her mother's stores for the past couple of years. But Crystal really wanted her to have an education, which could give her the opportunities she herself had missed out on when she was younger. That way Candice could make an informed decision. It was convenient for Candice to work there too as they now lived in Altrincham close to Crystal's best friend, Ruby, and her partner.

'I'm just having a meeting with Deanna to discuss the store and then I'll take you to lunch.'

'Great!' said Candice. 'Can we have pizza?'

'Course we can.' Crystal laughed. 'But don't expect me to be taking you out to lunch every time you're at work. I have got two other stores to look after too, y'know.'

Candice gave a mock grimace and Crystal laughed again. 'Right, I'll see you in a bit,' she added, following Deanna to the back of the shop. 'Then you can tell me all about your morning.'

*

While Crystal was busy at her Altrincham store, in Withington Amber had only just got out of bed after working most of the night. She went into the living room to find her mother and Nathan having a conversation, which was becoming heated.

'Why the fuck should I pay the full whack? I'm not even here half the time,' Nathan yelled at his mother.

'Because you live here,' Loretta said. 'And don't you dare swear at me like that!' Nathan gave her a contemptuous glare and tutted dismissively. Amber could see that her mother's hands were shaking. 'It's not my fault you spend a lot of time with your fancy girlfriend,' Loretta continued. 'And the bills still have to be paid whether you're here or not.'

'But they're not my bloody bills, are they? It's not my house.'

Loretta seemed to run out of steam in the face of his hostility. She grabbed her packet of cigarettes with trembling hands and lit one then took a calming pull on it. As the smoke hit her lungs, she started to cough.

But Nathan had no sympathy. 'Look at the fuckin' state of you!' he complained. 'Wrecking your health smoking that shit. And it's no wonder there's never any fuckin' money in the house with all the money you spend on booze and cigs.'

When Loretta's coughing subsided, she looked at him for a moment, seeming exasperated. Then she changed tack.

'You are such a disappointment to me, Nathan. I worked so hard to give you a good education. And now that you've got a decent job you seem to have forgotten about your poor old mother.'

'You've got no fuckin' idea what the word "work" means,

Mother. All you've ever done is spread your legs. You just use men as a meal ticket and you're not fuckin' using me!'

Loretta's mouth dropped open wide in shock and Amber quickly chipped in. 'Eh, that's enough.'

Nathan swivelled around and turned his angry glare on her. 'What the fuck's it got to do with you?'

'You've gone too far this time, Nathan.'

'I haven't even fuckin' started yet!'

Amber could see her mother becoming distressed as she spoke in a pitiful tone. 'I wouldn't have to bother with men if you looked after me like a good son, Nathan.'

'Oh, I've had enough of listening to this shit,' raged Nathan, and he barged past Amber as he marched out of the room.

Loretta shouted after him, bringing Amber into the argument to garner support. 'At least I can rely on my daughter. She always pays her way.'

But Nathan didn't respond. Presumably, he was now too far away to hear his mother's comment. Amber was glad because she didn't want to be dragged into yet another of their arguments. Nathan was full of resentment towards his mother and could be nasty at times.

She sat down and flicked through a discarded newspaper, peeping over the top of it at her mother. She could see that by now Loretta's lip was trembling and she was on the verge of tears, but she didn't go over to comfort her, knowing that Nathan had a point. Her mother's dependence on men for money and other gifts was all they had ever known from being children, so it was no wonder that she herself had turned to prostitution.

When Loretta could see that Amber wasn't about to get

involved, she also went out of the room leaving Amber with just her thoughts for company. Although she was used to her mother and Nathan having arguments, it was the first time Loretta had compared her favourably to him. For as far back as Amber could remember Nathan had always been the golden child who Loretta had nurtured with pride and affection.

She, on the other hand, had been expected to fulfil her mother's idea of a woman's role, handed down from generations of subservient women. Amber had been fed up of Nathan always being treated better than her and, in a way, it was good to hear that he had been such a let-down.

All her life Amber had sought approval from her mother and her various men friends. Now, it seemed like she had finally found it. Her lips thinned into an ironic smile. She might have finally found favour with her mother, but she'd had to go through a hell of a lot to reach this point.

27

July 1999

It was three months since Loretta's suicide attempt, and it hadn't taken her long to slip back into her old ways. Amy might have been only eleven years old, but she was a sensitive child who was very aware of what was happening around her. She had noticed the way her mother's drinking had started off slowly at first then gradually increased until she was drinking nearly every night again. Sometimes she went out, usually bringing one of her men friends back with her, but other times she stayed at home getting drunk while watching TV.

Amy was pleased when, at first, her mother had taken her and Nathan to visit her grandparents regularly. Although Amy had no desire to live there again, she didn't mind the visits because her grandparents made a fuss of her. But, as time went on, and Loretta became more slovenly once more, the visits became less frequent.

And she guessed it wasn't her grandparents' fault because her grandma had asked her on the phone to come and visit. Loretta had always promised her they would, but she never got round to it. Amy couldn't understand why her grandparents never came round to their house either, but she presumed it was because her mother didn't want them there. Although they had taken her and Nathan in for a few days, she could tell by the heated telephone discussions that their mother still didn't get on with them.

Amy knew her mother was expecting company this evening as she had enlisted her help earlier to do some cleaning and tidying, something she only did when one of her men friends was due to call round. They had all been in the living room watching TV for a while and Amy noticed the way her mother kept looking at the clock as she gulped wine from an opened bottle of red. She also noticed the way her mother was becoming more talkative as the level of alcohol in the bottle sank.

Loretta was almost at the end of the bottle when she took a giant swig and plonked the glass back on the coaster. Her drunken moves were clumsy, and the glass landed unevenly. Realising it was lopsided, Loretta grabbed at it, aiming to steady the glass. She managed to straighten it but not before some of the liquid had spilt, leaving a crimson pool on the coffee table.

She continued to watch TV then, noticing Amy's curious look, she said, 'I'll wipe it up later. I don't want to miss this.'

Amy knew that would never happen so, heaving a sigh, she got up from the sofa and went into the kitchen to fetch a cloth while her mother and Nathan carried on staring at the screen in front of them.

'Good girl,' said Loretta when Amy came back and wiped up the spilt wine. 'Don't forget to rinse the cloth out when you go back to the kitchen. It's all red.'

Amy did as she was told and was just coming back into the hall when she heard the doorbell. That would be her mother's visitor.

'I'll get it!' called Loretta and by the time Amy walked into the living room her mother was up out of her chair and tottering unsteadily towards the front door.

Amy tried to refocus on the programme she had been watching, aware at the same time of the sound of her mother's effusive greeting coming from the hallway.

'Hiya, Cliff. How are you?'

When Amy heard her mother and the man walk into the living room, she turned around and looked. The man caught her eye straightaway and she could see his face light up with a cheery smile.

'Who's this then?' he asked.

It was obvious he was referring to her. Nathan hadn't even bothered turning round to acknowledge him. Amy took in his appearance. He was about forty or maybe more and wasn't particularly tall, just above average height she thought. His features were weather-beaten but in a rugged sort of way and probably what someone of her mother's age would have considered good-looking. He was also slightly bald and had dark, brown eyes but they were happy eyes and, although he didn't look like Dale, his apparently affable nature made her think of him.

'That's our Amy,' said Loretta.

'And how old are you, Amy?' he asked.

She hesitated to reply. Although she was flattered by his interest, his overenthusiastic nature unsettled her a little.

'She's eleven,' said Loretta.

'Almost twelve,' said Amy, preening at the attention when she noticed that Nathan had turned around to see what all the fuss was about, and he was glaring at her.

'Really? Well, well, you certainly take after your mother for looks.'

This time it was Loretta's turn to preen. 'Oh, Cliff, you're such a charmer,' she said, and he rewarded her with a cheeky grin as he tickled her in the ribs.

'That's just one of the things you love about me,' he said, winking at both Loretta and Amy.

Amy felt uncomfortable. Although the man was jolly, his intense gaze embarrassed her, and she could feel herself blush. She felt sure he had picked up on her embarrassment, which seemed to amuse him more and he let out a hearty chuckle.

'Sit down, Cliff. I'll get you a drink,' Loretta said. 'What would you like?'

Her mother left the room, searching for the lager Cliff had asked for and he plonked himself on the sofa next to Amy. She felt his leg brushing next to hers and moved up slightly, but the man moved close to her once more and then there was that gaze again.

'So, what have you been up to at school today, Amy?' he asked. She shrugged, still feeling awkward and very self-conscious.

'Come on, Amy, no need to be shy with me. I don't bite.'

'Just stuff, English and that.'

He laughed. 'And what's *that*?'

Even at her age she had spotted the innuendo and her blush intensified. 'Dunno. I've forgot.' Then she switched her eyes back to the TV all the time sensing him still watching her.

Amy was relieved when her mother walked back into the room and uttered a variation of the line Amy was so used to hearing. 'Right, kids, me and Cliff need to talk so go on up to your rooms.'

'Aw,' said Nathan, stomping moodily from the room but Amy was glad of an excuse to escape from the man's scrutiny.

July 1999

Loretta walked over to the sink and poured herself a large glass of water. She had a raging thirst and her head was pounding. Maybe she'd overdone it with Cliff last night. She tried to recall just how much she had drunk but wasn't sure, so she went to the cupboard where she kept the red wine and found it was empty. Jesus! The discovery panicked her, and she became aware of her racing heart and twitchy limbs.

She hated that feeling when she was all tense and jumpy and the slightest thing heightened her anxiety. A hair of the dog was the only thing that would really calm her down when she felt like this, but she tried to resist. Drinking in the day wasn't a good idea. She didn't want to end up an old alcy. No, she'd have a cup of tea with one of her tablets and try to eat something instead. That should settle her if she could manage to keep the food down.

Loretta took a teabag from the few remaining in the packet and plonked it inside a cup and then switched the kettle on. She pulled the fridge door open to reach for the milk and was glad to find a carton almost full. Her thoughts turned to food. The kids would want something to eat even if *she* couldn't face it.

There was an opened tin of beans at the back of the fridge. She couldn't remember putting it there and she instinctively pulled it out and peered inside, recoiling when she saw a layer of mould round the top of the can. That wouldn't feed the kids. But there were two eggs there and a bit of butter. Maybe she could give them an egg each and some toast. But when she checked the bread bin, she found that was empty too.

Then her thoughts switched to something else. There was no alcohol in the fridge. It was all gone; all the lager and the bottle of white wine she'd put there too. Surely, they can't have drunk that much between them! But then memories of last night began to surface. Cliff encouraging her to have a beer. Cliff telling her the lager was gone. Her telling Cliff to open the wine. Discovering the red was gone. Opening the white.

Oh no! Did they really drink that much? But her throbbing head, thudding heart and trembling limbs told her that, yes, they did.

Loretta cursed silently, knowing she'd have to nip to the shops and at least get some food in. She toyed with the idea of sending one of the children but decided to go herself knowing she needed to check her bank balance while she was out. Last time she'd taken any cash out she had been overdrawn but she couldn't quite remember by how much. Cliff had given her some money last night but that wouldn't go far, not when she was behind with so many of her bills.

But there was another reason she wanted to go to the shops herself. She needed to get some more booze in. Promising herself it would just be there in case she fancied a drink tonight or in case a visitor called, her decision was made. She got herself ready, running a brush quickly through her hair and cleaning her teeth but not bothering to shower. That could wait till she returned.

An hour later she was back home. The money from Cliff was spent but at least she had some food in and some booze. She tried not to think about the bottles stacked inside the cupboard. It was still too early in the day. Loretta also tried not to think about her growing overdraft. The amount she owed was even more than she'd thought.

When the last of the shopping was tidied away, she popped some bread in the toaster. The aroma must have alerted Nathan who stumbled into the kitchen just as she was spreading some butter on the toast, her hands still shaky.

'Mum, I'm starving!' he said, his voice loud and whiny. 'When can I have something to eat?'

The sound startled Loretta who was already unsteady and her hand slipped with the knife leaving her other hand smeared with a layer of greasy butter. By this time Nathan was at her side, leaning over to see what she was doing, his head too close to the food. 'Ooh, is that one mine?'

'For God's sake, Nathan!' yelled Loretta. 'Can't you bloody wait? Look what you've made me do.'

She reached over for some kitchen roll to wipe the butter away but was perturbed to find she hadn't bought any. It hadn't featured highly on her list of priorities at the time. Knowing she wouldn't be able to get the grease off properly under the tap she decided to go to the bathroom and find some toilet paper.

As she walked away Nathan reached for the toast.

'Don't you bloody dare!' she yelled. 'I haven't finished yet. And if you don't stop pestering you won't get any at all. Now go to your room until I shout you.'

By the time she'd come back to the kitchen Loretta was already feeling guilty for yelling at him. Who could blame him for being hungry? But she was too het up at the moment to put up with any nonsense.

She continued buttering toast, in between stirring a pan of beans on the hob. As she occupied herself, more memories from last night surfaced and, in particular, what Cliff had said about Amy. But she'd baulked at the suggestion straightaway. Now though, she began to think about the huge sum of money he'd offered her. It was tempting. She could really use that right now. But no, she couldn't do it. Amy was her daughter and it was her duty to protect her.

She put the food onto the table and called the children down from their rooms. She still couldn't face it. Instead, despite her earlier resolve, she reached inside the cupboard for the booze and poured herself a glass of wine. Just a small one, to take the edge off, she decided. Then she went through to the living room and left the kids to it.

Taking hold of the remote control she switched on the TV and flicked through the channels. But she couldn't settle to anything. She gulped down the wine then put a stopper on the bottle promising herself that was the last till tonight. And as she sat there feeling a bit more relaxed her thoughts turned to last night once more and the huge sum of money Cliff had offered her.

28

July 1999

A few days later they were in the kitchen and Amy was washing up while her mother sat at the table watching her. She had a curious look on her face and Amy could have sworn that she was about to say something but then stopped herself.

Her mother seemed ill at ease with her for some reason. At first Amy thought it was just her usual irritability after she'd been drinking the previous night. But then she realised it was something more than that.

Eventually, she did speak but her voice sounded tentative, as though she wasn't sure she should be saying this. 'What did you think of Cliff?' she asked.

It was the first time her mother had referred to him since his visit a few days previously although she had heard her talking to him on the phone. The mention of his name took Amy by surprise. She felt the blood rush to her cheeks as she recalled the way he'd stared and how he'd spoken to her.

She glanced around at her mother momentarily but then her eyes darted back to what she was doing, hoping her mother hadn't noticed her blush.

'He's alright,' she said.

'Alright. Is that all? I think he's a lovely man and fun to be with. He always cheers me up anyway.'

Amy carried on washing up and didn't comment. She really didn't want to be having this conversation.

'Anyway, he likes you,' Loretta continued. 'In fact, he'd like to get to know you better.'

Alarmed, Amy swung around and glared at her mother, temporarily forgetting her embarrassment.

'Why?' she demanded.

'Oh, no reason. He just likes you, that's all. Anyway, I want you to be nice to him next time you see him. Like I say, Cliff's a lovely guy and I'd like him to stick around for a while.'

The thought of spending time with Cliff didn't appeal to Amy and she was confused as to why he'd want to spend time with her. But any doubts were suppressed by her mother's next words.

'Dale liked you too, didn't he? It's because you're a good girl. That's why everybody likes you. Cliff's not short of a bit of money, y'know. If you play your cards right, he could be good to us.'

Amy kept her back to her mother while she rubbed a ragged flannel over the last of the dishes and stacked it on the drainer with the others. Then she wiped her hands and made for the door. But she had to pass her mother on her way out of the room. Amy noticed the harsh expression on her face, which warned her she might become argumentative. She was often like that when she'd drunk too much the night before, and Amy couldn't wait to get out of her way.

'Well?' Loretta asked as Amy headed towards her.

'What?' snapped Amy.

'Don't give me that attitude, lady! I'm only asking you a question. You know what I'm talking about. Are you going to be nice to Cliff, or what?'

'I suppose so,' said Amy and then she dashed from the room, glad to escape from her unpredictable mother.

It wasn't long before Cliff visited them again. In fact, it was only two days later. Amy had been sitting in the lounge with her family, her mother drunk and belligerent, picking holes in everything anyone said whether it was a comment from Amy or Nathan or something on the TV.

'Turn the bloody telly over. I don't want to be watching nonsense like this.'

'But I like it, Mum,' Amy protested.

'You would. Small things amuse small minds. Anyway, I don't like it so do as you're told if you know what's good for you.'

Amy hated it when her mother was like this. She could be so volatile when she was drinking and, although she stopped short of using violence, it made her feel belittled when she spoke to her like that.

Amy could tell it was a man at the door as soon as she heard the change in her mother's tone of voice. First, she heard her saying thank you, her tone ingratiating. Then she heard Cliff's voice; it was loud and confident and carried easily from the hall to the living room. She felt herself tense as he laughed and joked with her mother then popped his head through the living room door.

'How's my favourite girl?' he asked.

Amy humoured him by turning around, seeing him smile and wink. Behind him her mother hovered until she managed to bustle past, holding out a lavish bunch of flowers and gushing. 'Look what Cliff's bought for me. See, I told you he was a lovely man, didn't I?'

'That's nothing,' said Cliff, and Amy could tell he was addressing his comments to her. 'Wait till you see what I've bought for you.'

He reached inside his jacket pocket and pulled out a box, which was wrapped neatly in gold paper.

'Well, aren't you gonna come and get it?' he asked.

Amy got up off the sofa and walked over to Cliff who handed her the present, his hand lingering on hers for a moment too long.

'Eh, that's not how I've brought you up,' said Loretta. Amy looked at her, perplexed. 'What do you say, Amy?'

'Oh, thanks,' said Amy who was so unsettled by Cliff's presence that she had forgotten her manners. 'I'll take it upstairs.'

'No,' said Cliff, barring her way through the door. 'I want to see you open it first. I'd like to see the look on that pretty little face of yours when you see what it is.'

Amy felt herself flush – something she always seemed to do when he was around. While he watched she fumbled at the wrapping paper, which revealed a neat blue box etched with a gold trim. She pulled open the lid and, despite herself, she was thrilled to find a silver bracelet inside with a heart-shaped locket and various charms. Her eyes lit up with joy and she couldn't resist a smile.

'Oh, Cliff. You shouldn't have,' said Loretta, patting him gently on the back. 'Isn't it lovely, Amy?'

Loretta's tone had changed from earlier. Now, instead of being aggressive, she was all friendly and flirtatious. Amy looked up and smiled at her mother but then she suddenly became self-conscious again, embarrassed at all the attention as they both stared avidly at her.

'Come here, I'll help you put it on,' said Cliff.

He took the bracelet out of the box and lifted Amy's tiny wrist, draping the bracelet around it then securing it with the clasp. 'Perfect,' he said, beaming at her.

Amy obliged him with a smile then sat down on the sofa, turning away from them both. She heard him whisper something to her mother but couldn't catch what was said. Then Loretta cleared her throat.

'Erm, Amy. Cliff would like you to show him your room. He wants to have a chat with you and get to know you more.'

Amy could feel her heart plummet. She didn't want to be alone with Cliff. He gave her the creeps. She turned around and glared at her mother.

'Come on,' said Cliff. 'I want to find out all about you.'

Her eyes remained focused on her mother, her expression filled with doubt.

'Go on, it's alright,' said Loretta. 'I told you, he's a lovely man. Look what he's bought you. He wouldn't have bought you that if he wasn't such a lovely man, now would he?'

Amy felt nervous without fully understanding why. All she knew was that she didn't feel comfortable with Cliff. There was something about him that unsettled her. But she was also worried about going against her mother. She got up unsteadily from the sofa and trudged back across the lounge and then up the stairs, sensing Cliff's presence behind her, then feeling his closeness when she walked into her room and stood facing her bed.

'Sit down while we have a chat,' he said, and she could feel his breath on the back of her head.

When she sat on the bed, he snuggled up close to her and spoke. 'Y'know you're a really nice girl, Amy. I thought that as soon as I met you.'

She smiled self-consciously and he leaned over, putting his arm around her shoulders. 'In fact, you could be my favourite girl. Would you like that?'

Amy wasn't sure. She liked the idea of being a favourite girl; it had been so special with Dale. But the prospect of Cliff taking on that role filled her with uncertainty.

'Well, what do you think?'

She shrugged. 'Dunno.'

He lifted his other hand and traced his finger affectionately down the line of her nose. His hand then hovered over her while he continued to lean across. 'You'll enjoy being my favourite girl. I'll make you feel really special and buy you lots of nice things.'

Then he lowered his hand and ran it over her breast, grazing her nipple. Amy felt a shiver and a tiny thrill shot through her, causing her alarm. Her feelings soon changed to intense guilt as well as the ever-present embarrassment and discomfort in his presence. She was all too aware that it was wrong.

Amy pulled away. 'No, I don't like it.'

'You sure?' he asked. 'Only, you looked to me like you were enjoying it.'

'No, I don't. I mean, I'm not,' Amy protested. 'I don't want to. You shouldn't be touching me there.'

Her head had dropped, and she found it impossible to meet his characteristic intense gaze. Cliff wasn't like Dale at all. He may have seemed nice and he was always kind to her but there was something about him. Something she couldn't fully comprehend. But something that made her feel embarrassed and nervous and as though she just wanted to run away whenever he was around. And what he was doing to her now validated all her distrust of him. She knew it was bad, but she felt helpless against a man who seemed so determined and sure of himself.

'Who says I shouldn't be touching you?' he asked.

Amy shrugged.

'Why shouldn't you do it if it feels nice, Amy?'

Her eyes clouded over with tears now as a feeling of helpless acquiescence overwhelmed her. 'I just shouldn't,' she said, but, in her powerlessness, she couldn't think of anything to substantiate her argument.

She wished he would go away and leave her alone although she was too afraid to say so. But he didn't go away. Instead he persisted. 'Why not? Who's to know what me and you get up to when we're alone?' He smiled, trying to sell the idea to her. 'If we want a bit of fun, why shouldn't we? No harm in a bit of fun, is there?' Then he leaned towards her and whispered, 'It can be our little secret.'

Amy was becoming desperate. She wanted to break away. She was frightened. But if she pushed him away, she didn't know how he would react. Desperately, she searched for the right words that would make him leave her alone. 'What about Mum?' she asked.

He grinned in a self-satisfied way and patted her leg. 'Don't worry about your mum. I'll see her right.'

For a few moments they remained silent, Amy clenching her muscles as she tried to shrink away from the constant glare of his eager eyes. Then she felt his hand graze her nipple once more and she reared back in shock.

'No, no don't,' she pleaded, her voice trembling.

Cliff got up off the bed and fixed her with a lewd smile. 'OK, I'll leave you for now. But I want you to think about it, Amy. We can have a lot of fun, me and you, and nobody needs to know. You can be my special girl.'

Once she was alone again it took Amy some time before she could calm her shaking limbs. The experience had frightened and upset her, and she was at a loss as to what to do about it. She was tempted to tell an adult but, at the same time, afraid. It was something she didn't feel comfortable discussing and what if they didn't believe her?

She thought about her mother and recalled his words, 'Don't worry about your mum. I'll see her right.' She wasn't sure what those words meant except that he seemed confident where her mother was concerned. And she knew her mum liked him because she'd told her so and asked *her* to be nice to him too. What if he convinced her mother that she'd been lying? Then she'd be in trouble. And she'd feel really ashamed because it would be a bad thing that she was accusing him of.

Amy thought fleetingly about telling her grandparents or a teacher or neighbour. But the thought of that bothered her even more than telling her mother. What if they didn't believe her either? She already sensed that they didn't think much of her mother and she didn't want them to think badly of her too.

A feeling of powerlessness swamped her once more. There was nothing she could do; she only hoped it didn't happen again. But the determined look in his eyes had told her that it probably would. And she dreaded his return.

29

July 1999

Loretta was feeling remorseful. She should never have agreed to let Cliff spend some time with Amy, but she'd been desperate for money. Cliff had been so persuasive, telling her that no harm would come to her daughter and, in the end, she hadn't been able to resist the huge amount of money he'd offered.

Now though, it was the day after his visit, and she was struggling with the harsh reality of her own complicity. Loretta had known what he was after but had blanked her mind to it, too focused on financial gain. She only hoped he hadn't gone too far. He'd assured her that he hadn't but had refused to share any details.

She walked into the living room that morning, dreading the look on her daughter's face. Amy looked up momentarily as she approached but then her eyes remained downcast, her face flushed.

'Are you alright, love?' she asked.

Amy shook her head slowly but didn't speak.

'What is it, love?' she asked, knowing what the answer would be but afraid of hearing it.

'I didn't like what Cliff did,' said Amy, her voice barely audible, and as she spoke a tear formed in the corner of her eye.

Loretta could sense that her daughter was afraid of telling her and she felt terrible. 'What did he do, love?'

'He touched me.'

'What do you mean?'

'Somewhere he shouldn't have,' said Amy, the tears now flowing onto her cheeks.

'Where?' asked Loretta. 'Show me where.'

Amy raised her hand and touched her own breast. 'There,' she said, quickly lowering her hand again.

Loretta gulped. 'Oh, I'm sorry, love. I didn't know he was going to do that. I'll have a word with him and make sure it doesn't happen again.' When Amy didn't respond, she asked, 'Is that alright?'

Amy nodded imperceptibly and Loretta instinctively raised her hand to her mouth. The guilt tore away at her, knowing that she had been a party to this. How could she have been so desperate to offer up her daughter like that? She rushed to Amy's side, taking her in her arms and whispering words of comfort, her own eyes now clouded with tears.

'I'm so, so sorry. I promise, it'll never happen again.'

And at that moment she meant every word.

*

August 1999

Cliff still came round to the house after that day, but he didn't ask to spend time with Amy alone anymore. She presumed her mother must have had a word with him and told him she didn't want him to. Amy couldn't understand why her mother still wanted to see him after what had happened until she spotted something in the hall that explained it.

Loretta was letting him out of the house one morning after he had stayed, and Amy happened to be passing through the hall on her way upstairs. She saw him pass something to her mother. She wasn't quite sure what it was at first, but it looked like a bunch of paper. Her mother was closing the door when she noticed Amy in the hallway and she quickly shoved whatever it was into her dressing gown pocket.

'What on earth are you doing, Amy?' she asked defensively.

'Nothing. I'm just going to my room.'

'Well go on then. Never mind standing there watching me.'

'I wasn't. I…'

'I know what you were doing. Now go on, get up. You're too nosy for your own good, young lady.'

Amy dashed up the stairs, eager to get away from her mother when she was in one of those moods.

It wasn't until she was in her bedroom that she realised what Cliff had passed to her mother. Money. Yes, it was definitely money. But why would he be giving her money? Then a recollection flashed through her mind. It was a few months previously when Nathan had asked if their mother was a prostitute.

The realisation hit her with startling clarity, and it made sense considering that her mother had previously told her Cliff would be generous to them if she treated him nicely. But then denial took over. No, that couldn't be right. Only bad people were prostitutes so she couldn't possibly be one. She was their mum and their mum wouldn't do something like that.

30

October 2015

Cora was pleased with herself. She'd finally managed to lure the object of her desire back to the squat where she was living. This wasn't a paying client; it was a freebie. She'd wanted this man for so long and now she had finally managed to persuade him to spend some time with her.

But Cora was no fool; she knew he was only after a quickie. But maybe after he'd spent the night with her and she'd worked a bit of her magic, he might come back for more. And, even if he didn't, she felt sure that the memory of this night would stay with her for a long time.

It was an old derelict office block, but Cora considered it almost luxurious compared to some of the squats she'd stayed in. There was a main area with pillars erected at intervals. The place must have been abandoned in a hurry for whatever reason because there were even some screens dotted about. These had previously been used to divide the main office into separate units but were now used by the homeless to section off an area that they could designate as their own space.

There were also still ladies' and gents' toilets. Although they were quite grubby-looking, the ladies' doubled up as a bathroom where she and the other girls could have a strip-down wash over the sink.

Cora had been one of the first arrivals as soon as the insurance company had gone bump and vacated the premises. So, not only did she have her own space, she had her own room. It was a small office to one side of the main area, which must have been occupied by somebody of managerial status.

The office wasn't completely private, but it was the next best thing. Although the door didn't have a lock, she could still shut it and prop something behind to stop intruders. She'd also fixed a padlock to the outside so she could lock the door when she was out to discourage people from stealing her things.

On the side of the room that met the main office there were windows, which stretched from the door to the opposite wall. There was also a smaller window on the other side looking out onto the city. She'd done her best to make some curtains from old discarded cloth she'd found in the bins outside a fashion warehouse. Unfortunately, they only covered about two-thirds of the windows on the inner side, but she had plans to cover the whole of them in time.

As she withdrew the key from her pocket Cora smiled at her man friend. She slid the key into the padlock and opened it. Then she pushed the door open, revealing the interior where she had a mattress pushed into one corner and covered with a duvet and several scatter cushions adorning the top end. There was an office cabinet in another corner where she kept some spare clothing and toiletries, and there was an empty upturned crate next to the mattress, which she had fashioned as a makeshift bedside table.

'Da daaah,' she said, in a sing-song voice as the man peered inside, but he didn't look particularly impressed.

Regardless, the room had everything she needed so she ignored his lacklustre response and focused on what they were here for. She lunged at him, her lips puckered, but he held her off.

'Hang on!' he said. 'What's the rush? Why don't we do a couple of lines first?'

'We can have that later. Let's have a bit of fun first. We have got all night, y'know. I've decided to give work a miss.'

Cora decided on a little gentle persuasion to start with. She got down on her knees, grasping his genitals in one hand while undoing his trousers with the other. She looked up fleetingly, seeing the look of readiness on his face, and knew she had him.

After working on him for a while she pulled away, leaving him wanting. Then she flung herself on the bed and waited for him to join her. He obliged and Cora helped him as he hurriedly tore off her clothes.

She had somehow expected that sex with him would be so much different than with her clients. She'd actually dreamt of this moment for weeks, fantasising about him and building up the event in her own mind. But up to now it had been a let-down. No kisses. No warm embrace. No tenderness. And his lack of feeling was starting to get to her.

'You might try some fuckin' foreplay first,' she complained when he tried to enter her.

'Why the fuck should I for a slapper like you?' he argued.

'Right, fuck you then!' she yelled, attempting to push him off, but the man wasn't having any of it.

For several seconds they fought on the bed with Cora trying to prise him away and shutting her legs tightly while the man pinned her down and tried to force her legs apart. Cora could feel him getting the better of her, so she clawed at his face.

He thumped her hand away and she yelled as her fingers began to throb. Ignoring the pain, she pummelled at his face, head and shoulders. The man pulled her hands away again then slapped her face till the stinging brought tears to her eyes. By now the idea of having sex with him had turned from a dream into a nightmare.

'Get the fuck off me or I'll scream rape!' she shouted.

But she was too late; he was already aroused. 'No, I fuckin' won't!' he yelled. 'That's what you brought me here for, isn't it?'

He put his hand over her mouth to stifle her screams while he managed to force her legs apart. She could tell he was enjoying this. When he entered her his fingers slipped down to her throat and pressed hard. As she struggled to push him off, his grip on her throat tightened and his eagerness intensified. Cora could feel him thrusting savagely and saw the look of exhilaration on his face; his eyes alive and his lips contorted into a wicked sneer.

At first, she continued trying to push him off, but she was pinned to the bed. She thrashed around, her legs kicking haphazardly and her fingers clawing at his face once again. He raised himself up, dodging her talons while his hands remained closed around her throat.

Cora wanted to yell for help, but her throat was too

constricted. She could feel the pressure building. Extreme pain pounded inside her head until it felt like it was going to explode. She carried on kicking and scratching, desperate to break free. To shout. To breathe. But his grip became stronger with his mounting excitement. She was losing strength. Her limbs slackened as the pain reached a peak, then all went black.

The last thing she spotted before she died was an image at the window. Her attacker had his back to the main office, but she could just about make out the vision set back from the hazy space that hovered behind her attacker's angry head. It was the horror-stricken face of a young man who had been watching.

31

Amber was feeling fed up, so she popped into the Rose and Crown hoping to have a few drinks and cheer herself up before work. As she walked inside the pub, she found Sapphire and Angie sitting at their usual table. They greeted her effusively and Amber noticed straightaway that Angie was really drunk.

She joined them and tried to strike up a conversation, but every time she and Sapphire were in the middle of a discussion, Angie butted in, waffling on in a drunken drawl. It was difficult when she was like this. None of what she said made much sense and it stopped the flow of conversation with whoever else was present.

They were just talking about the perils of unpredictable clients when Angie chipped in. 'Eh, I've got sssomething to tell you. And you'll want to hear it.'

'Go on then, what is it?' asked Amber.

'In a minute. I need a drink.'

Angie got up unsteadily and staggered to the bar. Sapphire looked across at Amber and shook her head.

'I know,' said Amber, in acknowledgement. 'She's really pissed tonight.'

By the time Angie had come back from the bar, Amber guessed that she had forgotten what it was she was going to tell them.

'Place isss dead,' she said. 'Not like the old days...'

Then old Angie looked about her wistfully. She was at an advanced stage of alcoholism, which meant that she didn't think or speak in a logical sequence like most people. But she seemed to think there was something the girls would want to hear so Amber pressed her for the information.

'What was it you wanted to tell us?'

'What? Oh that! Yeah...' Her voice had become livelier as though she was about to share a bit of juicy gossip. Then she spotted a man walking past them. 'Ooh, haven't ssseen him for a while.'

Amber raised her eyes at her, inquisitively.

'What?' asked Angie who suddenly seemed to remember what Amber and Sapphire were waiting to hear. 'Oh yeah. 'Bout things not being the same. You're not safe on the ssstreets now y'know. Look at that latessst killing.'

Amber had almost switched off but when Angie started going on about a killing, she sat up straight in her chair, paying rapt attention.

'Killing? What killing? Not one of us lot I hope?'

'Yeah. That nasty one. Erm, what was her name now? Karen? No... no... Carol. No, not Carol. Something like that.'

'You don't mean Cora, do you?' suggested Sapphire.

Angie stared back, her eyes glazed and unfocused.

'Big girl?' Sapphire asked. 'The one that had a go at you a few weeks ago and said you'd nicked a tenner?'

'Yeah, that'sss the one.'

'Shit! I don't believe it. What happened?'

Angie leaned into them both conspiratorially and Amber got a whiff of the vinegar-like stench of stale alcohol on her breath. She pulled back and waited for Angie to speak.

Angie leaned back as well and seemed to forget what she was going to say for a moment but then she spoke. 'Ssstrangled.' She bent forward again. 'In a squat. Her own room ap… pa… rently.'

Amber raised her hand to her mouth in shock. It was hard to believe. 'Why? Who did it? Do they know?'

Angie shook her head. 'Not a clue. One of the other sssquatters found her.'

'Shit!' said Amber and Sapphire in unison.

For a few minutes Amber tried to glean more information out of Angie with the morbid curiosity of someone who has just encountered the dark side of life. But it soon became obvious that she wouldn't find out anything more. Angie either didn't know or she couldn't remember and all she did was impart the same information repeatedly.

'I wonder who it could be?' asked Sapphire.

Amber shrugged. 'Dunno, maybe a sicko client. She might have taken him back to the squat and then he turned nasty on her.'

'Jesus! It's fuckin' scary, isn't it?' said Sapphire. 'Especially when you get them clients that take all their sick fantasies out on working girls, like the fuckin' Yorkshire Ripper.'

Amber just nodded then changed the subject. It was worrying to think that a killer might be targeting the girls. After a while she finished her drink and set off for work. She felt like going less than ever now that she'd heard about Cora. But then she reassured herself that at least she had a degree of protection now, if she went on the assumption that Kev Pike was doing what she paid him for.

She wished there was somebody she could confide in about her worries, but Angie and Sapphire were the only girls who hung out in the pub now. The old crowd had moved on, and Amber wasn't as close to Sapphire as she had been to Crystal. Angie was a waste of time, but she had been right when she'd said that things weren't the same. As she trudged to work, Amber felt lonely. But, more than that, she was scared.

32

September 1999

Loretta was in the kitchen fixing her and Cliff a drink while Nathan was upstairs in his bedroom, which left Amy alone in the living room with Cliff. Even though he hadn't touched her since that time many weeks ago, she still felt uncomfortable with him.

When he came to visit, he often brought presents for all of them, including her, and she had noticed how hers always seemed better than Nathan's and more grown up. Last time he had given her a toiletry set and she'd been overjoyed. But it had been difficult showing her gratitude to a man who she really wanted to distance herself from.

Now, as she watched TV, she could feel him examining her, making her cheeks flush and her heartbeat speed up. She tried to ignore him and keep her eyes fixed on the screen. But when he spoke to her, she turned around.

'What have you been up to at school, Amy?'

She shrugged. 'Nowt special.' Then she turned back and focused on the TV screen once more.

'You're turning into a fine-looking girl. I bet you have all the lads after you, don't you?'

Turning her head once more, she glared at him. 'No, I don't!' she raged.

'Come on, don't tell fibs, lovely-looking girl like you.' Then he reached inside his pocket and pulled out his wallet. He took a five-pound note from it and handed it to her. 'I've not treated you today, have I?' he asked, walking over to her. 'Here, have this.'

He held out his hand, so she stood up and reached for the money. As soon as her fingers touched it, he covered her hand with his other one. 'You deserve it,' he said. 'You're a good girl.'

His hand lingered and Amy was becoming uncomfortable and wary about what he was going to do next. She stood there awkwardly for several seconds, relieved when she heard her mother coming back into the room.

'Well, what's going on here then?' she asked.

Cliff laughed. 'Not what you think, you dirty-minded mare. I was just treating Amy, that's all.'

'Oh, Cliff, I've told you, you don't have to give them money and presents every time you come here.'

'I know. I do it because I want to. Amy's a good girl and she deserves treats. Isn't that right, Amy?'

Amy blushed and nodded, perturbed on realising that he was deliberately trying to embarrass her.

Cliff's attention switched to the bottle of wine Loretta had brought into the room and the two glasses she was clutching. 'Lovely,' he said, taking the wine from her. 'I'll pour.'

Loretta laid the two glasses down on the coffee table and

took up a seat next to Cliff on the sofa while Amy was seated on the armchair across from them. 'There,' he said, lifting both glasses and handing one to Loretta. Then he chinked his glass next to hers. 'Here's to us. Let's make it a good night, eh?

Later Amy had gone to bed. She would have liked to have watched some more TV, but it had become embarrassing sharing the same room as her mother and Cliff. As they downed the bottle of wine and started on the next one their conversation had become increasingly risqué and Cliff was slobbering over her mother.

He had started by putting his arm around her then graduated to patting her on the leg. That would have been bad enough in itself but Amy could sense Cliff watching her as though he was waiting for a reaction each time he touched her mother.

It was three hours later when she was awoken by the sound of them on the upstairs landing. Cliff was saying something with a note of amusement in his voice and her mother was giggling. Eventually her giggling ceased. 'Shush,' she said. It sounded like she was trying to whisper but was failing miserably. 'You'll wake the children up.'

Cliff said something else and her mother giggled again but quieter this time. For a few minutes Amy heard the running of taps, the flushing of the toilet and the closing of doors until the noise died down and all she could hear was faint chatter coming from her mother's room.

Their chatter didn't last long, and Amy presumed they must have fallen asleep. Thank God! Now perhaps she could get some sleep too. She turned over in bed, her face to the wall, and snuggled down into her duvet, pulling it over her ears in case the noise started again.

She was tempted to grab one of the soft toys that sat at the foot of her bed, knowing it would enable her to get back to sleep more easily. But she resisted. Nowadays she kept them for display, feeling too grown up to have them inside her bed, especially after Nathan had teased her. She'd had them since she was a toddler and was reluctant to part with them, especially Barney, a large brown cuddly bear with shaggy fur and one eye missing. He was the oldest and her most treasured.

It took her a while to get back to sleep and she was just nodding off when she woke up, startled, sensing a presence in the room. She turned and saw Cliff in his underwear hovering next to her bed. The sight of him without his clothing alarmed her and she shot up in the bed ready to shout for her mother. But Cliff reached down and clamped his hand over her mouth.

'Quiet!' he warned. 'You don't want to wake your mother up, do you?'

Amy stared at him, her eyes wide with terror, but it was impossible to speak with his heavy hand covering her mouth.

He seemed to take her silence as a sign of acquiescence and he climbed into the bed beside her, pulling her towards him with his free hand and wrapping the duvet around them both.

Then he whispered to her. 'I'm not going to hurt you, I promise. I just want to snuggle up next to you. You're not going to stop Uncle Cliff cuddling up with his favourite girl, are you? Isn't that what all uncles and dads do?'

Then he removed his hand from her mouth but before Amy had a chance to speak, he threatened her. 'Don't you dare say anything to anyone, especially your mum, because if you do, I'll have to stop coming round! And you know what'll happen if I stop coming round, don't you?'

Amy noticed his menacing tone and she listened while he elucidated. 'No more presents for you or your mum, that's what. And your mum wouldn't be happy with you if I stopped bringing presents, would she? Not to mention all the other nice things I do for her. In fact, she'd probably blame you and you'd be in big trouble.'

His words hit home when she thought about how happy her mother was whenever Cliff was around and how he made sure the family never wanted for anything. Then she thought about how sad her mother had been when the relationship with Dale had ended. Her thoughts relayed a distressing medley of scenes:

Her mother's sorrow after Dale's last phone call. Finding her unconscious one day after school. The neighbours' reactions to Loretta's suicide attempt. Being rushed to her grandparents'. Sitting in their house worrying whether her mum was going to be alright.

She didn't say anything, but she lay still in the bed, her body foetal with Cliff wrapped around her, as she unwillingly accepted her fate.

When she felt his hands graze her breasts, she flinched but he carried on. This time he delved deeper, his hands travelling down her body and his fingers probing as he explored her nubile flesh. She could feel his penis pressing ardently against the back of her. Amy had heard about the things men did, and she feared that it might be about to happen to her.

She shut her eyes and pretended it wasn't happening, her mind numb and her body stiff and unresponsive. Amy was glad when it was over and relieved that he hadn't tried to put his thing inside her.

As he got up from the bed, he issued a warning, 'Not a word of this, do you hear?'

Amy nodded her head, feeling the sting of tears.

'Right, I'm going now but I want you to be ready for me next time I come. And no crying. You're a big girl now. I need you to do as you're told and no squealing to anyone or you know what will happen, don't you?'

He waited for Amy to nod again before he added, 'Your mother will be furious with you!'

When he left the room, tears flooded her eyes. She felt invaded, dirty, ashamed, and for a long time she lay there reliving her ordeal, sobbing desperately and unable to sleep.

Seeking comfort, she grabbed at her favourite teddy, Barney, and pulled him into the bed with her, clinging to him and stemming her tears against his mangy fur. He was old and ragged, but he was also unthreatening and at this moment Amy needed to feel safe.

33

October 2015

It was late at night and Amber was standing in her usual spot having decided that she'd service another client before going home. She had been fearful ever since being attacked by Cora and Jack a few weeks previously. But, following Cora's death, she was even more frightened. Ideally, she could have done with making some extra cash but the longer she stayed out the more afraid she was, and it was becoming increasingly difficult to carry on working.

As she stood there, she felt persistently jumpy. Every car that stopped, every person who passed by and every sound presented a threat. In fact, she didn't know which was worse: standing at the mouth of the secluded railway arch or getting in a car with a complete stranger. With all those anxieties whirling around inside her head she was glad that it was almost the end of the night for her.

Apart from being frightened, Amber was hungry. As

usual her mother hadn't bothered getting any shopping in, so she had come out to work with hardly any food inside her, promising herself that she'd call at the late-night kebab shop before she went home.

She comforted herself with the thought that not only would she soon be able to leave the red-light district for the night, but she'd also get something to eat even if it was yet another kebab.

She saw a group of young men walking towards her. They looked animated, possibly a bit drunk, and she prepared herself to do battle. As they advanced, she gazed intently at them, trying to gauge the opposition. She saw them approach another street girl and a verbal exchange took place, but they didn't hang around.

They were drawing closer and the other street girl had since got into a punter's car. To Amber's consternation, there was nobody else around apart from two people who she could just about spot far off in the distance. She couldn't tell whether the couple were male or female, but they were heading towards her. She realised, however, that it would be a while before they drew level.

The young men were now only a few metres away and she noticed how they glanced at her and then chatted and giggled amongst themselves. It wasn't a good sign and instinct told Amber that they would be a problem.

She counted five of them altogether. At the front of the group was a short, stocky lad and next to him was one of average height with ginger hair. These two looked more animated than the rest of the group and she guessed that they would be the chief troublemakers.

Even as they approached, she was thinking of witty put-down lines she could use. This often helped to switch the focus of the group from herself to the men who she was ridiculing, rather like a comedian dealing with hecklers in the audience.

As she had predicted, the short man was the first to make a move. He broke away from the group and walked nearer to her, grabbing his crotch and bending his knees as he put each foot forward in turn, like a parody of a primitive dance.

'Fancy a bit of this love?' he asked.

'Not if that's all you've got to offer,' quipped Amber.

His mates roared with laughter, but the stocky man came back at her: 'I've got a good eight inches there, love.'

'I doubt it,' said Amber, attempting to look bored, 'Not if your height's anything to go by.'

As his mates laughed again, he countered, 'Good things come in small packages and what I've got is too good for a fuckin' prossie like you.'

'He's saving it in case he cops off,' shouted one of the men at the back, seeming to enjoy his friend's humiliation.

But, as he spoke, the guy with the ginger hair joined in their fun, scuppering Amber's idea of shifting the attention away from her. 'Show us your tits!' he said. 'Come on, let's see what you've got. I want to know if it's worthwhile shelling out my hard-earned cash.'

Then he fished around in his pockets, drawing out a few pound coins. 'This enough for you?' he asked. ''Cos I don't think you're worth any fuckin' more.'

Amber tried to put on a brave front but inside she was

quivering, 'I wouldn't even give it away to you, you fuckin' ginger minger. Now do one!'

For a few seconds they exchanged insults but as they argued she kept observing the short, stocky man. She could see him looking around and guessed that he was up to something. The breath caught in her throat when she realised what he was doing; he was checking for CCTV.

He must have been satisfied that there were none because, suddenly, he ran at her and clasped her buttocks tightly. 'Come on, love. You heard what he said. Let's see what you've got.'

Amber spun around and slapped his hand, but she could feel panic setting in. His hand flew back, this time grabbing her crotch. 'Phwoar!' he shouted, his fingers pulsating backwards and forwards as his friends jeered in the background.

She shoved his hand away and stepped off the pavement, so eager to escape from the men that she failed to notice a car that was hurtling towards her. She jumped back onto the pavement, crashing into the stocky man and pushing him aside.

'Fuckin' do one, you dirty little bastard!' she yelled.

As the driver's door slammed shut, she saw Kev get out of the car. 'What the fuck's going on?' he yelled.

At the same time, Amber noticed the couple approaching, and the group of men, not wanting to hang about while there were witnesses around, ran off laughing. Kev ran round to the passenger side of the car and took hold of Amber by the arm. 'You OK?' he asked.

'Yeah,' said Amber who was thankful that Kev had come

to her rescue. 'They were just acting cocky, that's all,' she added, trying to be brave even though she was shaken up.

He nodded and let go of her arm. Not wishing to discuss the matter further, Amber reached inside her pocket for some money, presuming he was here to collect. Kev was unpredictable and she never knew when he would turn up for his protection money. But whenever he did so, he was always nice to her. And, on this occasion, despite her bravado, she was relieved that he had shown up just at the right time.

As she took out the cash, the couple walked by. They slowed down as they passed her, obviously curious about what had taken place. She saw that they were eating from polystyrene trays and smelt the tempting aroma of chips. Amber couldn't resist turning round to look at them, her eyes lingering on the contents of the trays. She salivated, forgetting for a moment that Kev was waiting for his payment.

'Oy!' he called, and Amber's attention shot back to him.

'Sorry,' she muttered, passing him the money.

'You hungry or summat?' he asked, taking in her slight frame.

'A bit, yeah. But I'm going to the kebab shop after.'

He smiled and it transformed his face, emphasising his good looks. She noticed at once that other side to him and his charisma held her captive.

'Come on, I know somewhere better than a kebab shop. Get in,' he said.

'But I've not finished work yet.'

'That's OK.' He smiled. 'As long as you've earned enough to pay me, I'll get the meal. You look as though you need a good feed and it'll save you paying for a kebab.'

She pushed her caution aside and got in the car, partly because it didn't pay to cross Kev Pike but also because she was tempted by both the food and by Kev himself. He might have had a bad-boy reputation, but he also had a way with women that drew them in.

34

October 2015

Once Amber was inside Kev's car, he put his foot on the accelerator and drove across the city centre till they reached the financial area close to King Street. He parked the car in a side street and led her inside a modern restaurant. Amber didn't notice the name, but she probably wouldn't have known it anyway as she rarely ventured into this part of the city.

Inside she found that it was full of young, trendy types, probably office staff who worked nearby, she thought. As well as a restaurant, it doubled up as a cocktail bar. Kev got them a table and a waitress brought over the menus. Amber was spoilt for choice.

'Have whatever you want,' said Kev, as her eyes roamed up and down the menu. So, Amber made the most of it, ordering a starter, main course and dessert.

It was nice to feel spoilt and, as Kev entertained her with amusing tales of his life of crime, she realised that she was seeing a different side to him. He was witty and full of charm and seemed to command respect from the restaurant staff.

Later, when she was feeling replete after a three-course dinner with wine, Kev led her to the bar area where they ordered a cocktail each.

'Bet you've never been somewhere like this before, have you?' he asked.

'No.'

'Well, make the most of it then. You can have another cocktail after that if you want. I saw you looking at what that girl is drinking over there. I can get you one of them if you like.'

Amber smiled and said 'thanks' but she wondered what she had done to deserve this special treatment, and from Kev Pike of all people. Perhaps he did genuinely like her. Amber's other thought was that it had all been paid for by girls like her anyway so she might as well have what she wanted.

Her musings were addressed when he said, 'I've had my eye on you for a while. You're not like a lot of the other girls, all cocky and mouthy. You seem alright.'

She smiled again, lost for what to say. But she did recall his concern when Cora and her associate had beaten her up, which made her think that perhaps he did actually care about her.

Looking over towards the gents', he said, 'Be back in a minute.' Then he left her sitting at the bar on her own while he went to the toilet.

He was so enigmatic, and she liked that about him too. Anybody else would have announced that they were going to the toilet but not Kev Pike. He preferred to be vague about where he was going even though it was obvious. Amber had had a fair bit to drink by now and was becoming dreamy. She had failed to notice that while she was sitting on the barstool her short skirt had ridden up till it was nearly revealing her underwear.

Amber snapped out of her reverie when she saw a young, red-haired man at the bar who was peering intently at her. He spoke when she looked up at him.

'I fuckin' know you. You're one of them tarts that hang about at the back of Piccadilly. Me and my mates walked past you earlier tonight.'

With a sinking feeling Amber recognised the man and recalled the unpleasant encounter that had taken place earlier. The man turned to his friend who was standing the other side of him. 'Hey, Ant, have you seen this? She's that fuckin' whore that we walked past before. Do you remember?'

Ant, who was showing the first signs of baldness despite his youth, stepped around him so that he could have a good look at Amber. 'Fuckin' hell, yeah,' he said. 'What's a slapper like you doing in this place? Shouldn't you be lying on your back somewhere, love?'

'Piss off!' said Amber, too drunk by now to exercise caution.

'How much for you to suck my cock?' Ant asked while his friend laughed raucously.

'Just fuckin' do one, will you?' Amber snapped.

'Or else?' said Ant, sidling up to her till she could feel his hot breath on her face.

She pulled her head away but was saved from having to respond as Kev returned just at that moment. Without stopping to ask questions he grabbed Ant from behind and wrenched his arm up his back, pushing him into the bar and applying pressure till he was yelling to his friend for help. The red-haired man looked as though he was about to get involved but he was stopped when Kev released Ant's arm and switched his attention to him, taking hold of his shirt lapels and ramming his fists up against his windpipe.

'Don't even fuckin' think about it!' he warned.

The man was clearly terrified; his eyes were wide open, and his bottom lip drawn back at the corners.

Ant struggled to turn around in the narrow space between Kev and the bar. Once he was on eye level with Kev, he seemed to deliberate over what to do. The sight of his petrified friend and his own throbbing arm were making him indecisive.

The red-haired man tried to shake his head to warn him off but only managed to flicker his eyes from left to right.

'Alright, alright, we don't want no trouble, mate,' Ant said to Kev who glared at him but retained his hold of the other man.

'You alright, Amber?' Kev asked.

'Yeah, nothing I'm not used to,' she said.

By now the other customers had backed away and the barman had noticed the fracas. 'Calm it down or you're out on your arse and I'm calling the cops!' he shouted but his voice had a panicked edge to it.

Kev let go of the man and glared from one to the other of them. 'You're lucky we're in here,' he said. 'If we'd have been outside, I'd have kicked the fuck out of the pair of you! Now, piss off, and don't you dare fuckin' hassle one of my girls again.' Then he turned to the barman as the two young men distanced themselves. 'It's fine,' he said. 'It's sorted.'

The barman looked at him and, seeming to think better of taking things further, he walked away.

Kev sidled up to Amber and rested his hand on the small of her back. 'Are they the same guys who were hassling you tonight?'

When she nodded, he asked, 'You sure you're alright?'

She giggled, waving her hand with an air of nonchalance. 'Sure, I'm fine.'

Kev laughed. 'You're more than fine, you're pissed.'

He looked across the bar area to where the two young men had joined their friends a few tables away. They were now deep in conversation and he recognised another of the men from earlier; the short, stocky one. He would have loved to have taught him a lesson but knew he couldn't handle five at once. 'Come on, let's go,' he said to Amber.

'But I haven't finished my drink,' she protested, her drunkenness making her bold.

'I'll get you one another time,' he said, grabbing her jacket and draping it across her shoulders.

Sensing his determination, Amber jumped down from the bar stool and followed him out of the building.

'Where are we going?' she asked when they were outside, expecting him to take her to another bar somewhere in the city centre.

'Back to mine,' he said. 'Get in the car.'

35

November 1999

It was Amy's twelfth birthday party and she had been allowed to have some friends round, which was unusual in her house. She was currently in her bedroom with her two best friends, Rachel and Brooke, while her mother was in the kitchen preparing a buffet. For once she hadn't asked her to help. Amy thought it was probably because of her friends being there. She had helped her mother to clean and tidy beforehand though as she didn't want her friends to think she lived in a tip.

Amy had enjoyed showing her two friends the new clothes her mother had bought her. It was always good when her mother had money spare and she grudgingly admitted to herself that she had Cliff to thank for that. She and her friends were playing around with some makeup Brooke had bought for her birthday when Loretta called upstairs letting them know the buffet was ready.

They dashed down to the kitchen and Amy was thrilled to see all the food laid out on the table: sandwiches, sausage rolls, cocktail sausages, coleslaw, pickled onions, pizza and chicken legs and, at the end of the table, a strawberry gateaux and some chocolate biscuits.

'Wow! Thanks, Mum,' said Amy walking over to her mother and hugging her.

The three girls and Nathan sat down at the table to eat but Loretta didn't join them. Instead, she took a bottle of wine from one of the cupboards and poured herself a drink. Amy presumed it was her first glass of the day as it was a new bottle and she didn't seem tipsy yet. She was thankful for that and hoped her friends would be gone before her mother became drunk.

Amy was so busy enjoying herself, laughing and chatting with her friends and tucking into the delicious food, that she didn't notice her mother's constant eye on the clock. She hadn't realised her mother was expecting a visitor till she heard the doorbell ring.

'I'll get it,' Loretta said.

She left the room, and Amy was disturbed to find that when she returned, she was accompanied by Cliff. She turned to see him walk into the kitchen with a smarmy grin on his face, eying the girls appreciatively. Then he grinned lasciviously at Amy.

'Happy birthday to my favourite girl. You *are* looking all grown up,' he announced. 'I've got something special for you.'

'Thanks,' said Amy, turning back to her friends, and subconsciously putting a hand over her face to hide her embarrassment.

For a while he remained transfixed, frozen to the spot,

and Amy could feel his eyes roaming all over her. It was Loretta who broke the tension in the room.

'Well, aren't you gonna tell us what it is?' she prompted.

Cliff's grin grew wider as he withdrew a present from his pocket and handed it to Amy.

'Thanks,' she repeated, keeping her eyes downwards as she took the small package and placed it on the table.

'Aren't you gonna open it?' asked Loretta.

'Yeah,' said Cliff. 'I'm dying to see your little face light up when you see what it is.'

Amy reluctantly picked up the box and removed the packaging with a sense of déjà vu when she revealed the small box inside. It reminded her of the one that had contained the silver charm bracelet he'd previously bought for her, and she knew it was going to be jewellery.

But she was still unprepared for the exquisite gift inside the box. It was a gold chain fitted with gold lettering in the centre that formed the word 'Amy' in a fancy scroll.

'Wow!' said Amy's friends in unison and Amy's jaw dropped as she held the necklace and examined it.

'Bloody hell!' exclaimed Loretta. 'Those don't come cheap. You are good to us, Cliff.' Then she turned to her daughter. 'What do you say, Amy?'

'Thanks,' said Amy for the third time, resisting a smile. She was thrilled with the gift but not with the giver.

He laughed. 'I'm bloody glad it's only a short name anyway. Here, let me put it on for you,' he said to Amy, and before she could protest, he had taken it out of the box and was trying to find the clasp.

Amy felt a shudder of revulsion as he draped it around

her neck and fiddled with the fastening. Then he reached in front, running his hand over the letters as though smoothing them down, his fingers lingering on her décolletage. She sat, stiff as a sentinel, wishing he would go away.

'Stand up, let's have a look at you,' he said, and Amy obliged while he stood back and admired his handiwork. 'Perfect,' he uttered, and Amy sat down as quickly as possible, noticing the uncomfortable expression on Brooke's face.

Once he had finished making a fuss of Amy, Cliff joined her mother at the other side of the kitchen, and she handed him a glass of wine. As he stood chatting with her mother, she could still feel his eyes on her and, despite the extravagant present, she couldn't wait to escape the table and go back to her room.

Rachel seemed to toy with her food for ages and Amy was glad when she had finally put the last morsel into her mouth. 'Come on, let's go up to my room,' she said, getting up from the table and dashing to the door without waiting for her friends' response.

The girls followed her, and they were soon seated on Amy's bed again.

'Wow!' Rachel repeated. 'Your necklace is gorgeous. Isn't your uncle nice?'

Amy was thankful at not having to answer when Brooke chipped in. 'I think he's creepy,' she said.

As Brooke spoke her eyes were fixed on Amy who could feel her face burning with shame. She could see Brooke scrutinising her for what seemed like an age as though she knew her dirty little secret and was challenging her to confess.

Her blushes were saved when Rachel reached towards

the necklace and held up the lettering. 'Can I try it on?' she asked, and Amy willingly agreed, relieved that the focus had now shifted from her to Rachel.

For the rest of that evening Amy couldn't relax, worried that Cliff would do something else inappropriate or that her mother would become drunk and embarrassing. She was relieved when it was time for her friends to go home.

Amy should have been thrilled with the beautiful necklace, but she wasn't. It was obviously expensive and over the top considering he wasn't even her dad. But it was more than that; it was a symbol of what she had had to do to earn it.

Later that night Amy heard the familiar sound of Cliff creeping inside her bedroom. She had expected it. The way he had looked at her and the fuss over the necklace told her what he had in mind. She mentally prepared herself for what was about to take place, familiar by now with the scenario.

Cliff would jump in bed beside her, hugging her from behind. Then his hands would roam up and down her body while he panted, and she felt his breath on the back of her neck. Then he would want to lie with her for a few minutes before finally leaving her alone.

As he nestled behind her, she found herself willing the time to pass until she could be alone once more and seek comfort by snuggling up with her trusty old teddy bear, Barney. But tonight, he wanted to talk as well.

'Did you like your present, Amy?' he whispered while his hands travelled along her body.

'Mmm,' she muttered, noncommittally.

'I bet your friends were jealous, weren't they? I bet they'd like a necklace like that. Nice girls, aren't they? Good-looking. But not as pretty as you. I've told you, you're special, Amy.'

He seemed to wait for her to respond but when she didn't answer he said, 'That's why I've got you something really special for your birthday.' He chuckled then added. 'I bet you thought the necklace was your special present, didn't you? But it wasn't. I've got something else lined up for you. You're getting a big girl now and I think it's time.'

Before Amy could even begin to imagine what he was talking about, he had rolled her over, clamped his hand over her mouth and was lying flat out on top of her with the weight of his body pinning her to the bed. Then he used his free hand to wrench up her nightshirt and prise her legs apart before forcing himself on her.

'You're a good girl,' he said as he entered her.

Amy felt a sharp pain shoot through her insides, and she screeched. But her screams were stifled by the weight of his hand gripping tightly across her mouth. Heedless of her pain or distress he carried on until he had climaxed, and then he got up off the bed.

'Happy birthday, Amy,' he said as he turned and walked out of her bedroom.

36

October 2015

Crystal breezed into her Altrincham store with an air of confidence wearing the smart clothing that had now become standard for her, together with her perfect hair and makeup. It was a Saturday and she was in search of her store manager, Deanna, while also trying to catch a glimpse of Candice.

Candice had been working at the store on Saturdays for a couple of weeks now and Crystal was eager for a progress report on her daughter. She spoke to Deanna regularly in relation to business and mentioned Candice in passing but they hadn't gone into detail. Deanna's usual comment was to confirm that Candice was doing well but Crystal wanted to hear more.

She was at the back of the store when she spotted Deanna.

'Hi, how are things?' asked Crystal.

'Fine.'

'Where's Candice?'

'On her break.' Deanna smiled. 'Don't worry, she isn't skiving.'

Crystal laughed. 'Fancy a coffee and a catch-up?'

'Yeah, sure,' said Deanna who asked one of the junior staff to bring some drinks through to her office.

They sat down in Deanna's office and made small talk while they waited for their coffees. Then, once the junior assistant had brought their drinks through, Crystal asked Deanna for an update regarding the store. She was pleased with the feedback. Profits were up on last month and the latest member of staff they had recruited was shaping up well.

'Talking of staff,' said Crystal, finally reaching one of the main topics she was here to discuss. 'How's Candice getting along?'

'Wonderful,' said Deanna. 'Sorry I haven't been able to tell you too much on the phone. It's because I'm usually in the shop where the other staff can overhear but you've got no worries with her, Crystal. She's so hard-working, she loves the job and she's even a wiz at maths. I've had her in the office counting the takings. She's definitely cut out for a career in fashion.' Then she laughed. 'I'd better watch my job, I think.'

Crystal returned her laughter. 'Brilliant,' she said. 'That's great to hear.'

It was good to know that Candice was capable in the world of work as well as being intelligent, and Crystal felt confident that one day her daughter would go far.

*

October 2015

It was the morning after her night with Kev and Amber was feeling happy. She'd had a lovely meal with him and a great night at the cocktail bar. Then they'd gone back to his and Kev had joined her for a drink before they'd gone to bed. As far as Amber was concerned, he was pretty good in the sack too and easy on the eye.

It felt good to be with a man who was protective. Amber realised that prior to last night Kev hadn't been protecting her so much, just taking the money and leaving her to cope alone on the beat. Cora's death and her own loneliness had left her feeling vulnerable but now things would be different.

She was going to be his girl; he'd said as much last night. Just thinking about that made her feel safer especially when she thought about how he'd dealt with the men at the bar who were making a nuisance of themselves.

She hadn't gone back to Kev's because she was drunk; she'd done it because she'd weighed up her options. In this game you did what you had to do. Besides, she was attracted to him, especially now he had shown his nicer side, and she was also flattered by his attention.

As she lay there reflecting on her decision, she glanced over at him, realising that he was starting to stir. 'Oh hello, sleepyhead,' she teased.

Kev managed a weak smile. 'Jesus! How can you be so fuckin' cheerful after what you drank last night? My head feels like someone's hit it with a fuckin' sledgehammer and I didn't even start drinking till we got back here.'

She laughed. 'You soon caught up though.'

'Go and get us a coffee and some paracetamols, will yer?'

Amber began to protest. 'But I don't know where everything is.'

'All the drink stuff is in the first cupboard on the left, milk's in the fridge and there's a box on the top shelf with medicines in it. Go on, get yourself a drink while you're at it.'

The thought occurred to Amber that as she was a guest in his home, he should really have been making the drinks. She was about to say something further but then she saw the look on his face and thought better of it. The grimace had returned and, although she still felt attracted to him, the violence he had displayed last night made her wary too, so she did as he ordered.

Her mind was in conflict. On the one hand, he had been so nice to her and on the other he had this whole other side to him. But Amber had made her decision now. She was his girl and she reasoned to herself that it would be much safer to be involved with him than to risk walking away.

37

December 2015

It was several weeks later and Amber was sitting inside a tapas bar with Kev. She'd never had tapas before or any other type of international cuisine apart from the odd Chinese from the local takeaway. She couldn't believe how tasty it was, especially the patatas bravas with various sauces, which she was tucking into with gusto.

When they'd arrived at the restaurant, she hadn't had a clue what to order but Kev had taken care of everything, reading through the menu and telling her about the various dishes. Then he'd ordered a high-end rioja, which was delicious. The staff seemed to have a respect for him too and were quick to attend to his every wish. Apparently, from what he had told her, he was a regular.

Amber was really enjoying herself as she sat there eating the food and getting pleasantly tipsy. That day had started with him taking her clothes shopping. It was lovely to have a man fuss over her, and she'd enjoyed his comments on the various outfits she'd tried on, telling her how gorgeous she looked.

This particular night out was typical of others she'd had with Kev since she'd started seeing him and he didn't seem to mind taking her out once or twice a week as long as she worked on the other nights. He knew some good restaurants and seemed switched on about the right wines to drink. Because of all the fine dining she'd put on a couple of pounds since they'd been together, but she looked better for it.

On the nights when they stayed in at Kev's apartment, he was willing to share his coke supply with her. His generosity was just one of the things she liked about him. He was also witty at times and good fun to be with. He had a dominant side to his personality and would sometimes order her about when she was in his flat, but it was something she was coming to accept. She didn't mind helping out around the flat when he was letting her stay for free.

But as the weeks had gone on, she was realising that Kev had a moody side too. When they were getting towards the end of the meal, Kev ordered some Prosecco and they stayed at the table chatting and getting to know each other better. The staff didn't seem to mind that they were hogging the table.

'What kind of mum was yours when you were growing up?' asked Kev.

Amber was taken aback at first, wondering what had made him ask that question. Bad memories of her mother's part in what she had been through flashed through her mind, but she didn't want to spoil the meal by confiding in him about all the secrets of her past just yet.

'Oh, she tried her best,' she said. 'She wasn't perfect by any means but then, I suppose she had her problems.'

Amber deflected before he asked any more awkward questions about her childhood. 'Why? What was your mum like?'

Kev smiled. 'She was perfect. I often wish she were still here.'

'Why, what happened to her?'

Kev looked as though he was about to speak but then she saw tears forming in his eyes, and he shook his head.

Amber was intrigued as to why it made him upset to talk about his mother so instead of backing off, she asked, 'Was it really bad?'

Kev nodded and she reached out, putting her hand on top of his. 'I'm sorry. I didn't mean to upset you.'

He snatched his hand away. 'Well you fuckin' have so just leave it, will you?'

Amber was alarmed at this rapid change of mood. 'OK, like I say, I'm sorry.'

For a few minutes they stayed silent, both lost in their own thoughts. The mention of Kev's mother made Amber think of the recent killing of Cora. It was scary to think that one of her crowd had been strangled to death and Amber shuddered subconsciously. If she was honest with herself, she'd never really liked Cora, but she still didn't deserve what had happened to her. It could just as easily have happened to any one of them, and Amber considered herself lucky that at least she now had Kev to watch over her.

After a while Kev spoke. 'Y'know, Amber, you're really special to me. In fact, I don't know what I'd do without you.

I can't stand the thought of losing you as well.' She could see that he was becoming upset again.

'Eh, it's OK,' she said, taking his hand once more. 'I'm not going anywhere, don't worry.'

They carried on chatting, but the mood had changed. Kev could be so unpredictable that it unnerved her. But she did enjoy his company most of the time and, on balance, his good points outweighed the bad. Besides, in her world it was all about survival and Kev now made her feel safer out on the streets. She was therefore much happier with him than without him.

She eyed the level on the bottle, willing the time to pass so they could leave the restaurant and go back to his place. Maybe he would be in a better mood once he'd had some sleep. She happened to look up when she was confronted by a man who was making his way out of the restaurant. It was a face from the past, and she visibly flinched. Cliff!

Why hadn't she noticed him before? He must have been sitting at a distant table with his back to her. The sight of him struck terror into her and she could feel herself burning up as she recalled all the abusive things he had done. Her insides churned and for a moment she thought she was going to vomit. Amber felt a desperate urge to flee from the restaurant. But it was too late. Cliff had already seen her.

Despite her alarm, Cliff tried to act normal. 'Oh hello, Princess, fancy seeing you here,' he gushed. Then he turned to the man who was following behind him. 'This here's a little friend of mine,' he said, smirking. 'Lovely girl, but I haven't seen her for years.'

He turned back to Amber again. 'How are you keeping? I often think of you and the good old times.'

His smarmy grin together with his words made her recoil but she tried to act normal for everyone's sake. What had happened to her wasn't something she wanted to share so publicly.

'I'm OK,' she said. Despite her attempt to act normal, her voice was shaky, and she quickly lowered her head, hoping he would take the hint and just go.

Amber's flushed complexion, wide eyes and furrowed brow gave things away, and she could tell Kev had picked up on her discomfort. She was relieved when Cliff added, 'Oh well, we'd best be off. We're going to the pub over the road if you fancy joining us later.'

He winked out of sight of Kev then made for the exit with a lewd grin on his face.

'Who the fuck's that?' demanded Kev even before Cliff had gone through the door. 'And why the hell is the cheeky bastard calling you "Princess"? Isn't it fuckin' obvious you're with me?'

'Shush,' said Amber looking over at the couple at the next table who were watching them ardently. 'I'll tell you, but I don't want anyone else to know.'

Amber knew she had to tell Kev something because he'd keep on at her until she did. And, right now, she didn't want to keep it from him any longer because to do so would make it look as if she had something to hide. And she wasn't the guilty one.

She therefore lowered her voice to a whisper and quickly divulged the fact that Cliff had abused her when she was a girl. It was the first time she had told anyone, and reliving her ordeal brought a tear to her eye. She could also see the rage building in Kev as the shock revelation registered.

'Drink up, we're going,' he said.

'Where to?'

'To sort that bastard out, where do you fuckin' think?'

'But there's two of them, Kev.'

'Yeah, two out-of-condition, middle-aged fuckin' losers. D'you really think they'll bother me?'

Kev grabbed the attention of a waiter. 'Bring me the bill, I wanna settle up. Quick as you can!' he demanded. 'And bring the card machine too.'

The waiter brought the bill and Kev paid it straightaway. Then he walked out of the restaurant without another word, leaving Amber trailing behind. When they got to the door of the pub, he spoke to her.

'Right, I don't want him to see us so when we get inside, I want you to find a seat out of the way, OK?'

'Alright,' said Amber.

She did as she was told, scanning the room to see if there was any sign of Cliff and his friend. Even the thought of being in the same vicinity as that man made her shiver. The pub was busy with pre-Christmas revellers, their lively chatter at odds with the mood surrounding Amber and Kev. The crowds made it difficult to spot Cliff at first but then she saw him, and she quickly changed tables to one behind a pillar so that he and his friend couldn't see her. Kev walked over with the drinks and she was relieved that Cliff hadn't spotted him either.

The next half hour was excruciating. They hardly spoke as Kev kept peeping out from behind the pillar to see what Cliff was doing. Amber was sitting with her back to the pillar, so she couldn't see anything. But she was aware of his presence and that was enough. She couldn't shake off the uneasy feeling that now dogged her.

All of a sudden, Kev rose from the table and dashed away. Amber got up from her seat and watched him stride across the pub in pursuit of Cliff who was on his way to the gents'. Her first thought was that at least Cliff was on his own so Kev would only have him to deal with. She didn't spare any concern for her abuser; he deserved what was coming to him.

Amber nibbled on her bottom lip as she waited for a few anxious moments, knowing there would be a confrontation taking place inside the men's toilets. When Kev didn't return, she grew increasingly worried. In the end, she decided to approach the gents' but was nervous about going inside. She hoped to peek through the door if somebody opened it.

It wasn't long before a young man walked into the gents'. He came straight back out again, shaking his head and muttering to a guy who he passed. 'I wouldn't go in there if I were you, mate. Someone's getting a right fuckin hiding. The guy beating him up has really lost the plot and I wouldn't risk getting involved.'

Amber's unease turned to alarm. Maybe Kev had gone too far, and she didn't want him getting into trouble. She dashed inside the gents' and stopped by the door, gasping with shock at the sight of Kev standing over Cliff, who was bent double. He had his hand on the back of his head and was bashing it repeatedly into the sink. Even from where she was standing, she could see the blood spatter.

'Shit, Kev. No!' she yelled. 'You've gone too far. He isn't fuckin' worth it!'

For a moment Kev didn't seem to register her presence and he continued his vicious assault till Amber grabbed his arm. 'Kev!' she yelled. 'We've got to get out of here before someone calls the cops.'

Mention of the police seemed to bring him to his senses, and he stopped what he was doing. Instead he pulled Cliff's head upwards so he could assess the damage. The sight of his misshapen nose and bloody face made the bile rise to Amber's throat and she brought her hand up to her mouth. Cliff looked piteously across at her and she felt sickened. She may have been shaken by the assault but that didn't mean he deserved her mercy.

'She's right,' said Kev, looking into Cliff's swollen and bloodshot eyes. 'You're not fuckin' worth it. You pervy bastard!'

Then he rammed Cliff's face into the sink one last time and turned to go.

'Don't stop to finish the drinks. Go straight out,' Kev ordered as they walked across the pub.

They stopped at another pub so Kev could get himself cleaned up, and he bought them both a drink. Amber was glad of the brandy to settle her nerves, and it wasn't long until they left and hailed a cab.

They made the silent journey back to Kev's place. Amber was deep in thought about the night's events. Seeing Cliff again after all these years had upset her. He was a traumatic reminder of all she had been through, and now she felt enraged by the woeful look he had given her. How dare he look to her for compassion after what he had done! She had stopped Kev for his own sake, not Cliff's. But she didn't feel any remorse for Kev's actions. Although he could be violent, he was doing it for her.

Amber could never have dealt with Cliff on her own, and she was satisfied that he had got his comeuppance. She had no regrets about being in a relationship with a man as violent as Kev. She just needed to tread carefully and learn how to play him to her advantage.

38

December 2015

Angie held up the wine bottle. The lighting wasn't brilliant inside the Rose and Crown and it was difficult to see if there was any wine remaining. She tipped the bottle upside down and held it over the glass, disconcerted when nothing but a tiny dribble slipped from it. She tried to drink from the empty glass anyway before conceding that she needed to go back to the bar for more drink.

She was alone inside the pub tonight and was already feeling drunk. As Angie sat there a series of random notions floated around inside her alcoholic brain. How had she come to this? Her life had been alright once. Years ago. She giggled to herself, recalling some of the fun she'd had in the past, and remembering it like it was yesterday. But then her thoughts switched course. Everything had changed now.

She hated her life, hated the clients and knew the other girls didn't have much time for her. It wasn't surprising really as even her own kids rarely acknowledged her these days. Poor old Angie!

When she returned from the bar, Angie continued to indulge in this disjointed thinking. She found it difficult to understand why her life was the way it was. Inside her head she was still a young girl: pretty, vibrant and slim. Life and soul of the party. Always was. Everybody wanted to join in when Angie was letting her hair down. And all the handsome young men made a beeline for her.

She began to voice her thoughts out loud. 'Poxy bloody clients!' She coughed. 'Bloody cough! Let's have a drink.'

Angie lifted the bottle and filled her glass again. 'Cheers,' she said, holding her glass up into the air and trying to catch the eye of a good-looking young man on a neighbouring table. She spoke out loud again. 'Not your type, eh? Like 'em curvy, do ya? Sssome men do.' Then she mumbled to herself, 'Not his type. Bloody fat that's what they are. Curvy? Phut! I can ssstill get the men. You just don't want your girlfriend to find out, do you, love?'

One of the young man's friends overheard her chunnering. He glanced over momentarily then turned to his friend and sniggered.

She sat there for some time, drinking the wine and muttering to herself until she eventually announced, 'Need the toilet!'

Angie stood up and stumbled her way past the young men on the neighbouring table, not stopping to acknowledge them. She'd already temporarily forgotten they existed. Angie staggered into the ladies', did what she had to do, heedless of the continuing stream of urine as she pulled up her briefs. Then she made her way to the mirror, her moist underwear clinging to her buttocks.

She was about to touch up her makeup when she was

seized by a coughing fit. Angie put up her hand to cover her mouth and, as she did so, she caught sight of her reflection in the mirror. An old hand, bony and weathered. Yellowing teeth inside a mouth with thin lips, criss-crossed with tiny lines. Wrinkles beneath sunken eyes. Thick makeup clogging the creases and emphasising them. Dull hair. Pale skin. Grey and lifeless. Past it!

'No, I'm not bloody passst it,' she shouted into the mirror. 'And you can fuck off. You lying bastard!'

She attempted to top up her lipstick, which seeped into the fine cracks along her lips. Angie failed to notice that she had smudged it at the corners. 'There, that's better. Ssstill got it,' she muttered as she pushed up her breasts till the crinkles gathered in her cleavage.

Unperturbed, she did a half-turn and pushed out her right hip towards the mirror. 'Still got a tight arse,' she announced to the mirror, smacking her own backside. 'Not fuckin' lying now, are you?'

Angie staggered back to the table intending to finish the last dregs of wine that she thought were inside her glass. But it was empty. She picked up the bottle and, in a repeat of her earlier action, held it over the glass. 'Gone!' she complained.

After plonking the glass back down onto the table she fished her purse out of her handbag and searched around for some money. But all she found was a fifty-pence piece and some coppers. 'Shit!'

Angie noticed the two young men on the neighbouring table again. 'Bloody youngsters... Don't want to know old Angie... Sssuppose they think I cramp their style.' Then her mutterings became louder. 'Just you wait, love!' she shouted. 'You'll be old one day.' She lowered her voice again and mumbled into her now empty wine glass, 'Fuck 'em! All the sssame.'

She stood up and almost tumbled back down again. 'Let's see who can turn a trick or two.' Then she passed the young men once more; this time she remembered her earlier comments and she left them with a parting remark, 'Old Angie's still got it, love. You ssstick with your fat girls. There's plenty where you came from.'

Then she went from the pub, leaving a cacophony of laughter ringing out from the other customers.

39

April 2000

Amy was in the kitchen washing up while her brother sat at the table doing his homework. He was preparing for a spelling test the following day and Loretta was helping to test him.

'Brilliant,' she said. 'You're doing really well, Nathan. You know most of them already so if we can just get those other couple of words right, you'll get full marks again.'

Amy turned around, envious, as Loretta fawned over him, patting him on the back and smiling. She never did that with her and as Amy was in secondary school now, she got more homework than Nathan. Often, she struggled with it and could have done with a bit of help, but her mother never offered.

Five minutes later her mother and Nathan had gone over the remaining difficult words several times while Amy was still standing at the sink trying to get the stubborn marks off one of the pans.

'Wonderful!' said Loretta. 'I think you've nailed it,

Nathan, but we'll have a little refresh later just to make sure.'

She was patting him on the back again. 'The way you're going on you'll end up going to university and getting a good job. Then you can look after me when you're older just like your father did.'

As Amy finished what she was doing and wiped her hands on the towel she could see that her mother was becoming all dreamy-eyed. 'Y'know, you take after your father a lot, Nathan. He was clever as well and he always made sure we didn't want for anything.'

Nathan just grunted and left the table with his slip of paper containing the words he had learnt. Amy didn't blame him for not wanting to listen. They'd heard these reminiscences many times before.

She walked over to where her mother was sitting. 'Can I go to university, Mum?' she asked.

Loretta stifled a snigger. 'You? Why do you want to go to university?'

'So I can get a good job too.'

'University's not for everyone, love. I don't think you're gifted like your brother.'

Amy felt suddenly upset, her mother's insensitive words getting to her. It didn't seem fair that her mother should be so encouraging with Nathan when she wasn't with her.

'Oh, but don't worry,' Loretta quickly added on seeing she was upset. 'You're clever in your own way. But, if you really want to go to university then you'll have to improve on your school marks, love. I don't know what's got into you lately. You didn't seem to be doing too badly but recently your marks haven't been so good.'

Amy didn't reply but a kaleidoscope of troubled thoughts was whizzing around inside her head. She just felt so tired lately that she couldn't put her mind to her schoolwork, often drifting off in the classroom when she should have been concentrating. Her teachers had told her off about it several times, but she couldn't help herself.

It was ever since Cliff had started visiting her bedroom late at night, usually two or three times a week as he had taken to calling round more often nowadays. Not only did he wake her up when he came into her room, but she also lay awake for some time afterwards crying into her pillow while she clung to Barney. On a couple of occasions, she'd even had to take time off school as she had woken up with pains in her stomach.

Amy didn't know if her mother was aware of what was happening, but she remembered the first time he'd ever touched her and the likelihood that her mother had condoned it. She was tempted to confide in her until she also recalled Cliff's warning that he'd have to stop coming round and her mother would be furious. The words she was about to say got stuck in her throat as worry and shame overwhelmed her, and she knew she couldn't do it.

Everything had changed since the night of her twelfth birthday and Amy felt perpetually miserable. Prior to that, she had become used to what Cliff was doing even though she still knew it was wrong. And the nice gifts had been some sort of consolation for all her shame and misery. But none of this was nice. It was painful both physically and emotionally, and he always seemed insensitive to her pain.

After the night of her birthday the presents had stopped too. They had gone along with her innocence.

40

December 2015

Amber enjoyed staying at Kev's flat. It was a private rented one and was a step above the home that she shared with her mother and Nathan. Situated in Didsbury, it was part of a large Victorian house with many of the charming original features such as ceiling roses, cornices and decorative fireplaces.

Despite being from the Victorian era the flat appeared modern and stylish, making the most of the high ceilings and the light that flooded in through the large sash windows. The kitchen and bathroom were also modern in design as well as being clean and well-kept although Amber had noticed that, even though she didn't live with Kev full-time, most of the cleaning seemed to fall on her now that she and Kev were a couple of months into their relationship. She didn't mind though; it was a small price to pay.

The best thing of all about staying at Kev's was that he always had food in. Currently Amber was enjoying learning to cook. Previously she had been used to grabbing something quick from the meagre contents in the kitchen cupboards at home, which usually comprised of something on toast or a can of soup.

Tonight, she was making a curry, using a recipe she'd found on the Internet. It was the first time she'd tried it, but things were going well up to now. She was letting the curry simmer while she waited for the rice to cook when she heard Kev shouting in the other room, and she presumed he was on the phone. Curious, she went to the living room to see what was going on.

But, as she approached the door, Kev's angry voice told her it wouldn't be wise to venture further so she stayed in the hall. She couldn't resist listening in but as she stood there, she felt like a naughty schoolgirl and it was reminiscent of the times when she used to listen in on her mother's conversations as a child. It was a bad habit that she couldn't seem to shake.

'I don't give a fuck about your sick kid!' he shouted. 'Don't think you can come at me with your bullshit excuses. You'd better have the fuckin' money next time I come calling or else.'

Amber felt her heart thundering in her chest on hearing this other side to Kev. It was one thing being told about his reputation by others but now she was witnessing it herself. She carried on listening and was even more disturbed by his next words.

'Don't fuckin' try me. You know I'll do it so unless you wanna end up in a fuckin' wheelchair you'll do as I say.'

She heard him curse to himself and guessed that he'd finished the call, so she dashed back to the kitchen. Amber knew he was caught up in other dodgy dealings apart from pimping, but she had turned a blind eye to it. Most of the men she knew were shady in some way or another. It was just the way it was and, as long as it didn't harm her, she didn't usually get involved.

Amber had been so busy listening in to Kev's conversation that she had forgotten about the food simmering on the hob. The smell of burning curry alerted her and she dashed over to the pan and lifted it away. Then she did the same with the rice.

A quick examination of the food told her that the curry was burnt at the bottom and the rice was overcooked. The curry she could deal with; she would just scoop the bulk of it out and leave the burnt bit in the pan to be disposed of later. But the rice was soggy. She tasted it twice, weighing up whether to start another batch or whether to go for it. But then she didn't want the problem of having to keep the curry warm while the rice was cooking and, besides, it would mean dinner would be late.

In the end she decided they could live with it. After all, it was no worse than some of her earlier efforts while she'd been living with Kev and he'd just laughed them off telling her not to give up the night job. She dished out the food, deciding to keep quiet about her culinary disaster and hope he didn't notice. After all, the curry still tasted good and the rice wasn't that bad.

They ate in the lounge with the plates on their knees. Amber could see that Kev was still worked up from his phone call. He wasn't saying much, and his face was set in a scowl. She decided not to ask what the problem was as she didn't want him to guess she'd been listening at the door. At least he seemed to be enjoying the curry, so she was glad of that. But then he tasted the rice.

'What the fuck is this shit?' he demanded.

'Curry and rice. I thought you liked curry and rice.'

'Not rice like this. You've fuckin' overcooked it.'

'Sorry!' she said, with attitude. 'It's just a bit soft that's all.'

'Soft? It's like fuckin' spunk it's that soggy.' He toyed around with the rice on his plate pushing it to one side. 'I can't eat this shit. Have we got any naan bread?'

'Oh yeah, I forgot to put it out.'

'You're fuckin' useless!' he yelled storming out of the room.

When he returned a couple of minutes later, he was carrying some naan bread on a plate. Amber could smell the fragrant aroma and guessed that he'd quickly cooked it in the toaster.

'Ooh, that smells nice,' she said. 'Can I have some?'

'No, you fuckin' can't! I'll teach you to go messing up the dinner. I noticed you burnt the curry as well. I hope you don't think I'm cleaning that fuckin' pan out after the mess you've made!'

'No, I'll do it,' she said. 'It's no biggie. What's wrong with you?'

Kev glared at her. 'Don't push your fuckin' luck!'

Amber had never seen him this moody and she wondered if it was because of his use of cocaine. Having been used to his softer side, she miscalculated her response. Instead of keeping quiet she reached over to where he was sitting next to her on the sofa and her hand perched over the naan bread on the side of his plate.

'Go on,' she said. 'There's enough for both of us.'

As Amber made a grab for it, Kev pulled his plate away. The food shifted with some of the curry spilling over and landing on the fabric of the sofa. 'Now look what you've done. You dozy cow! That's gonna fuckin' stain. Go and get a fuckin' cloth and clean it up.'

'In a minute,' said Amber, shovelling a forkful of curry into her mouth.

'You what?'

'In a minute. I said I'll go in a minute. I want to finish my food first.'

'You need to do it now. The longer you leave it the worse the fuckin' stain will be!'

By now Amber was realising just how angry he was. 'Kev, calm down, will you? A few minutes won't make a difference. I'll put some stain remover on it or summat.'

Rather than replying, Kev slammed his plate down onto the coffee table and stormed out of the room again. He returned carrying the kitchen cloth and a bottle of stain remover. Amber glanced up then quickly averted her eyes when she saw the fierce expression on his face.

'Don't think I'm doing this my fuckin' self!' he said, slinging the cloth at her.

But Amber was enjoying her curry. 'I've said I'll do it,' she said between munches. Then she patted the seat next to her. 'Come and sit down and have your curry.'

'I've lost my fuckin' appetite now. I'm not eating that shit.'

Amber ignored him and carried on eating her food, but she could sense him hovering like an angry bull. Still he took her by surprise when he grabbed the plate out of her hands and slammed that down on the table too.

'That can fuckin' wait till you've cleaned the mess up,' he raged. 'You greedy cow!'

The irate look on his face told Amber she'd better do as he said and she got up from the sofa, grabbed the cloth and began scrubbing at the curry stain.

'That's more like it. And in future, don't take the piss, Amber. You're lucky you're a woman or you'd have got a fuckin' good hiding for what you've done tonight.'

'Sorry,' said Amber. 'I didn't mean to ruin the dinner. I just…'

But her words were lost on him. He had already left the living room and she listened as she heard him stomping about, presumably looking for something in the bedroom. A few seconds later she heard the heavy slamming of the front door and let out the breath she had been subconsciously holding. Thank God he was gone!

Despite her relief, Amber carried on trying to remove the curry from the sofa, prepared to let her dinner go cold. Having seen that other side to Kev she was wary of him coming back and finding a stain. She didn't want a repeat of tonight's performance or maybe even worse.

Something had obviously upset him tonight and it hadn't taken much for him to go overboard. She pictured him, apoplectic with rage, his eyes bulging and the lines on his face strained, and she shuddered. Perhaps it would be wise for her to tread more carefully in future now she had seen how angry he could get with her.

His behaviour had shocked her but, if she was honest with herself, she had seen an indication of his mood switches, apart from the incident with Cliff, and she knew it was only a matter of time before she would be on the receiving end.

The previous week, they'd been getting along fine and were staying in one evening drinking wine and watching a music channel on the TV. They'd just had sex on the sofa, and she was snuggled up to him feeling mellow as they listened to Ed Sheeran's 'Thinking Out Loud'.

As they sat there, they became lost in conversation. He'd just been telling her tales about some of the mischief he'd got up to when he was a teen when he asked, 'What about you? What were you like as a teenager?'

'Me? Well, I had a couple of mates, but they stopped coming round the house. I think they felt a bit awkward 'cos of my mum and her boyfriends, especially the one called Cliff. He was the one you beat up the other week, the one who took my virginity. I can't blame my friends for not coming round really; he was a creep and a perv.'

'How old were you? You never told me the details.'

'Twelve.'

'Twelve? Fuck! You didn't tell me that. Did your mum know?'

Without being able to help herself Amber told him the whole sorry tale. It felt strange to unburden herself in this way and it was something she had never done before. His questions were coming thick and fast and she carried on talking until she'd told him everything. The night-time visits. Her tiredness. The stomach pains. Her mother's constant need for money.

Once she'd finished talking, he became silent too. And,

although he didn't say anything for some time, she could feel a change in the atmosphere. She felt his eyes on her and looked back at him.

'So now you know.'

He smiled awkwardly. 'Fuckin' hell! Yeah, I'm shocked. I never knew you'd started so young.'

Amber tried to ignore his insensitive comment. It seemed like he'd totally missed the point that she was the victim, not a willing participant. Then the conversation was over, and they carried on watching the music channel. The only time the silence was broken was when one of them passed comment on the music or to discuss the state of their drinks. But the conversation was stilted, and she no longer felt relaxed.

Amber could sense the change in him after her revelation. It felt as if he'd turned the blame from her abuser to her. Perhaps it was one thing for him knowing she was a prostitute who had been molested as a child but another matter to be confronted with the stark details.

She recalled him telling her that she was different from the other girls. Maybe he had built up some sort of ideal in his mind, which was now shattered. Because now he realised that she was no different from all the other girls who plied their trade to earn a living so that people like him could turn a profit and live in relative luxury.

From that moment onwards Amber feared that she'd lost his respect, and her supposition was confirmed by the scene that had taken place tonight.

41

December 2015

Amber was relieved that she'd managed to remove most of the curry from the sofa by the time Kev returned to the flat quarter of an hour later carrying a takeaway pizza. Avoiding the damp patch, he plonked himself down next to her without speaking, the hostile expression still on his face. Then he took hold of the TV remote control and switched channels from what she was watching.

Once he had opened the box and begun eating the pizza, he turned to her. 'You getting ready for work or what?' he asked.

Amber was about to argue that she had been going to finish watching her TV programme first. But then she thought about his attitude earlier and thought better of it. 'Sure,' she said, getting up.

'Hurry up then. I'll be ready to drop you off once I've eaten this.'

Amber got ready quickly then returned to the living

room where Kev was still sitting down with the discarded pizza box beside him.

He nodded at it. 'Shift that, will yer?'

Amber did as she was told, noticing that there were a few crumbs on the sofa too and scooping them into her hands before depositing both in the kitchen bin.

They made the twenty-minute trip to Manchester and Kev dropped her in the red-light district. It wasn't until he was about to drive away that he muttered, 'See you later.'

Amber took up her usual spot at the mouth of the tunnel, relieved to be free of Kev for a while even though her usual trepidation at the prospect of a night on the beat swiftly returned. With customary caution she glanced around her and noticed that another two girls were also out plying their trade tonight. They were standing a few metres away from her and seemed deep in conversation.

Amber recognised the two girls who regularly worked this beat and nodded at them. They returned her greeting enthusiastically and Amber preened realising for the first time that her status among them had become enhanced since she'd been seeing Kev. Despite the way he had treated her tonight, she was still happy to be with him and hoped that by the time she saw him again he would be in a better mood. After all, he wasn't often like that; he was normally great fun to be with.

It was later that night when Amber was faced with another problem. The other street girls were no longer there, and she was alone apart from a man who she could see in the distance. She watched him as he approached. He was young, only around mid-twenties, and had a cocky swagger. Amber saw the way he was looking intently in her direction and knew that he was heading for her. Instinct told her this wasn't going to be a friendly confrontation.

'Alright, love?' he asked once he had reached her.

Amber nodded and waited to hear what he had to say.

'How much for a blow job?' he asked.

Amber gave him a price and he reached into his pocket, withdrew a twenty-pound note and waved it in front of her face. Then he grabbed her by the arm. 'Come on then. What you waiting for?' he said, pulling her inside the tunnel.

'Hang on! You sure you want to do it here?'

'Yeah course, it's darker down there. No one will see owt.'

He let go of her arm and she followed him into the tunnel. Amber felt relieved. She had expected abuse but maybe the man only wanted a bit of business after all. And this should be quick and easy cash. She wouldn't even have to leave the area. But then he stopped and turned around, making a display of tucking the money back inside his pocket. He stepped up to her and grabbed her arm once more but this time he was rough, clenching it in a vice-like grip.

'Ouch,' she yelled, trying to tug her arm free. 'There's no need for that.'

'Shut the fuck up! Do you honestly think I'm gonna pay for it? I want a fuckin' freebie.'

He lifted his other hand and grabbed her by the hair, letting go of her arm while he undid his flies. Then he pulled her head viciously down towards his crotch.

'Come on then. Get on with it!'

Amber struggled, trying to pull away from him but he tightened his hold on her hair, digging his fingers into her scalp. If it was just a matter of doing it for free, then Amber might have acceded to his wishes to avoid a beating. But there was no way she was doing it without a condom. It just wasn't worth the risk.

'Let go of my fuckin' hair,' she yelled while she continued to struggle, and her scalp screamed out in pain.

For a few seconds she fought against him, bunching her hands into fists and punching blindly and ineffectually above her head. She could feel most of her punches landing in mid-air although the odd one made contact with his body. But she was losing the fight and she felt her head being dragged closer towards his crotch area till she could see his engorged penis and smell the cheesy odour that it gave off.

Amber kept her mouth shut tight while he sank his nails further into her scalp and pressed her head down with his other hand. She didn't even scream because she didn't want to risk opening her mouth.

Then she heard footsteps running towards them. She couldn't see anything, but she desperately hoped it was someone coming to help her. Suddenly, the pressure on her head eased and she saw the man's feet shift away from her. She looked up to see Kev grabbing the man by the throat.

'You fuckin' cheeky bastard!' he yelled. 'What the fuck do you think you're playing at?'

The man tried to say something, but his words made a choking sound. Without releasing his grip Kev propelled himself forward, overpowering the man and hammering into him till his head hit the wall. Amber's first reaction was one of gratitude. Thank God Kev had arrived when he did!

For a moment she stood and watched, revelling in the

fearful expression on the man's face. He deserved it after what he had done to her.

'Fuckin' arsehole!' she yelled. 'See how you like it.'

But then Kev carried on. Not content with slamming the man against the wall once, he did it repeatedly. The sound of his head impacting the solid brick and his agonised screams filled Amber's ears and she grew tense. As she watched in horror blood began to spatter against the wall and she could see a look of sheer terror on the man's face.

At first, she was wary of intervening, recalling Kev's earlier mood. But as the blood spatter thickened to a dense crimson patch and the man's screams became more desperate, she knew she had to do something.

'Kev, that's enough!' she yelled. But he didn't seem to hear her. 'Kev, Kev, please stop. You're going too far.'

'Help!' pleaded the man who was now in tears.

Amber had visions of Kev beating the man to death. Desperate to stop him she rushed forward and grabbed his arm. 'Kev, Kev no!' she yelled again.

Kev swung around, tugging his arm out of her hands then swiping her across the face with the back of his hand. He glared at her and she could see the madness in his steely eyes. Amber raised a hand to her chin, which was throbbing from the angry blow, but her concern was more for the other victim. 'Please, Kev! You've gone far enough. You're gonna kill him.'

For a moment he gazed through her then a light seemed to ignite in the back of his eyes, and they softened. But he was still irate. 'Bastard deserved it!' he yelled.

He turned back towards the man who was cowering, afraid to move. Kev raised his hand and pointed his finger into the man's face. The man shrunk back, squeezing himself tightly against the wall and then grimacing as his damaged head pressed against the bloody patch on the bricks.

'You're fuckin' lucky she stopped me,' Kev ranted. 'If she hadn't been here, I'd have finished you good and proper. Don't ever fuckin' think of doing anything like that again! You can fuckin' pay for it like everyone else.'

Then he walked away, leaving the man slumped against the wall, and Amber followed him to her spot on the corner. With his back to her, he spoke as he walked away, but his words were rushed as though he felt obliged to utter them. 'Sorry for hitting you. It was that bastard's fault! He made me do it. Y'know I don't normally hit women.'

Amber clutched at this meagre show of remorse, hoping he'd take her back home after her ordeal. But he didn't. Instead he jumped inside the car, started the engine, and pressed down hard on the gas.

'See you later!' shouted Amber as he tore off down the road.

Once he was gone her usual anxiety returned. She peered down the tunnel to see the man heading towards her once more. Amber stepped away, wary in case he tried to drag her back into the tunnel. But she could tell by the way he was walking that there wasn't much chance of that. He appeared disorientated and battle-weary and, once he'd reached the mouth of the tunnel, he headed off in the other direction with his head slumped and his wound dripping blood onto the back of his clothing.

Amber was glad the incident was over, but she didn't entertain any thoughts of Kev being her heroic knight in shining armour. She was steadily getting to know Kev, and she realised that the reason he beat the man up wasn't in defence of her. It was because he was protecting his own reputation. Amber was now Kev's property and the man had taken liberties in trying to take it for free.

42

April 2000

Amy had noticed that Cliff hadn't been around the house for a couple of weeks. At first, she couldn't have been happier. Maybe it was finally an end to the shame and humiliation of his night-time visits. But her happiness was marred by the change in her mother.

The moodiness was returning, and her mother was irritable once more. She wondered what had made Cliff stop coming round and was tempted to ask her mother. But she was wary of being snapped at and, besides, she didn't want her mother thinking she missed his visits.

She was saved from having to ask when her mother raised the subject with her one day. They were in the living room watching TV as usual. Her mother had had a good deal to drink and was in one of her belligerent moods. Nathan seemed to grow tired of her constant interruptions while she waffled on about nonsense and, eventually, he stomped out of the room. Once they were alone, Loretta edged up to Amy on the sofa.

'I've been meaning to talk to you, lady,' she said, and Amy noticed that her eyes were unfocused.

Her wording was formal and unfriendly, and Amy's perpetual sense of guilt made her dread what her mother was about to say. She could feel the adrenalin pulsating around her body as anxiety took hold. Amy stared at her mother's stern face, her eyes pleading for leniency while she waited for her mother to get to the point.

Then Loretta came out with it: 'I know what you and Cliff have been up to.'

Her accusatory tone disturbed Amy and the blood rushed to her face as shame overwhelmed her. Inside she felt a nervous flutter in her stomach, her mouth went dry and she could sense the tears building in the backs of her eyes. She was finally encountering that moment of horror when all her humiliating secrets were laid bare like a festering wound with the dressing removed.

Amy was anxious about how her mother would react now that it was out in the open. Would she blame Amy, Cliff, or herself? But there was no apology nor a comforting embrace with her mother begging her for forgiveness, no bitterness against Cliff for robbing her daughter of her innocence, and no reproachful words against her. Instead, she said, casually, 'I had an idea, y'know. I'd seen the way he looked at you, but I didn't know for sure until he came out with it recently. I'm surprised you let him do it though. I thought you were a good girl.'

Amy stared at her mother, bewildered by her reaction. 'But I am a good girl,' she pleaded.

Her mother patted her drunkenly on the thigh.

'Don't worry. Your secret's safe with me, love. I promise

not to tell a soul.' Then she paused to sniff. 'We've all done things we're not proud of and I'd be the first to admit it. But if you do things right by me then I'll do things right by you.'

Amy refrained from heaving a sigh of relief. She somehow knew that there was more to come. Her mother sniffed again.

'Course, it leaves us in a bit of a fix, y'know. Cliff was very generous with his money and now that he's gone, I don't know what we're going to do.'

Amy shrugged, wondering where this was leading until her mother carried on. 'I've got another friend who's interested in you actually. He's a lovely man and very well to do, and he's asked after you a few times.'

Amy stared at her mother, horrified. 'What, you mean…? No! No, I won't do it.'

Loretta took hold of Amy by the wrist. 'Look, love, it's no different than you're used to doing, y'know. Just think, we'll be well off again. You'll be able to have all those nice things like Cliff used to get you…'

The tears that had been building now filled Amy's eyes. She couldn't believe her mother's betrayal. 'No!' she repeated. 'It was horrible and I'm not doing it.'

Loretta's tone of voice changed. 'Do you think money grows on trees? Don't you think I've had to do a lot of things I didn't like over the years to keep you and your brother clothed and fed? Do you think I enjoyed it? Eh? Eh?'

By this time Amy was crying openly. 'But, Mum, it was horrible!' she repeated.

'We all have to do horrible things, Amy. That's life. I

don't think you've got any idea what it takes to keep a roof over our heads but it's about time you learnt.'

Amy couldn't take any more. She sprang up off the sofa and dashed from the room to the sound of her mother shouting after her. 'You'll do it, lady, unless you want us all to end up on the streets. Imagine how that would feel, knowing you could have prevented it.'

Then her mother stopped shouting and Amy dashed into her room where she sobbed helplessly into her pillow. She couldn't believe what her mother was asking her to do but she was determined that this time she wouldn't put up with it.

Amy hoped that her mother was just being unreasonable because she was drunk; she'd known for a long time how drink affected her mother's judgement and how irrational she could be under the influence. Maybe tomorrow when she'd sobered up, she would realise what a terrible idea it had been.

43

Sapphire was walking through Piccadilly Gardens on her way to the Rose and Crown for a swift drink before work when she thought she saw someone she knew except he now looked even thinner than she remembered. He was also accompanied by a girl she vaguely recognised. She was about to grab his attention when he spotted her too and she realised it was definitely him. There was no mistaking those piercing blue eyes, which were his only redeeming feature.

'Skinner!' she shouted, giving him a hug and trying to ignore the unwashed smell that emanated from him. 'Is it really you?'

He pulled away from her and laughed. 'Well it ain't any other fucker.'

He turned to the girl who was with him. She had dark hair and well-defined features with full lips and a prominent nose. Sapphire realised where she knew her from; she had seen her on the beat. 'This is Elena,' he said. 'She's from Romania.'

'Hi,' said Sapphire, still laughing at Skinner's previous comment.

Skinner had that way about him that always made you want to laugh. He had gained his nickname because of his skinny frame and, because he was so tall, the lack of flesh didn't sit well on him. He hadn't been blessed in the looks department either. His nose was huge and was exaggerated by his sunken cheeks, which also emphasised his sharp cheekbones. He was the nervous type, always cautious around strangers, but to those who knew him, his sense of humour was wicked.

'Bloody hell! I can't believe it. How long has it been?' asked Sapphire.

'Not long enough away from you, you scally,' he teased.

Sapphire laughed and pretended to cuff him on the ear. 'I see you've lost none of your cheek. What are you up to now?'

'Not much, just moved out of a squat so I'm on the streets now.'

'Aw! How come?' asked Sapphire.

Skinner shrugged. 'Some bad company in there.'

For a moment Sapphire was tempted to offer him her sofa but then she recalled what a thieving bugger Skinner had been. They'd shared a squat with some other youngsters years previously when Sapphire had been homeless. He was a great lad to get along with but when it came to pilfering other people's possessions, he didn't seem to be able to help himself.

'Anyway,' he said. 'What you up to these days? You still working the streets?'

'Yeah, that's me,' said Sapphire.

'Ooh, well in that case, you need to watch out.'

Sapphire felt that he was about to add something else but stopped himself. 'Watch out?' she asked. 'Watch out for what?'

'Oh nothing, just, y'know, it's a dangerous place out there.'

Sapphire wondered if he was referring to Cora's death but that had been weeks ago and there'd been no recurrences since. But Sapphire knew Skinner of old and she could tell he was hiding something. His tell-tale jumpiness had shifted up a notch and he couldn't meet her eyes. 'Come on, Skinner, what is it you're not telling me?'

'Nowt, like I said, it's dangerous out on the streets.' As he spoke, he glanced across at Elena, but his eyes didn't settle on her.

'It's OK, I already know,' said Elena.

'No, you don't!' he snapped back.

'Look, Skinner,' said Sapphire. 'Don't you think I deserve to fuckin' know if I'm working the streets and there's summat iffy going on?'

'No, I can't, Saph. It could land me in a lot of shit.'

By now it was becoming obvious to Sapphire just how nervous Skinner was and she adopted a more sympathetic tone. 'This is summat bad, isn't it, Skinner?' He nodded, his eyes wide with fear. 'Look, Skinner, you've always been able to trust me. You can tell me anything and you know it won't go any further. Who was it that always had your back when we lived in the squat?'

Skinner appeared shamefaced and for a while she could see he was weighing up his options. Again, he looked over at Elena who had been listening to their conversation; her impatience obvious from her folded arms, rolling eyes and heavy sighs. 'Elena, can I catch up with you later?' he asked. 'Only, I need to speak to Sapphire about something.'

Elena tutted. 'If it's about that prostitute who got killed then I already know. Everybody knows. It was ages ago, so I don't know why you're acting like it's something new.' Then she left them, and Sapphire couldn't resist a grin as she watched her stomping across Piccadilly Gardens.

'Is she the jealous type by any chance?' she asked.

'Oh, don't worry about Elena. She'll soon come round. She just doesn't like being left out of anything.'

Sapphire nodded then waited for Skinner to get to the point.

He peered around him shiftily then nodded at her. 'Not here.' He pointed to some benches on the other side of the gardens. 'Let's go and sit over there.'

Once they were seated on a bench some distance from anybody else, Sapphire prompted him. 'Go on then, spill. What is it I need to know?'

Skinner peered around again then lowered his voice. 'Elena was right. It is about that killing but there's a bit more to it and I don't want Elena to know. She might mouth off.' He hesitated before finally opening up. 'It was a girl called Cora who got killed. She used to work the beat.'

'Yeah. I know. I knew Cora. Somebody found her dead in the squat where she was staying.'

Then something dawned on Sapphire. 'Shit! Is that the squat where you used to live? Is that why you moved out?'

Skinner grabbed hold of her hand. 'Keep quiet for fuck's sake! Then he lowered his voice again. 'Yeah, it was.' He leaned in conspiratorially till his head was only centimetres from hers before he whispered, 'I saw the whole fuckin' thing.'

'You're joking! What the fuck?' she said, pulling her hand away and staring at him in shock.

Skinner nodded. 'You're the first person I've told. I swear I fuckin' shit myself. She was in her room with this guy and I just happened to look through the window.'

Sapphire couldn't resist a slight smile. Knowing Skinner, he was looking for an opportunity to lift some of Cora's stuff without being detected. She listened as he told her more.

'She'd took this guy back and when I looked through the window, he was fuckin' strangling her and she was choking, man, I swear. She saw me looking but I just fuckin' legged it.'

'What about him? Did he see you?'

'No. He had his back to me. He was on top of her, strangling the fuckin' life out of her. At first, I thought they were just shagging. But then I saw his hands round her throat. And her face. Fuckin' hell!' He stopped and shook his head from side to side as if trying to chase the memory away. 'I swear, her fuckin' eyes were popping out of her head.'

Sapphire placed a hand gently on top of Skinner's. 'Jesus! That must have been bad.' She knew he had more to tell her. In view of what Skinner had already said, it occurred to her that there was possibly a further link to the beat. She wasn't wrong.

Skinner dropped his head and muttered, 'I know who the guy is.'

'Shit, who?'

'He's someone I'd not seen around before, but I did see him go into the room with her. Later I wondered if they were still there; that's why I looked in the window. Anyway, I don't think anyone else saw them arrive apart from me. Then I saw him again one day in Piccadilly and I shit myself. I was with a mate who let on to him, so I asked him who he was.'

'And?'

'He's a glorified pimp. He doesn't call himself that but, apparently, he collects protection from a lot of the girls. You might know him. He's a good-looking guy called Kev.'

Sapphire grew even more alarmed. 'Kev? Kev who?'

'Pike. Some people call him Pikey.'

'Shit!'

'What? Do you know him?'

Sapphire had recognised the name straightaway. She remembered Amber telling her about him a few weeks ago. She'd seemed really chuffed with herself for bagging this guy with his own nice flat and a bit of cash.

Sapphire had only seen him the once as he never came into the Rose and Crown and she worked a short distance away from Amber. But she just happened to have been walking across town when she bumped into the two of them together. Amber looked like the cat that had got the cream, but Sapphire noticed that, despite his obvious good looks, his face wore a grimace.

Sapphire resisted the urge to tell Skinner everything. Instead, she just said, 'Yeah. I know of him. He collects protection from one of the girls I know.' Then she quickly shifted the focus. 'Have you told anyone?'

'What, about what he did? Have I fuck! I shit myself. I tell you, after that night I couldn't get out of that fuckin' squat quick enough. I dragged my stuff together and I've been on the streets ever since.' Then he seemed pensive for a moment before he added, 'Sapphire, promise me you won't tell anyone what I've told you. He's a right nasty bastard and I don't want it coming back on me.'

'No, course I won't,' she said. But even as she said it, she knew that she needed to find Amber. She had to be warned what Kev Pike was capable of, as soon as possible.

44

October 2000

After Amy's mother first suggested entertaining other men, she hadn't mentioned it again for several months. Amy had hoped that it was just a drunken notion. But then Loretta had raised it again a few weeks later and this time it was in the morning when she was hungover.

'Look at this,' she had said, showing Amy the bill that had just landed on the doormat. 'Three bloody months we owe on the rent now. We're going to have to do something, Amy. We're behind with all the other bills too and I can't bloody raise all that money on my own. Have you thought any more about what I said to you before? He's still asking after you, y'know.'

Tears of bitter disappointment sprang to Amy's eyes. 'Mum,' she pleaded. 'I don't want to. It was horrible.'

'OK. Then I suppose we'll have to carry on as we are. But it'll only be a matter of time before we lose the house. The landlord's already threatened me with eviction. And when that happens, I don't know what the bloody hell we'll do.

'You and Nathan will probably end up in care. And me... well, I don't know what will become of me. I'll probably end up on the bloody streets. And when that happens, Amy, just think, you'll be able to tell yourself you could have prevented it.'

Amy thought about what her mother had previously told her regarding children's homes. She was about to plead with her again but as she opened her mouth her lip trembled, and she was worried that she'd burst into tears. She walked away and tried to occupy herself with other things, so she didn't have to think about it.

But the thoughts wouldn't go away, and Amy felt a disturbing mix of feelings: shame because of what she'd had to do and unwillingness to get involved with that again. But then guilt took over along with a sense of responsibility for getting the family out of their current predicament so that they could all stay together in this house.

She also thought about the wider implications. Apart from the unappealing prospect of being taken into care she had concerns over her mother. Not only was there a chance of her becoming homeless but Amy also worried about how her mother would cope with that. A vision of her mother lying on the sofa with an empty packet of pills on the coffee table flashed into her mind and she subconsciously bit down on her bottom lip.

Despite all that, Amy fought the feelings of guilt that were gnawing away at her and kept to her resolve not to agree to her mother's wishes. She knew deep down that it was wrong, and she dreaded getting dragged into that situation again.

But her mother continued to work on her. A few days later Loretta showed her a final demand for an overdue telephone bill and reiterated that they didn't have money for anything more than necessities. It was obvious to Amy from her mother's tone of voice that she was becoming frantic with worry.

A week after that Nathan had asked what they were having for tea.

'I don't know, love. We've got no food and no money for any, have we, Amy?' said Loretta, flashing her daughter a look of despair.

Amy shrugged but her mother's eyes remained fixed on her for several seconds. The implicit meaning was obvious to Amy who squirmed under her mother's penetrating gaze.

Somehow it didn't occur to Amy that her mother must have found a way around the arrears problems if they were still living in the house. Neither did she consider that the food situation was no different than it had been before Cliff came on the scene, and they'd managed alright then.

It took a few more months for Loretta to succeed in her intentions where her daughter was concerned but eventually Amy acceded to her mother's wishes, beaten down by overwhelming guilt and worry about the future.

45

January 2016

Sapphire should have been at work, but she was desperate to find Amber and warn her about Kev Pike before it was too late. Unfortunately, she didn't have Amber's phone number, so she hoped to catch her in the pub. She dashed into the Rose and Crown and had a quick glance around the place but there was no sign of her or any of the other working girls. She wasn't surprised given the time. Most of them would be at work by now but she'd called in on the off chance.

She raced up to the bar and shouted over to Moira who was at the optics pouring a drink. 'Moira, Moira, I need a word.'

'Oy, wait your bloody turn,' said a man standing further along the bar, clutching a ten-pound note between grubby fingers.

'It's urgent!' said Sapphire.

'Just a minute, Kenny,' said Moira, placing the whisky on the bar and walking over to Sapphire. 'What is it, love?'

Sapphire leaned over the bar. 'Have you seen Amber? I need to find her urgently.'

Moira looked alarmed but she didn't ask questions. 'She was in earlier, but she left about an hour ago, maybe more. Why, what's wrong?'

'Sorry, I can't tell you,' said Sapphire, 'but thanks.' She patted the bar in acknowledgement then fled out of the pub door.

Once she got outside, Sapphire deliberated. She wanted to get to work and wondered whether she should wait till she saw Amber in the Rose and Crown again and then tell her about Kev. But what if something should happen to her in the meantime? She would never forgive herself.

She decided to see if she could find Amber on the beat. Her friend worked a different street than her, but Sapphire knew the red-light district well. She therefore reasoned that if she searched around the place, she would hopefully come across her.

Within five minutes Sapphire had arrived at the back of Piccadilly and she raced up the main thoroughfare, panting. She spotted someone straightaway, instantly recognisable as a working girl due to her scanty dress and look of desperation.

'Hi,' she said. 'Do you know a girl called Amber who works around here?'

The girl shook her head. 'Nah, never heard of her. But you could try further up the road.'

'Cheers,' said Sapphire who carried on until she spotted another of the working girls and asked her the same question.

The second girl had never heard of Amber either and it

wasn't until she reached the third girl that Sapphire realised it would be best to give a description of Amber too in case they didn't know her by name.

'Short, only slim and with blonde hair,' she said to the third girl she encountered.

'Yeah, I think there's a girl like that whose patch is further up there. See that tunnel over there...' She pointed to a railway tunnel in the distance then added, 'She stands there most nights.'

'Thanks,' said Sapphire, pausing to regain her breath before carrying on towards the tunnel.

She was a few metres away when she spotted Amber. 'Thank God for that!' she muttered out loud, relaxing her stride now she was within sight of her.

Unfortunately, before she had chance to catch up with her a car appeared, seemingly from out of nowhere and pulled up on the road next to the tunnel. Amber walked over to the passenger window, still unaware of Sapphire's presence.

'Shit!' Sapphire cursed then she shouted, 'Amber! Amber, hang on.'

But Amber either didn't hear her or she was too intent on bagging a customer. Sapphire watched in disappointment as the car set off with Amber inside it. The vehicle passed her, and she waved frantically at Amber who was sitting in the passenger seat. Amber turned her head as she went by and Sapphire hoped for a moment that she would get the driver to stop. But she didn't.

'Shit!' said Sapphire again.

She carried on walking slowly and it was only a few seconds later when she arrived, panting, at the spot where

Amber had been standing before she got inside the car. For a moment Sapphire wondered what to do next but then decided to wait till Amber came back. She lit a cigarette, taking anxious puffs while she waited for her friend to return. With a bit of luck, it shouldn't take too long.

After a few minutes of waiting she saw another car approach, but she hung back away from the pavement as she wasn't looking for business at the moment. She hoped the driver might stop next to one of the other girls instead but, to her dismay, he pulled over near to her. She ducked back into the tunnel, hoping he would take the hint and go away.

It was then that she noticed who the driver was. Although she was obscured by the shadow of the tunnel, he was lit up by the streetlight next to the car and she recognised him from that one encounter. It was Kev Pike. Sapphire could feel her heart thundering as he peered around him and she shrunk further back, pressing tightly against the tunnel walls and hoping he wouldn't see her.

To her relief, after a few seconds he started the car and drove off. She presumed he must have been looking for Amber, and she wanted to find her before he did. She took another drag of her cigarette, checked the time on her phone and waited. But, unfortunately, after a further twenty minutes, Amber still didn't show. So, she reluctantly decided that she would have to leave it till another night.

46

July 2001

Amy was feeling miserable and sore. It was Sunday morning and she'd just got up after the man she'd spent the night with had left. The experience had been horrid, even more so than usual.

The man was old and repulsive to look at. As soon as he entered her room Amy could smell a mix of body odour, beer fumes and stale cigarettes. He had been rough with her and, once he'd had his way, he'd fallen straight asleep, snoring loudly all through the night with his greasy, offensive-smelling body pushed up uncomfortably against her.

She walked into the bathroom and examined herself using a cosmetic mirror prised between her legs. She could see that she was swollen down below, which would explain the soreness. There was also some bruising at the tops of her thighs where the man had used his hands to wrench them open. Amy knew she'd have to tell her mother she was swollen otherwise she would line up other men before she'd had a chance to heal.

She dreaded telling her. Even though Amy had now been entertaining men for several months, at the behest of her mother, she was still ashamed about what was happening. She also felt embarrassed every time her mother brought up the subject.

Amy walked into the kitchen to find her brother doing his homework at the table. He was so engrossed in what he was doing that he didn't even look up to acknowledge her presence.

When Loretta entered the kitchen, Amy was pouring some cereal into a bowl. She decided to confront her mother as soon as possible to get it over and done with. 'Mum, can I have a word with you?' she began, her voice shaking.

Loretta didn't look her best. Her hair was messy, and she still had remnants of last night's makeup daubed on her face. After her excesses of the previous night, Amy guessed that her mother must have been feeling as bad as she looked when she snapped at her, 'Yeah, what is it?'

Amy glanced across at Nathan. 'Not here, it's private. Can we go in the living room?'

Nathan tutted and carried on with his homework while Loretta followed Amy into the lounge.

Once they were in the other room, Amy checked to make sure her mother had shut the door then lowered her head and said quietly, 'I'm sore and swollen down below.'

'Bastard!' muttered Loretta but Amy didn't know whether she was referring to the potential loss of income or the man who had damaged her. Her meaning became clearer when she said, 'OK, I'll make sure he doesn't come round again.'

'Thanks,' said Amy. 'But... well...'

'Come on, Amy. Out with it.'

'Well, I was thinking, I'll be too sore to do it again tonight.'

'OK, I'll cancel. But you need to get a salt bath, twice a day, then we'll see how you go on.'

Amy was relieved. That would give her a few days' reprieve at least and she decided that she might even carry it on for a bit longer.

Amy had been seeing two to three men a week since not long after she'd finally agreed to her mother's wishes, and she was still only thirteen. She was regularly taking time off school because she was so exhausted from the night-time activity.

Consequently, Amy found herself getting more and more behind with her schoolwork, and often felt out of place in the classroom as she struggled to keep up with her peers. She'd been tempted many a time to confide in someone about the abuse, but several things prevented her from doing so.

Firstly, it was the overpowering sense of shame at confiding in anybody else about what she did. Secondly, it was the fear of losing the family home and the knock-on effects of that; her and Nathan in care and her mother on the streets or maybe even committing suicide if she couldn't cope with things. And thirdly, she was frightened of encountering her mother's wrath. Loretta was an unpredictable drunk who knew Amy's dirty little secret and Amy was afraid that she would reveal it to the world if she did anything to upset her.

Amy hated what she had to do. Apart from the shame and humiliation, she was often tired and sore, and always felt envious of Nathan who was being given a better chance in life. She'd been tempted on a couple of occasions to end it all. It seemed like the only escape from the life she was trapped in. But she didn't feel brave enough to do it.

The only consolation was that by doing what she was doing she was keeping her mother happy. Whenever she had entertained a man her mother would be extra nice to her. And, despite what she had to do, it was good to receive the approval she had always sought. It made her recall the time when Dale had been around, and she desperately wished it could be like that now.

47

January 2016

When Amber walked into the living room that afternoon, her mother and Nathan were arguing again. Amber was glad she sometimes got a break from all the tension by staying at Kev's despite his mood swings although it was usually by invitation only. She wouldn't dream of turning up at his place unannounced, sensing that he wouldn't be happy with the lack of control.

This time Amber was surprised to find her mother having a go at Nathan rather than the other way round. She had obviously had a drink, which had given her the confidence to tackle him, but she hadn't yet reached the stage where she was incoherent.

Nathan gave Amber a cursory glance as she walked into the room, but her mother's focus was on him. Her words told Amber that it was probably because she was after money, which he was unwilling to give.

'Y'know, Nathan, you've been such a disappointment to

me. I always thought you would take after your father, but I was so wrong.'

'Save it, Mother. The emotional blackmail won't work anymore.'

'I'm not trying to blackmail anyone; I'm just pointing out the difference. Your father was a real man and a very generous one too. He always saw to it that we didn't go without; Dale too for that matter, but not you, oh no!'

'Have you ever stopped to consider that I might not want to take after either of them. They were both mugs for putting up with you. No wonder Dale fucked off back to his wife if all he saw was you pissed out of your head half the time.

'How dare you talk to me like that!' said Loretta, putting her hand to her head and pretending to swoon like a golden age movie star, the drama heightened by her struggle to catch her breath.

Amber chipped in, 'Nathan, that's well out of order.'

'You can butt out as well. You're as bad as her, nowt but a pair of fuckin' slappers! When are you going to get a real job like the rest of humanity?'

The familiar feeling of inadequacy struck Amber and she didn't know what to say for a moment. But then she thought about the injustice of it all and found her words.

'It's alright for you,' she shrieked. 'Just because you've been to university, you think you're too fuckin' good for us. Well you're not.'

'Amber, watch your language!' yelled Loretta, deflecting from the real issue concerning Amber's lack of opportunity.

Amber was just about to walk out of the room and leave

them to it. She was sick of the endless rows and couldn't be bothered wasting her time and energy on them. But before she could make a move, Nathan spoke again. 'Y'know what? I don't even know why I'm putting up with you two. The house will be through any day now so I might as well stay with Chloe while we're waiting to complete.'

'House? What do you mean, house?' asked Loretta with a look of confusion on her face.

'Yes, you heard right, Mother. Me and Chloe are buying a house. We've been saving up for months. It's what working people do in the real world, rather than living in a dump and defaulting on the rent. I might as well stay with her and her parents while we're waiting for it to come through. They won't mind. They've already asked me a couple of days ago. In fact, the only reason I turned them down was because I didn't want to move all my stuff twice. But, thinking about it, it'll be worth the trouble just to get away from you two.'

Then he marched out of the room, leaving Loretta staring after him, dumbstruck.

She turned to Amber. 'Did you know about this?'

'No, I had no idea.'

'Oh my God! What are we going to do?'

'Not a lot we can do,' said Amber, shrugging. 'Anyway, he wasn't giving you so much money lately, was he? Now we know why, it was because he was saving for a house.'

'Well I hope you're not going to bloody leave me too.'

'No, Mum, I've promised you I won't, haven't I?'

'He can't just leave things like this,' said Loretta who then went out of the room in search of Nathan to remonstrate with him once more.

Amber left them to it. If Nathan wanted to leave, who was she to argue? He hadn't been very nice to be around lately anyway. And if he was buying a house then there was no way her mother would be able to talk him out of leaving.

January 2016

It was the night after Sapphire had unsuccessfully searched for Amber, and she was inside the Rose and Crown once again waiting for her friend to show up. Sapphire knew there were no guarantees that Amber would come into the pub, but she decided to wait for her anyway as she was so desperate to tell her about Kev and Cora.

The place was dead and the only one of the girls who was in was Angie who was sat drinking alone. Sapphire was occupying herself by standing at the bar and engaging in conversation with Moira and a couple of the regulars who came and went.

'What the bloody hell's wrong with you?' asked Moira. 'You're like a cat on hot bricks.'

'Oh, nothing much,' said Sapphire. 'I just need to speak to Amber about something, that's all.'

'Didn't you find her last night?'

'No.'

'Oh dear. Aren't you normally in work by now, anyway?' asked Moira.

Sapphire checked the time on her phone. 'Well yeah, but... I could really do with seeing Amber, that's all.'

'Well, if you want to get yourself off, love, I'll tell Amber you were here looking for her if she comes in.'

Sapphire knew she really ought to get to work so she said to Moira, 'Okay, would you please?' She toyed with the idea of leaving her phone number with Moira but decided against it. She preferred to speak to Amber directly rather than on the phone.

'Course I will, love,' said Moira. 'Do you want me to give her a message?'

'No, it's okay. Just let her know I was looking for her. I'll try to catch her again.'

Before she went, Sapphire decided to see if old Angie had seen anything of Amber. Hopefully, at this time of night she would still be sober and wouldn't therefore start making a nuisance of herself. She stopped by her table and said, 'Hi, Angie. You don't know if Amber's been in, do you?'

'What? In here? No, I've not seen her for a while.'

Just then Angie started coughing hard. Sapphire could hear the rattling in her lungs, and she became concerned. 'Bloody hell, Angie! Your COPD's bad tonight, isn't it? I've not seen it that bad for ages.'

Angie took a moment to regain her breath before replying. 'Yeah, the doctor says I've got a chest infection on top of it.'

'Well, it doesn't sound too good to me. You take care and keep warm.'

'Oh, I intend to,' said Angie, raising a glass of some kind of spirit and smiling. 'This'll help to warm my insides.'

Sapphire smiled and left the pub. She started making her way to work but she couldn't shake the nagging feeling that Amber might be in danger so she took a slight detour and headed instead for the area where she might find Amber. It wasn't long before she arrived, but she was perturbed to find there was no sign of her friend. Again, she decided to wait for her, hoping it wouldn't be too long this time before Amber showed up.

48

January 2016

Amber arrived at the Rose and Crown determined to have at least one drink before her night on the beat.

'Bloody hell, you've just missed Sapphire,' said Moira. 'She's been looking for you again. She was in here last night too. She seemed to think it's urgent, whatever it is.'

Amber was intrigued. 'Really? Any ideas what it's about?'

'No, she wouldn't say but, like I say, she seemed to think it's urgent. Anyway, she's gone now so why don't you give her a ring and ask her what she wants?'

'Thanks,' said Amber. 'I will do in a minute.'

Then she realised that, actually, she didn't have Sapphire's number. She'd had no need for it before. Up to now Sapphire had just been one of the girls who she hung out with in the pub, and their friendship hadn't progressed beyond that stage.

'You seem frazzled,' said Moira. 'Are you alright, love?'

'Yeah, it's just… my mum and Nathan have been arguing

as usual and they've made me late for work. She's not very happy because he's just told her he's leaving home.'

Moira smiled. 'Families eh?' Then another customer grabbed her attention and she didn't have chance to comment further.

Amber managed a swift double whisky and then set off for work. She had wanted more but it was getting late. As she felt the whisky warming her insides, she was glad that it should at least quell some of the anxiety she always felt when she worked the beat these days. She'd rely on her usual drugs to do the rest.

She had almost arrived at her patch at the back of Piccadilly when she noticed it was occupied by another girl. She sped up, determined to let this interloper know that she wasn't welcome on her spot. It was only when she drew nearer that she realised it was her friend Sapphire who noticed her at about the same time.

As soon as Sapphire spotted Amber she dashed towards her. Straightaway Amber felt ill at ease. For a start, she knew that Sapphire worked in another part of this beat so it was strange that she should even be here. Then Amber remembered that she had also seen a girl the previous evening when she was in a punter's car. She'd thought at the time that the girl bore a remarkable resemblance to Sapphire but she dismissed it, knowing that Sapphire worked a different area of the beat, and presuming it must have been somebody else who looked like her. But maybe it had been Sapphire after all.

Amber was also alarmed by the speed at which Sapphire was hurtling towards her and the fact that Sapphire had been looking for her two nights in a row. It struck her that Sapphire must have something urgent to tell her if she was going to all this trouble. A street girl desperately wanting to tell another something of huge significance was never a good sign and she felt a flutter of nerves inside her tummy.

'Thank God I've found you!' said Sapphire when she reached her. Then she bent forward with her hand resting on Amber's shoulder while she paused to regain her breath.

'Shit, Sapphire! What the fuck is it?' asked Amber. 'You've got me really worried.'

Sapphire straightened up, took a deep breath, and said, 'It's about Kev but you need to promise me first that you've not heard this from me.'

Amber was so eager to find out what the problem was that she would have agreed to anything, and the mention of Kev's name made her feel even more alarmed. 'Yeah, sure. You know me, I won't tell a soul.' She looked at Sapphire, expectantly.

Sapphire looked around before breaking the news to her. 'It's him that did Cora.'

Amber's first reaction was one of alarm and she could feel the flutter in her stomach turn into a grumble. Then she became defensive. The notion was so ridiculous that she refused to entertain it.

'No! No, you're fuckin' joking. Kev wouldn't do that. He'd never hurt a woman. Who the fuck's told you this?'

'Straight up, Amber, it's true. A mate of mine told me.'

'And how do you know she's not lying?'

'It's not a she; it's a he. And he isn't. I can't tell you his name. He's shitting himself already in case there's any comeback. But take it from me, he ain't lying. He saw it with his own eyes.'

'No chance! What did he see? And where?'

Sapphire took another deep breath and to Amber it felt like she was becoming exasperated with her. 'He used to live in the same squat as Cora. She had her own room there, an old office that she'd made nice with all her stuff. There were some windows in it that looked out onto the main office area. My mate just happened to be peeping through a gap in the curtains when he saw them.'

'No! Hang on,' said Amber. 'I don't like the sound of this. Why the fuck would he be looking through the window unless he's a fuckin' peeping Tom or summat?'

'I don't fuckin' know, do I? Look, Amber, I've gone to a lot of trouble to tell you this. I should be at work now, not trailing you all over Manchester. So, don't shoot the fuckin' messenger.'

'Sorry, Sapphire, but this mate of yours doesn't sound reliable to me. Where is he now? Can I have a word with him?'

'No, I've already told you, I can't tell you who he is.'

'Aah, I know, I bet he's staying at yours, isn't he? Don't worry, I won't tell Kev. I just want to hear it from the horse's mouth, that's all.'

'No, he isn't staying with me. I wouldn't have him living with me.'

'Why not if he's so reliable?'

Amber was still in denial, but Sapphire surprised her when she grabbed her by the arm and pulled her closer before speaking directly to her. 'Trust me, Amber. I'm telling you all this for your own fuckin' good! If my mate says he saw it, then he saw it. I know him and he might have his faults, but he wouldn't lie about summat like that. And if you'd seen the look on his face, you'd know he wasn't lying too. I'm telling you, Amber, he's fuckin' shitting himself.'

Sapphire's action coupled with her words made Amber more amenable to what she had to say. 'W-w-what did he see?' she asked again.

Sapphire stared at her for a moment, her stern expression telling Amber she was running out of patience with her. 'He said he thought they were having sex at first but then he noticed that Kev had his hands round Cora's throat. He swears Cora saw him looking through the window, and her fuckin' eyes were bulging out of her head apparently.'

Amber instinctively raised her hand to her mouth as she felt a tremor of fear surge through her body. Then her legs grew weak. This time it was her who grabbed hold of Sapphire's shoulder to steady herself.

'*Now* you believe me!' announced Sapphire.

Amber shook her head although it was obvious from her reaction that she thought Sapphire was telling the truth. Even if she didn't want to acknowledge it, the shock had hit her like a slap in the face, and a hidden instinct told her that it probably was true.

'Are you alright?' asked Sapphire as Amber took her hand from her shoulder and tried to steady herself.

'Yeah sure,' said Amber but her bravado sounded hollow.

'Right, I'll have to leave you then. I've got to go to work.'

Amber didn't say anything; she just stared at Sapphire as she walked away. It occurred to her that she had been a bit off with her friend and should have at least thanked her.

But maybe Sapphire would understand that it was because of the shock.

As she tried to come to terms with Sapphire's revelation, thoughts began to flash through her mind with alarming clarity. Kev's barely concealed anger with her. The way he had handled the guys in the wine bar. And his uncontrolled beating of Cliff and the guy in the tunnel.

She shuddered at the recollections, knowing how close she had come to getting a beating from Kev. The only reason he hadn't done so was because of his own belief that it was wrong to hit women. But even though he suppressed that urge, it was still there, and she was troubled knowing that he had been fighting it all this time.

49

November 2001

Loretta was on her way back from the shops, her arms laden with shopping bags. It felt good to be able to buy the things she wanted for her and the kids, and she knew she wouldn't have been able to do that if it hadn't been for Amy entertaining two to three men per week for the past year.

She was in one of her sober, reflective moods when the guilt at what she was doing ate away at her. There were many times when Loretta regretted letting Cliff and all the other men take advantage of her daughter, and she had decided yet again that she would put a stop to it.

But in the back of her mind was the nagging doubt that her resolve might cave once she'd had a bit to drink. As usual, the lure of the money would prove too much and she would give in to her alcohol-induced reasoning again, telling herself that the additional money wasn't just for her; it was to give the kids a better life too.

Secreted inside the shopping bags were a few bottles of

red wine and a bottle of brandy, and Loretta was already craving for a drink as soon as she got home. She had overindulged the previous night and knew she needed something to calm her shaky hands and racing heart.

When she turned into her street, she saw Mrs Wiley outside her garden gate chatting to Mrs Griffiths from over the road. They watched her as she approached. Their expressions were grim, and they kept turning back to each other and saying something. Loretta suddenly felt self-conscious and was convinced they were talking about her. Despite how long she had lived here, she still didn't quite fit in.

The fact that she had taken a step down when she had moved to the area was enough to alienate her in their eyes without anything else. But Loretta knew that her suicide attempt a couple of years ago could only have given them more reason to take against her. The two women were resilient types who had rushed to her rescue and that of her children, but she somehow knew that on reflection they would have seen it as a weak and selfish act.

It was difficult to feel grateful for what they had done when she felt so indebted to them. She also knew that they would have derided her for leaving the children to fend for themselves when things got too much for her. In their eyes, she had done a bad thing and she would always be scorned because of it. Despite all that, they managed to rub along. None of the women had ever spoken to her about what happened that day, nor she to them, but Loretta knew that it was always there, like an invisible barrier between them.

Before Loretta reached her neighbours, Mrs Griffiths went back to her own house, but Mrs Wiley remained, leaning on the gate, her large frame making it appear diminutive in comparison. Her eyes were roaming along the street but straying back to Loretta at intervals.

Loretta knew she was waiting for her and wondered what she wanted. Whatever it was, she hoped it wouldn't take long as she was anxious to get back home and pop open a bottle of red while she cooked the tea for her and the children.

As she drew to within a few metres of Mrs Wiley, she noticed that her neighbour was now staring directly at her. Mrs Wiley's gaze was unwavering, and Loretta became concerned over what the other woman was about to say. For a moment, her anxiety about the imminent encounter overrode her desire for a drink.

'I've been wanting a word with you,' Mrs Wiley announced, matter-of-factly, once Loretta was in hearing range.

Loretta turned up her chin and raised her eyebrows in an expression of curiosity then stopped and put down her shopping bags. Nathan must have been watching for her return because he dashed out of the house and raced over.

'Have you got any biscuits, Mum?' he asked.

'Yes.'

'Can I take them in?' He was pawing at the bags trying to find them.

'No, you can wait till after your tea, but you can take a couple of these bags inside.'

'Aw, Mum.'

'Do as you're told, Nathan, and then wait inside for me.'

All the time she was speaking, Loretta could feel Mrs Wiley's eyes on her, watching, waiting and judging.

Once Nathan was indoors, the woman spoke again. 'It's about all these strange men that keep calling round,' she said.

Loretta felt her heart thump as the words struck home. She'd never had to answer for her actions before.

'I'm all for live and let live,' continued Mrs Wiley. 'What you choose to do behind closed doors is your own bloody business as far as I'm concerned. But when there's children involved, it's a different matter altogether.'

Loretta opened her mouth to speak but she couldn't think what to say. A feeling of dread assailed her. What if the neighbours knew about Amy? That would be the end of everything!

But Mrs Wiley hadn't finished admonishing her yet. 'It's been going on long enough and it's about bleedin' time you put a stop to it! At first, I thought it was just the odd boyfriend but not now. I think there's more to this than you're letting on, isn't there? And Mrs Griffiths has seen it too – different bleedin' men coming and going at all hours.

'Those children are at an impressionable age, y'know. It's not bloody right! So, either you put a stop to it, or I'll make sure you do. I don't like telling tales, but I'll be reporting you if it carries on.'

Mrs Wiley's lengthy diatribe had given Loretta a chance to think of a defence. 'There's nothing untoward going on; they're just friends. I like a bit of company from time to time, that's all.'

'Tell that to the cat!' spat Mrs Wiley. 'If you reckon it's all so bloody innocent then perhaps you'd like to explain it to the police.'

Mrs Wiley folded her arms under her huge breasts and

turned around, ready to go back into her own home till Loretta stopped her.

'No, wait! Mrs Wiley, it's not what you think but I will do something about it. Please don't report us. It'll only affect the kids.'

'Aye, well maybe you should have thought of that before. I'll leave it with you but I'm warning you, if you don't do summat about it, and bleedin' quick, then I will!'

Loretta bent down and picked up the remaining shopping bags, eager to get away from the woman. Her eyes failed to meet Mrs Wiley's and she quickly turned and went through her own garden gate and into the house.

Once indoors, Loretta went through to the kitchen and began unpacking her groceries, the thoughts spinning around in her head as she placed items into the fridge-freezer and cupboards. She could feel her heart beating rapidly as she went over the encounter with Mrs Wiley.

Damn! It had been a close call. She cringed as she recalled Mrs Wiley's words, which made her feel so ashamed and inadequate. But at least her neighbour had given her fair warning before taking matters further and, more importantly, she didn't seem to have a clue about Amy's involvement.

Loretta wasn't worried about Amy telling anybody; she knew she wouldn't. But she was concerned about Nathan. She wasn't sure whether he knew about the men going into his sister's room. She'd taken care to make sure they only came when he was in bed and that they left before he got up. But you never knew whether he had overheard things. He was twelve now, two years younger than his sister, and a bright lad, and he might have arrived at his own conclusions.

It wasn't long before Nathan ran into the kitchen. 'How long will tea be, Mum?' he asked.

'For God's sake, Nathan, give me chance to get in the house first! I need to unpack the shopping and then I'll start it, and I'd appreciate it if you would stay out of the kitchen till it's ready.'

As soon as she spoke the words, Loretta regretted being so sharp with him. But the confrontation with Mrs Wiley and her guilt feelings over Amy, combined with her hangover, had left her shaken. She spotted the red wine in one of the shopping bags and pulled out a bottle, her hands shaking as she uncorked it and poured herself a large glass.

As she carried on unpacking the shopping, she took huge gulps of the crimson liquid to calm her nerves. The revelation that her neighbours were on to her had thrown up all kinds of complications. She knew she'd have to stop the men coming round or at least limit it to just one or two familiar faces. It was too risky otherwise. But how would she and the children cope with the loss of income?

There were still ways she could earn a bit of money herself. Perhaps she could go back to a client's place or a hotel rather than having them call home. But it was tricky. Men she met in bars didn't usually want to take her back to their place where they might have a wife or partner. And as for the cost of a hotel, not many would want that added expense especially when there were plenty of younger girls available for those who could afford to be extravagant.

Despite her earlier decision to stop men spending time with her daughter, Loretta knew that the loss of income from Amy would hit them the hardest. Men who preferred a younger woman were willing to pay handsomely for the privilege and, now that Loretta had no choice but to put a stop to it, she panicked over how she would cope financially.

As she puzzled over what to do, Loretta started to prepare their evening meal, chopping veg haphazardly in between taking gulps of wine. But her hands were still shaking, and she knew it would take at least a couple of glasses till she was feeling calm again.

Nathan dashed back into the kitchen but before he had a chance to speak, Loretta rebuked him again. She was so agitated that she couldn't seem to help herself. 'For God's sake, Nathan! Can you just leave me to get on with it please?'

Nathan adopted a sulky expression and trudged out of the kitchen. Loretta stabbed angrily at a red pepper and caught her finger. 'Ouch!' she yelled as her blood spilt onto the pepper, adding a moist sheen to the crimson veg.

She gripped her finger, trying to stem the blood flow, then dashed to the tap and rinsed both the cut and the pepper. She didn't have any plasters in the house, so she grabbed some kitchen towel and held it over her finger till the bleeding stopped.

Loretta was so absorbed in tending to her wound that her troubles were temporarily forgotten. But they soon returned and with them an idea had entered her subconscious. After a few glasses of wine, Loretta had started to see things differently and had thought of a way in which she could make even more money. She smiled as she topped up her wine and mulled the idea over in her mind. Yes, she thought, it could be the answer to all her problems.

50

January 2016

After Sapphire's warning, Amber had managed to avoid Kev. She didn't know whether he had turned up at her patch while she had been with a client, but she was glad she hadn't seen him.

It was the night after she had seen Sapphire, and Amber was once again on the beat. The weather was chilly and, as she stood there, Amber was shivering so much that her teeth were chattering. She didn't know whether it was because of the cold or whether it was fear as well. She was now more anxious than ever, knowing it was probably Kev who had killed Cora.

Before she had set off from home, Amber had received a text from him:

Hi babe, what time you at work tonight?

She ignored it. There was no way she was telling him when she was at work; she didn't want him turning up and inviting her back to his. But, on her way to work, she received another one:

Well?

The last text was followed by a phone call from him, which she'd also ignored and, by the time she arrived at work, Amber was becoming flustered. She kept a nervous look out for Kev's car, dreading the moment when she spotted it. He was bound to know something was wrong, but she was frightened that if she spoke to him, she'd make it even more obvious. How could she act normal towards him, knowing what he had done?

It wasn't long before a car dropped off one of the other girls, a tall peroxide blonde who spotted Amber and made her way towards her. Amber recognised her, having seen her on the beat many times before. She was one of the girls who had given her what Amber had thought of as admiring glances when she saw Kev drop her off at work. But she had her own friends and didn't usually come over to chat.

The girl came straight to the point. 'Hi. Kev's been looking for you.'

'What did he want?'

'He didn't say but he looked well pissed off. I'd tread carefully if I were you.'

'Thanks for the warning,' said Amber.

She expected the girl to return to her spot, but it seemed she wanted to talk some more. 'You been seeing him long?'

'A few months. Why?'

'You know about his rep then,' said the girl.

Amber didn't want to give anything away to someone

who she hardly knew. 'Yeah, I've heard stuff, but he's OK once you get to know him.'

'I wouldn't be so sure if I were you.'

'What do you mean?' asked Amber.

The girl hesitated and it seemed to Amber that she was already regretting saying too much. 'Nothing. And don't tell him I gave you the tip-off. Just watch your back, that's all.'

Before Amber had chance to say anything, she was making her way back to her own patch. Amber knew she could have shouted after her, but it was unlikely she'd tell her more. For some reason, the girl was just as wary of Kev as she was.

She heard her phone ping for the second time since she had been talking to the girl, so she switched it on and looked at the screen. There were two messages from Kev, the second only a minute after the first:

Where the fuck are you?

You're fuckin' annoying me now, Amber.

The aggressive words startled her, and she was about to put the phone away when it pinged again. Another text from Kev:

Why aren't you answering your phone?

Amber was relieved when a client pulled up. After negotiating the fee with him, she got inside his car. The sound of her phone ringing made her jump and she took it out and looked at the screen to see who was calling.

It was Kev again. She could feel her heart pounding and deliberated over whether to answer it or not. In the end, knowing he wouldn't stop until he'd made contact, she hit the call-receive button.

'Where the fuck have you been, Amber?' Kev blasted down the line. 'I've been fuckin' texting you all night!'

She smiled half-heartedly at the client whose eyes kept straying from the road to her and then back again. 'I was going to call you back, but it's been full on. In fact, I'm just with a client now.'

She hoped the urgency in her voice would send him away, but it didn't. 'What, for the last two fuckin' hours?' he demanded. 'Don't give me that bullshit! You probably weren't even at work two fuckin' hours ago.'

'Oh, I, erm, I've only just seen my messages. I was going to call you back as soon as I got a minute.'

'Like fuck you were! Anyway, you're coming back to mine later. I'll pick you up at three.'

He cut the call straightaway and Amber stared at the phone in her hand. She hadn't had a chance to wangle out of it. But she was so panicked that she probably wouldn't have been able to think of a good excuse anyway. His aggressive attitude had put her even more on edge. Maybe she should have told him she was too tired. But there was no way Kev would have settled for that. He was a man who was used to getting his own way.

For the rest of her shift Amber couldn't settle; the prospect of meeting Kev was dominating her thoughts. She kept checking the time on her phone, noticing that it was passing much quicker than usual. It would soon be three o'clock and Kev would be here.

The thought of seeing him petrified her. How could she sleep with him knowing what he had done? What would she say to him? How would she be able to hide what she now knew? He'd suss her out straightaway. She was no good at hiding things. It would be obvious from the look on her face. He might have even already guessed and for a minute she regretted that she had ignored his calls. She should have tried to carry on as normal.

But Amber would never have been able to do that. She checked the time on her phone again while she stood at her patch at the back of Piccadilly: 2.35 a.m. Shit! She spotted a car that looked like Kev's and dashed inside the tunnel, relieved when it passed, and it wasn't him.

But the thought of it had sent her into a panic. Her heart was thundering once more, and she felt breathless. Instead of coming out of her hiding place in the tunnel, she carried on to the other end, hoping to catch sight of a taxi before she spotted Kev's car.

To hell with it! She was going home. At least he wouldn't find her there. Amber was so ashamed of her home and her mother's behaviour that, in all the time she had been seeing Kev, she'd never given him her address. Thank God!

Amber had made a decision. This was to be her last night on the beat. She couldn't do it again, not when Kev could turn up at any minute. She'd have to think of some other way to find clients. Perhaps, for now, she'd just take the ones who rang her and arrange to meet them somewhere else. She couldn't risk hanging around in the same area anymore, knowing that Kev would be touring the streets of Manchester until he found her.

51

Fourteen-year-old Amy was sitting on her bed putting on makeup, the hand mirror balanced between her knees. She was applying some mascara when her mother walked into the room. Amy looked up and, as she did so, the mascara left a trail under her eye.

'Aw, Mum, look what you've made me do,' she complained.

It was her third attempt at putting on the mascara. She'd never been very good at it since her mother had introduced her to makeup the previous year but now, she was so nervous that her hands were trembling, making it even more difficult.

Loretta smiled at her. 'Do you want some help?' she asked.

Amy nodded and her mother walked over. 'By the way, Rick's downstairs waiting for us,' said her mother. When Amy looked at her, alarmed, she added, 'It's OK. He'll wait. I'll make it worth his while.'

Amy hadn't been alarmed because they were making Rick wait but because it underlined the fact that it was almost time to leave. And with that on her mind, her mother's words had wound her up even more than usual.

She hated her mother's innuendos. It was something she often did when she'd had a drink and, despite Amy's growing experience with the opposite sex, it still embarrassed her. Rick, a wiry-looking man with tatty hair surrounding a bald patch, was one of the few of her mother's regular men friends who still visited the house, and Amy wasn't too keen on him. Although he generally left her alone, he seemed to bring out a side to her mother that she wasn't comfortable with.

Loretta took a baby wipe and removed Amy's mascara, and then she stood back and examined her daughter's face. 'I think we're best starting again.'

'Why?' asked Amy.

She took up the mirror and held it to her face. Amy had been happy with her look up to now but when she looked with a more critical eye, she could see it was all wrong. She hadn't applied any foundation and her blusher was too thick, making her complexion appear ruddy. Her eyeshadow had been partially removed when her mother had wiped off the mascara, and her eyes were now slightly red-rimmed from all the prodding. She hadn't yet got round to applying her lipstick either.

'Well, love, you're not going to the school disco now,' said her mother. 'I think we need a different look. Leave it with me, I know what I'm doing.'

Amy let her mother apply her makeup, relieved in a way because she had been struggling with the mascara. She relaxed a little as she felt the bristles of the foundation brush sweeping along her cheeks followed by the blusher brush. Then she allowed her mother to apply some eyeshadow followed by mascara and some eyeliner. As her mother pulled her lower eyelid down and slid liner pencil along the rim Amy's eyes began to water and she was glad when her mother had finished.

'Right, just your lipstick to do now,' said Loretta, rummaging inside the makeup bag to find the right colour. She pulled out three and tried each of them in turn on the back of her hand, finally settling on a bright red one. 'I think this one will do. Open your lips, like this,' she instructed, showing Amy what to do.

She quickly applied the lipstick then stood back to admire her handiwork, singing, 'Da da!'

Amy grabbed the mirror to have a look for herself. She hardly recognised the person looking back at her and for a moment she stared open-mouthed.

'Well?' asked Loretta.

'It's... erm... a bit... I don't know. I look really old.'

'That's the idea,' said Loretta. 'Right, now I'm gonna leave you to get yourself changed while I go and have a drink with Rick. It'll stop him getting bored. Wear that outfit I got for you. And don't forget the heels.'

Amy put on her outfit and shoes then examined herself in the hand mirror. The girl in the mirror looked nothing like her. The short, tight-fitting dress clung to her, emphasising her figure, and the shoes gave her instant height so that, together with the heavy makeup, they made her look much older than her fourteen years. She was pleased in a way because she looked attractive but part of her felt a little intimidated by this new, grown-up version of herself.

She took the stairs, slowly, knowing she was going to elicit a reaction when she walked into the living room. But she was unprepared for how extreme that reaction was going to be.

'Whit woo!' shouted Rick as she walked unsteadily into the room on her high heels.

'Wow! You look stunning,' said Loretta.

For a few seconds they looked intently at her, making Amy feel uncomfortable. Their scrutiny also made her more nervous as it emphasised what she was about to do.

Nathan's reaction was a bit less enthusiastic. 'Where are *you* going?' he grumbled.

'Never you mind,' said Loretta. 'It's got nothing to do with you. Just you behave yourself while I'm out. I won't be long.' Then she turned to Amy. 'Right, let's go.'

Amy could tell by the way her mother spoke that she had drunk a fair amount. Earlier, Loretta had seemed hesitant about what they were going to do but now that she was drunk, that hesitation seemed to have disappeared. Rick also had an almost empty glass of wine in his hand but, unlike her mother, he still seemed relatively sober.

They all piled into Rick's car. As Amy sat on the back seat, feeling increasingly apprehensive, Loretta turned around and said, 'Don't forget what I've told you: if anyone asks, you're to tell them you're nineteen.'

'OK,' said Amy and she sat in silence for the rest of the journey while her mother and Rick made mundane conversation.

As they approached Piccadilly, Amy began to sit up and take notice. She could feel her heart beating so frantically that it felt like it was rising into her throat and she tried to swallow down the nerves that were threatening to overwhelm her.

Just before they reached Piccadilly station, Rick took a right turn. 'You sure this is the right way?' asked Loretta.

'Yeah, course I'm sure.' Then he turned his head to the side and winked saucily at Loretta, 'Been here enough times, haven't I?'

They drove to an area in the backstreets, which was more secluded, and Amy gazed, wide-eyed, at the scantily clad girls who hung about on the street. Then Rick stopped the car next to a tunnel opening.

'This'll do,' he said. 'There's nobody else here so she should be alright. She's best not muscling in on anyone else's patch. These girls can be right nasty bitches when they get going, y'know.'

'Shush!' Loretta warned, flashing her eyes over her shoulder to indicate Amy's presence.

But there was no point issuing the warning. Amy had heard what he said, and her nerves shifted up a gear till she was feeling intense anxiety. She tried to latch on to what her mother had told her earlier.

'You'll be fine. It's just the same as you've done before except most of it will probably be in cars.'

And those were the only words of advice she had given her apart from the need to pretend she was nineteen.

Amy sat there, numb with fear, until her mother said, 'Come on then, Amy. Let's have you out.'

Loretta climbed out of her own seat and opened the rear door for Amy to step out. She smiled at her daughter. 'Eh, you'll have to practise wearing those shoes. You could walk up and down a bit while you're waiting for customers.'

'But, Mum...' said Amy.

Her mother butted in, 'Now, come on, Amy, we've discussed this.

'I've not bleedin' come all this way for nothing,' Rick shouted from inside the car.

Loretta cast a worried glance over her shoulder. 'I've got to go. But I've told you, you'll be fine. It won't be any different from what you're used to. Just think of the money, love; it'll save us from losing the house. We'll be back here at two o'clock anyway.'

She gave her daughter a peck on her forehead, but Amy could see the pained expression on her face as she quickly got back inside the car and shut the door.

Panic set in as soon as Amy realised she was on her own. She stepped back towards the car and made to grab the door handle, but Rick pressed down on the central locking. Then he revved the engine and flew off up the street.

Amy let go of the handle and jumped back in shock. The momentum of the car, together with the dangerously high heels, made her stumble, and she landed on the pavement. It took her a moment to recover and she got up, straightening her dress and wiping bits of dust off the bottom of it.

Once she was on her feet, she assessed her bruises, checking the painful areas on her legs and holding her hand to her left buttock where it was smarting. She heard the slamming of brakes and looked towards the road, half-hoping that her mother had had a change of heart and decided to take her back home.

But it wasn't her mother; it was a stranger, and he was winding down his car window. 'You doing business, love?' he shouted, and Amy stepped forward, ready to take on her first client.

52

February 2016

It was the first time Amber had been in the Rose and Crown since her decision not to work the beat. For the past few days, she had been inundated with calls and texts from Kev, but she had ignored them, desperately hoping he'd lose interest and leave her alone, but sensing that that was unlikely.

She wouldn't have been there tonight if she wasn't due to meet a client later in a Manchester hotel and she figured that, as she was in the city centre anyway, she might as well have a few drinks beforehand. Amber couldn't remember if she had mentioned to Kev the name of the pub where she and the other girls hung out or whether she had merely referred to it as 'the pub'. But she consoled herself with the fact that she had never known Kev to go into the Rose and Crown. He seemed to prefer more upmarket venues.

Tonight was also the first time Amber had seen Sapphire since her warning about Kev, and the atmosphere was strained between them. She knew she owed Sapphire an apology for being so sharp with her; she had only been looking out for her after all. But she didn't want to mention it in front of Angie or anybody else. What Kev had done was best kept to as few people as possible. She didn't want it getting back to him that she had spread the word about his crime.

Apart from the strained atmosphere between her and Sapphire, Amber was also on edge in case Kev *did* turn up in the pub. You never knew what to expect with him and she only hoped that, if he did show up, he wouldn't do her any harm when there were witnesses around. The door swung viciously open and Amber jumped then swivelled around to see who it was. She gave an audible sigh when it wasn't Kev.

'What the bloody hell's wrong with you?' asked Angie. 'You're like a cat on hot bricks. And your phone's not stopped pinging. Is someone after you or summat?'

'No!' said Amber, glancing across at Sapphire who flashed her a warning look.

She remembered Sapphire telling her not to let anyone know about what Kev had done. But Amber wouldn't have, and she was a bit niggled that Sapphire's warning look seemed to suggest she would. She wanted to reassure her, but she couldn't while Angie was there.

'Why don't you switch it off if it's bothering you?' asked Angie.

As she spoke Angie started coughing. Amber was busy thinking about what she had said. She couldn't switch her phone off in case any clients rang. She needed all the business she could get now that she couldn't work the beat. Amber was missing the money; she'd had to reduce her drug intake and that was making her even more on edge.

She was so lost in her own concerns that she hadn't noticed how bad Angie's cough had become. She snapped to when she saw Sapphire get up out of her chair and slap Angie roughly on the back. Angie was wheezing and seemed to be struggling to get her breath. But, after Sapphire had given her a few slaps she coughed up the phlegm that had been blocking her windpipe and started breathing easier again.

'Shit, Angie! You had me worried there,' said Sapphire. 'That chest infection isn't getting any better, is it?'

Angie wheezed again. 'That's the trouble when you've got COPD, and it doesn't help when you're working in all weathers.'

'I've told you not to work when it's cold!' snapped Amber, still preoccupied with her own troubles.

'It's fuckin' freezin' out tonight,' said Sapphire. 'I'd sack it if I were you.'

'We'll see how I go,' Angie replied, sizing up the amount of whisky left in her glass.

Sapphire checked the time. 'I'm off anyway. You take care, Angie.' She looked at Amber and her voice had more of an edge to it when she added, 'You too.'

Once Sapphire had gone, Amber noticed the time. It wasn't far off her client meeting and she didn't fancy waiting around for Angie to become drunk and incoherent.

'I'm off too, I've got a client meeting,' she said. 'Don't forget what Sapphire said: you'd be best leaving it tonight.'

She dashed out of the pub, eager to be away, not only from Angie but also from the persistent worry that Kev might walk into the pub at any minute.

★

Old Angie stayed for a little while longer once the other girls had gone. Tired of going to the bar, she went just the once, buying three double whiskies. One of them she divided between the other two then left the empty glass on the bar. It was easier to carry them that way and made her drink problem less obvious to anybody watching. The barmaid, Moira, looked at her knowingly but didn't say anything. Nevertheless, Angie was quick to defend herself.

'It's for my bad chest.'

She returned to her table as quickly as her persistent tiredness and breathlessness would allow. Once she had put the drinks down and plonked herself in her seat the coughing returned. Angie felt a sharp pain in her chest and her lungs crackled. She shoved her change quickly inside her purse and grabbed a tissue from her handbag, which she held to her mouth. A large globule of phlegm worked its way up from her chest and she spat it out into the tissue.

Then she sat back and tried to regain her breath before she took a sip of the whisky. Her lungs were rattling as she breathed rapid shallow breaths and she put her hand to her chest to ease the pain. Angie's breathing was worse than ever, and she was becoming panicked as she gasped for air. She grabbed at the whisky and took a huge gulp, hoping it would calm both her and her chest.

Feeling curious, Angie examined the contents of the tissue and noticed that it was smeared with a large patch of thick green phlegm tinged with blood. She screwed it up tight and put it back inside her handbag. Then she took out her purse and checked her money, noting that she was now down to her last tenner plus some change.

Angie knew her state of health wasn't good. Despite her COPD, she had never felt this bad. And as she sat there swigging the whisky, she could feel herself burning up. 'Jesus, it's hot in here tonight,' she muttered as the whisky, combined with what she had already drunk, started to take hold.

It wasn't long before she had downed all six measures. She was becoming hotter although the cough had calmed a little, and she decided she needed to get outside. 'Too bloody hot in here,' she repeated. 'I need some air.'

She stood up and staggered. But it wasn't just the effects of the drink. She felt light-headed and didn't have any energy.

'You alright, Angie?' shouted Moira.

'Bloody dizzy,' mumbled Angie and she continued to wobble towards the exit, grabbing onto the tables and chairs for support.

Moira raced over and took hold of Angie, trying to steady her. She led her to a chair. 'Sit down here, Angie. You don't look fit to walk. Hang on while I order you a taxi.'

Angie was too weak to argue. It would cost but it would be easier than having to walk to her patch on the beat. So, she stayed where she was, deciding to shut her eyes while she waited for the taxi. Her head lolled forward and she thought she must have nodded off because, before she knew it, Moira had come back to tell her the taxi was outside, and she was trying to help her out of her seat.

Moira guided her to the door and waited while she got inside the taxi. 'You take care now,' she said.

'I'm only going to bloody Aytoun ssstreet,' Angie replied.

Moira shut the taxi door after Angie and went back

inside the Rose and Crown. As soon as she was inside the cab, Angie's cough returned, and she shivered from the cold air that had hit her once she stepped outside the pub. The driver looked over his shoulder at her, concerned by her obvious ill health.

'You sound like you'd be better off going to the hospital, love,' he said.

Angie tried to speak between gasps. 'No... need the money.' Somewhere in her drunken brain she decided that the taxi driver was having a go at her and, when the heat of the taxi began to permeate her bones and her breathing steadied a little, she snapped at him. 'I'm not drunk, y'know. I'm ill.'

'I can see that; you're as white as a ghost and shivering like buggery. All the more reason you should get some help, love.'

Despite Angie claiming to be sober, the alcohol had taken its toll and was affecting her judgement. She wrongly believed that, although still ill, she was now feeling much better than earlier. The cough was nothing more than a nuisance. As she sat back in the taxi, her jumbled thoughts took over and, instead of responding to his statement, her mind drifted to other things.

'I used to be sssomeone, y'know,' she said but the driver ignored her and kept his eyes on the road. 'Now I'm just old Angie, the prostitute.'

Picking up on the driver's disinterest, she muttered to herself instead. 'Nice figure, nice clothes. And *all* the men wanted me.'

She continued muttering to herself for the few minutes it took to arrive at the red-light district.

'We're here, love,' said the driver.

Angie looked out of the window, confused. Then she recognised her usual patch and nodded. She undid her handbag, slowly, her hands shaky and her mind unfocused.

'You sure you wouldn't be better off going to the hospital?' asked the driver.

'Nah,' said Angie, shutting her handbag again. 'I'm not going there.'

She settled back in her seat again, her head lolling once more. Suddenly, she had an urge to be home. She didn't want to hang about on the streets freezing. She just wanted a nice warm bed.

'Home…' she muttered. 'To bed.'

'Where's home, love?'

Angie quickly reeled off the full address then closed her eyes and fell asleep.

53

December 2001

It was Amy's third time on the beat. Each night had followed a similar pattern. Her mother and Rick had dropped her off, she'd waited on the same spot for clients and at the end of the night her mother and Rick had come back to take her home. But tonight, her mother had told her she'd have to make her own way home as Rick didn't want to keep driving into town.

Despite it being the third night, Amy was still terrified. As her mother had pointed out, it wasn't anything she hadn't done before, but for Amy it was the unpredictability of it that got to her. At home she felt as though she had a level of protection. If one of the clients got too out of hand and started roughing her up, at least she knew that her mother was only in the next room. But out on the street, anything could happen.

The sheer number of clients worried her as well. Instead of having the same regular two to three clients a week, she was now entertaining between six to eight clients each night she worked. She'd already had a few clients who gave her the creeps – old seedy men who were almost frothing at the mouth when she agreed to service them. But, if she turned down every client who repulsed her, she realised she'd have very little custom at all.

Apart from the clients, she found the other girls intimidating. On her first night she'd been approached by one of them.

'You new?' she had asked. When Amy nodded, she had added, 'Poor cow. I don't envy you. It takes some fuckin' getting used to. I'd sack it now if I were you before you get too used to the money.'

'I can't afford to,' said Amy. It was the only excuse she could think of.

Now, as she stood waiting, she saw a car approach and she stepped forward. But she was surprised when a girl got out of the car just a couple of metres away. She was a tall girl, with pointed features, and she stared venomously at Amy.

'Eh you, what d'you think yer playing at?' she demanded. 'Yer on my fuckin' patch!'

'But I was here last Friday and Saturday,' said Amy.

'Yeah, only 'cos I was ill. But I'm back now so you can fuck right off and find somewhere else.'

Amy was tempted to argue but, as she was new here, she didn't want to make enemies. So, instead of retaliating, she asked, 'Where can I go?'

The girl looked Amy up and down and she felt uncomfortable under her appraisal. But her facial features seemed to soften as she asked, 'How old are you anyway?'

'Nineteen,' said Amy, just as her mother had instructed.

The girl laughed. 'Ha, a likely story. I bet your pimp told you to say that... Listen, you'll be alright further up the road. Julie's the next one down but there's a big gap between her and the next girl. Why don't you wait there?'

'Thanks,' said Amy, walking away, and she thought she could detect relief on the other girl's face.

It was an hour and a half later. Business had been slow tonight and Amy had only had one client up to now. As she waited for a car to stop, she gazed around her, noticing the other girls who were also hanging around. In the distance she could see two girls chatting then one of them broke away and started heading in her direction.

Amy watched as she approached and, to her consternation, the other girl locked eyes with her. She felt a shudder of fear and dreaded having another confrontation. It seemed obvious to Amy that the other girl wanted to speak to her for some reason. She gazed away but was still conscious of the girl's approach. The sound of her high heels clattering on the pavement warned Amy that she had now almost reached her.

Curiosity made Amy turn around and she was relieved when the girl smiled at her. If it hadn't been for that smile, the girl's appearance would have put Amy on her guard. Aged around twenty, she was taller than Amy and had dyed red hair in a messy style. Her makeup was heavy, and she had a hard expression that screamed 'streetwise'. But what was most noticeable about her was her huge breasts, which seemed out of place on her slim frame.

'Hi, I'm Crystal,' she greeted. 'You new?'

'Yeah.'

'Aw, never mind. You'll soon get used to it. What's your name?'

'Amy.'

'Ooh, no. That's too prim and proper. You need to change it. How about Amber?'

'Why?' asked Amy, feeling a bit wary because of the girl's forcefulness but nevertheless warming to her.

'Well, for a kick-off, it's a rule never to tell a client your real name. There's some fuckin' weirdos out on the street and the less they know about you, the better. And secondly, you want something that sounds more exotic.'

'OK. I'll think about it.'

'How you finding it?' asked Crystal.

Amy was so taken by the girl's apparent concern that she felt tears pricking her eyes. Not trusting her voice to keep steady, she shrugged.

'Scary?' asked Crystal.

Amy nodded.

'That lot been giving you a hard time?'

Amy didn't want to say too much as she didn't know where Crystal's loyalties lay so she just said, 'A bit.'

'They can be like that sometimes. They feel threatened when they see a new girl, especially one as young and pretty as you. They're frightened of you getting all the business but don't worry, they'll soon get used to having you around. You got anyone looking after you?'

Amy was taken aback. She wasn't sure exactly what the girl was asking and was too ashamed to admit that her mother and Rick usually dropped her off. 'What d'you mean?' she said.

'The street's a dangerous place. Most of us have a pimp to protect us. It makes it less risky. You got one?'

'No.'

To Amy's surprise, Crystal put her arm round her. 'You stick with me. I'll make sure you're looked after. I know someone who really takes care of his girls. He'll make sure no one bothers you. He's called Gilly and he's alright. I'll take you to meet him tomorrow before work if you like.'

Amy already knew that this was going to be her life for years to come. She could tell by the way her mother and Rick had been so excited about her earnings from the first two nights on the beat. But the thought of it also terrified her and, if Crystal's friend was offering protection, she'd be a fool not to take it.

So, she shrugged and said to Crystal, 'Yeah, OK.'

54

February 2016

Nathan looked around his living room. It was late at night, much later than he had intended to go to bed, but he and Chloe had been working on their new house all day and by the time they'd finished it was too late to cook. They'd grabbed a takeaway and a bottle of wine then snuggled up on the sofa.

Although he was tired, he was content. The sight of what he and Chloe had achieved made his insides feel alive with pure bliss. The furniture had now arrived, and he had been able to ditch the deckchairs they had been temporarily using. It was wonderful to be able to put it amongst all the other items they had been stocking up while they had waited for the house to come through.

As he sat on the sleek dark corner sofa he gazed around the room. The polished floorboards looked fabulous as did the expensive rug and he was pleased with the quality curtains and cushions, which he and Chole had selected in earth tones with subtle dashes of colour to brighten the place up. He also loved the way Chloe had arranged the modern artwork so that it complemented the room rather than dominating it.

He looked over and smiled at her. He marvelled once more at just how wonderful she was. Chloe was everything he had ever dreamed of; with dark, glossy straight hair, perfect skin, dazzling eyes and a cracking figure. Unlike his mother and sister, who abused their bodies with drink and drugs, Chloe shone with health and vitality.

Nathan had met her at university and she now worked in finance for local government. She came from a respectable middle-class family and didn't mind that his past had been different to hers. As she had said, despite his upbringing he had still attained the same status in life as her. They were together now as a couple and that was what was important.

Chloe had taste and a wonderful creative streak that enabled her to visualise something even before they started decorating and buying household items. He knew it was down to her that the place looked so wonderful. It wasn't finished yet, but he knew that with Chloe's magic touch it would soon be looking fantastic.

'Happy?' she asked.

'Oh yeah, it's amazing.' He leaned across and took her in his arms then planted a chaste kiss on her lips. 'And I've got the best girl to share it with. Thanks for everything, Chloe. You make me so happy.'

Chloe smiled back at him. 'Don't go getting all soppy on me now.'

Nathan pulled away. 'No, I'm serious, Chloe. I'm so lucky to have you and all of this.' He waved his hand, indicating his surroundings. 'I've been dreaming of this for so long while I had to live in that dump with my mum and sister. And now I've finally got it, I'm the happiest man alive.'

Chloe beamed. 'Me too.'

After kissing her for the second time, Nathan spoke again. He was feeling emotional and had to take a deep calming breath before he could get his words out. 'I'll tell you something, Chloe… I'll always love you and I guarantee that I'm never going to let anything, or anybody spoil our happiness.

February 2016

Amber was standing outside a city centre hotel with a full purse. The client visit had gone well. He was average-looking and amiable, so when he had offered her a lot of money to stay most of the night, Amber had jumped at the chance.

It was now early morning and she was making her way to the taxi rank, which was only a couple of streets away. She assumed that Kev wouldn't be cruising the city centre at this time; he would normally be in bed by now. But with Kev you never knew, and Amber was taking no chances so she was glad that she could afford a cab back home.

It wasn't long before she reached the taxi rank. All the way there she had been looking around expecting to catch sight of Kev at any minute. She was reassured to find nobody else in the taxi queue at this hour and she gladly jumped inside the cab and asked the driver to take her to Withington.

Her relief was short-lived because as soon as she arrived home Amber sensed that there was something not right. The first sign of a problem was when she found her mother's keys still in the front door. Amber took them out and tutted, thinking that her mother must have been so drunk she had forgotten to take them out of the lock.

When she got inside the hall it was in its usual state of neglect. Apart from the stale odour, the old-fashioned wallpaper was grimy, the carpet had grease stains and the white skirting boards were yellowing and scuffed. But what made it look out of place was the fact that her mother's shoes had been left strewn across the hallway carpet. This was unusual because no matter how drunk her mother was, she always made a point of putting them on the shoe rack and had always drummed this into Amber and Nathan too when they were growing up.

The second thing Amber found strange was that the mirror was lopsided. Her first thought was that her mother's drinking must have descended to a new low if she couldn't even put her shoes on the rack and she had obviously been staggering if she had banged into the mirror on her way down the hall. She presumed she must have carried on drinking till late.

Something instinctively told Amber that she would find her mother in the living room rather than the bedroom. It was therefore no surprise to see her sprawled out on the living room sofa. The drunken fool must have been there all night. She appeared to be fast asleep, but Amber had no qualms about waking her.

'For God's sake, Mother! Anybody could have walked into the house. You didn't lock the bloody door and your keys were still in it,' she raged, as she walked across the room.

She noticed that her mother's head was slumped, her face pale. Amber's hand shot to her mouth, and her mind flashed back to that time when she was a child. Her mother was lying on the sofa then too, her head lolling and wine-stained spittle dribbling from the corner of her mouth. Alongside her had been the empty bottle, opened pill packet and upturned wine glass sitting in a pool of sticky red wine.

'Shit!' cursed Amber, dashing towards her, expecting the worst.

She was worried. How long had her mother been here like this? It might have been since the pubs shut, which was hours ago. And if she had tried to top herself again then her chances of survival would be slim.

But there was no wine bottle, no pill packet and no empty glass. Still, there was something not right.

'Mum!' she shouted, grabbing her shoulder and shaking her.

Small slits appeared between the heavy eyelids as her mother struggled to open them, and her mouth formed the shape of Amber's name, but no sound came out. *At least she was alive. Thank God!*

Amber could tell she was in a bad way and another recollection flooded her brain. It was from a long time ago when she had only been working the beat for a couple of years. This memory jabbed at her guilty conscience. She tried to push it aside while she grabbed her mother's wrist to examine her pulse. But it wouldn't go away, and Amber knew that if anything happened to her mother, she would never forgive herself.

55

March 2004

Amy had been on the beat for over two years, working under the name of Amber, and she was currently having a good time inside the Rose and Crown with her friends: Crystal and Ruby. While listening to 'Where is the Love?' by The Black Eyed Peas, she was also enjoying a bit of banter with the other girls before she set off for work.

Working the streets had now become a way of life. It was tough and wasn't what Amber would have chosen for herself, but she had been pushed into it by her mother when she had been too young to fight back. And now, she was stuck with it. She'd been sucked into the whole meaningless existence: the drugs, the cravings and that endless need to earn money.

In her more lucid moments, she felt a deep resentment that she had come to this. But the camaraderie with the other girls helped, and it usually enabled her to tackle work in a better frame of mind than the one she'd set off from home with.

Amber happened to look up at the door when she noticed her mother stumbling inside the pub. It was the first time she'd seen her inside the Rose and Crown, as Amber had taken great care to keep her away, and she was alarmed. The way Loretta was staggering told Amber she was already drunk. *Oh no!* she thought. *How the hell did she find me in here?*

Loretta had followed Amber to Manchester's red-light districts years previously when she realised that she could earn more money that way. It had also stopped the neighbours complaining as she kept her trade away from the home. But she worked a different beat than Amber, and they didn't usually socialise together.

From the age of twelve Amber had felt ashamed and her mother was a representation of that shame. She was the one who had condoned the men visiting Amber's room late at night and carrying out their vulgar acts. In fact, she had encouraged it for the money and to help finance her descent into alcoholism.

Amber shot up out of her seat and raced across to where Loretta was making her way across the pub. Without allowing her to get as far as the bar, she grabbed her by the arm and dragged her towards the ladies'.

'In here,' she hissed. 'I want a word with you.'

Amber was relieved to find there was nobody else inside. 'What's all the fuss?' asked her mother.

'What the hell are you doing in here?' she raged.

'I've been looking for you.' Loretta hiccupped. 'Can't a mother spend some time with her only daughter?'

'No! You can't. I don't want you here. But now they've already bloody seen you, so they'll know that I know you.'

'I just want to keep you company, love.'

Amber thought about her predicament. Even if she managed to persuade her mother to leave the pub, she knew she would return every time she was drunk. There would also be the inevitable questions from the other girls who had seen Amber race over to Loretta and pull her to one side.

'Right, you can stay,' she said. 'But on one condition... Don't you dare tell anyone who you really are!'

Loretta looked hurt and Amber immediately felt guilty. Why did her mother always have this ability to make her feel sorry for her? For a moment she wavered over her decision. Maybe she should acknowledge Loretta as her mother.

But she knew she couldn't face the other girls knowing. She was an embarrassment! And, as if her drunkenness weren't enough, she had also sunk to new depths in the services she was now prepared to offer to the seediest clients for a pittance. Time and alcohol abuse had taken their toll on Loretta's looks and she couldn't attract the men as easily as the younger girls so she settled for whatever she could get. In the eyes of other street girls, she was the lowest of the low.

So, Amber held fast. 'As far as they're concerned, you're just Angie the prostitute,' she added, referring to her mother by her street name.

'I know, I know,' slurred Loretta who was already drunk. 'Loretta's too posh for a street girl.'

Amber knew her mother's last point was irrelevant,

but she had reached that stage of intoxication when her thoughts and words became random and disjointed.

'Don't even fuckin' mention that you're called Loretta!' she hissed. 'Or that you're my mother. Because, if you do, I'll leave you and you won't see me or any of the money I earn ever again.'

'But, Amy!' Loretta said, trying to stare at her daughter but unable to focus. 'I'm proud to be your mother.'

Her last word was punctuated by a hiccup.

'Well I'm not proud to have an alcoholic for a mother and I don't want the other girls to know. You've no right to come in here drunk and showing me up. Don't you think you've done enough harm to me in my life? And my name's Amber by the way. Don't you ever call me Amy in front of the other girls! I don't want them sussing out that you're my mother.'

She fled from the ladies' leaving Loretta to follow behind, and desperately hoping that the threat of leaving home would persuade her mother to keep her secret. When she reached the other girls, they all looked up at her expectantly.

'What's the matter?' asked Crystal.

'Nowt. It's just Angie. She works the beat. She can be a bit of a pain but she's harmless enough. I've told her she can join us. I hope you don't mind.'

'No, it's fine,' said Crystal.

'We'll soon put her straight if she starts anything,' cut in Ruby.

Amber managed a half-hearted smile then watched her mother as she waited at the bar before staggering across the pub to join them.

'This is Angie,' said Amber once her mother had joined them.

The other girls shuffled their seats around to accommodate her and Crystal smiled amiably.

'Yes,' said Loretta. 'Old Angie the prostitute. That's who I am.'

56

February 2016

Loretta's pulse was rapid but weak, confirming Amber's suspicions that all was not well. She remembered how she had been in the pub – coughing uncontrollably until Sapphire had slapped her on the back. But Amber had been so preoccupied about Kev that she had barely noticed. Guilt ate away at her when she recalled how she had been eager to get off to her client meeting before her mother became a drunken menace.

Loretta's eyes opened and she tried to speak again. Her breath was shallow, and Amber could hear it rattling in her lungs. She was now fully awake, but her eyes were cloudy, and her pupils were like pinpricks.

'I told you not to go to work, you silly cow!' said Amber. Although her words were stern, her voice cracked with emotion.

'I didn't go,' said Loretta. 'I got a taxi back here.'

She paused to get her breath back and Amber put a hand to her head, which felt hot to the touch despite the room being chilly. 'Jesus, you're burning up! How long have you been lying there?'

Loretta wheezed. 'Dunno. I didn't stay in the pub long after you'd gone. I didn't feel so good.'

'OK. I'll get you a duvet and something to bring your temperature down,' said Amber rushing out of the room.

While she looked for the things, Amber also switched the heating on. Her mother may have been burning up, but she knew that the chilliness in the house couldn't have been good for her chest infection. No, it was best to let her sweat it out.

Fortunately, Loretta always kept a supply of paracetamol for hangovers, so they weren't difficult to find. It wasn't long before Amber was back in the room with the tablets, a glass of water and the duvet off Nathan's old bed.

'Mum, I need to sit you up so I can give you some paracetamol,' she said.

Amber knelt and reached over, putting her hands under her mother's arms to lift her. As she did so, the pungent smell of stale whisky hit her, and she recoiled. But this time she couldn't walk away and, as she picked her mother up, she noticed something else. She was light and easy to lift. In fact, she was all skin and bone, and she coughed and wheezed with the exertion as Amber lifted her. Why hadn't she noticed before just how frail her mother had become?

She managed to get her to take the tablets then she put her back in a comfortable position, wrapping the duvet around her.

'I'm too bloody hot,' Loretta complained.

'You'll cool down in a bit now you've had the paracetamols, but you need to keep warm because of your bad chest. It's bloody freezing in here. I'll get you a damp cloth to hold to your head. That should help to bring your temperature down.'

Amber raced to the kitchen and brought back a cold compress, holding it to Loretta's forehead. She knew that her mother should really be in bed, but she was far too weak to manage the stairs. As she looked at her pallid complexion and cloudy, red-rimmed eyes and listened to her laboured breathing, she realised that this was more than just a bad chest. She strongly suspected that her mother had pneumonia and she deliberated over what to do about it.

It was too early to ring the doctors or go round to the neighbours', but Amber felt that Nathan should know that their mother was so ill. She half hoped that he might also provide some moral support when she told him just how unwell their mother was.

'Mum, I'm just going to ring Nathan,' said Amber. 'She placed her mother's hand on top of the cold compress. 'Hold that there while I make the call.' Then she took out her phone and tried to stand up. 'I need to let him know you're ill.'

Loretta reached out a scrawny hand. 'No, stay here. Never mind him. I need to tell you something.' She paused to catch her breath.

Amber knelt back down next to the sofa and watched her mother take a deep juddering breath as she raised her head and prepared to speak again.

'I'm sorry, love,' she said.

'What for?'

'For... everything. I was a bad mother.' Amber wanted to reassure her that she was wrong. But she couldn't so she let her mother carry on between gasps of air. 'I did what I had to do to make ends meet... I was wrong too... it wasn't Nathan... you were the special one... always you.'

Loretta's head sunk back onto the pillow and she closed her eyes, exhausted. For some time, Amber stayed where she was, watching her mother's chest rise and fall and listening to her croaking lungs. She took hold of her hand and felt tears stinging her eyes.

Once she had watched her mother fall back to sleep and taken a moment to calm herself down, she got back up off the floor and walked into the hall. She needed to ring Nathan. They hadn't heard anything from him since he'd left home, and any attempts Loretta had made to contact him had all been ignored. But Loretta was his mother too and she was in a bad way so it was only right that he should know.

Nathan awoke to the sound of his mobile ringing. He glanced at the alarm clock: 6.08 a.m. *What the fuck? Who could be ringing at this time?* He reached over for his phone, which he always kept on the bedside cabinet. When he picked it up and saw his sister's name lit up on the screen, he was tempted to press the call-reject button. But curiosity made him answer it.

'Yes, what is it?'

'It's Mum, Nathan. She's in a really bad way.'

'Jesus! Don't tell me she's pissed again. Surprise, surprise! Why don't you just let her sleep it off like she...'

'No!' his sister cut in. 'She's not drunk. She's really ill.' Then he heard his sister's voice break as though she was upset. 'I think she's got pneumonia or summat.'

'Well get her to the bloody doctors' when they open then instead of ringing me at this hour.'

'I think she's on her way out, Nathan.'

'Look, don't think you can get to me with your emotional blackmail. I told you when I left home that I'd washed my hands of the pair of you. Now I suggest you take the hint and stop bloody ringing me; you and her!'

He cut the call before his sister had a chance to say anything further and put his phone back down. Then he pulled the duvet around his shoulders, hoping to get back to sleep. But as he grabbed hold of the bedcover, he felt Chloe stir next to him. Bugger! His silly cow of a sister had woken her up too.

'What's the matter?' asked Chloe as she forced her eyes open. 'Who was that on the phone?'

'Nobody,' he said, giving her a reassuring peck on the forehead. 'Nothing for you to worry about, babe. Go back to sleep.'

Amber was annoyed with Nathan. How could he just ignore what she had to say, knowing how bad the situation was? She could understand him having some ill feeling. Fair enough, their mother hadn't been a perfect parent. But, at the end of the day, she was still their mother and had tried to provide for them in the only way she knew.

Perhaps he couldn't accept the gravity of the situation, Amber thought. Maybe he thought it was just a ploy to get him to speak to them. She tried to put him out of her mind. She needed to get back to her mother. In a couple of hours when the doctors' surgery was open, she would give them a ring. Hopefully, once they had a diagnosis, Nathan would take things more seriously.

Amber went back into the living room and tiptoed up to the sofa, not wishing to wake her mother up. She knelt on the floor once more, keeping watch. But then she noticed something. Her mother's hand wasn't holding the cold compress anymore; it was lolling to one side of her head as though she had lost control of it and the compress was on the floor. Then Amber saw that her chest was no longer rising and falling either. '*Shit. No!*'

Feeling panicky, Amber took hold of her mother's wrist and felt for a pulse. She couldn't feel anything, so she moved her fingers about, desperately hoping to find a steady rhythmic beat. But there was nothing.

'No!' yelled Amber, breaking down and sobbing. 'Oh God, no!'

She stayed there for some time, weeping, her head nestled against her mother's breast. Then she came to. She had to do something. She couldn't just leave her mother lying there! Amber took out her phone once more and dialled 999.

While she waited for the ambulance she stayed with her mother, crying bitter tears. She thought about her mother's dying words, especially when she had told her she was always the special one. As she played those words over in her head, the irony of the situation struck her like a painful jab.

For most of her life she had sought her mother's approval and had always felt that she fell short compared to Nathan. Now, at last, she had finally told her she was special. But she had had to wait until her mother was dying before she heard it.

She felt a strange torrent of emotions:

Sadness. Because she was her mother. They had shared their lives together and, if Amber tried hard, she could conjure up a few brief happy memories with her.

Relief. Because she didn't have the burden of her anymore, that overriding sense of responsibility that had made her look out for her mother even when she didn't deserve it.

Guilt. For feeling relieved.

And worry. Because she now felt all alone in a world that was frightening.

57

It was three days since Loretta had passed away. The police and ambulance people had all been round to the house on the morning of Loretta's death. Amber's mind had been in a whirl, having to answer all their questions when the shock of her mother's death still hadn't fully registered.

Finally, a doctor had been summoned to pronounce Loretta dead. Amber had then rung an undertaker who had been recommended by Mrs Griffiths from over the road, and they had eventually arrived to take the body away.

Amber spent most of that day sleeping and sobbing intermittently. The following day had followed a similar pattern but on the third day she decided to start putting matters in order. She began by visiting the undertaker and was overwhelmed by all that was involved. She had rung Nathan to try to garner some support but all he had said was that he would see if he could get a day off for the funeral and then he'd asked her to let him know as soon as she had a date.

There was so much to do: a visit to the doctor and registrar, a funeral and wake to organise and relatives to notify. She had rung all the relatives she could think of, and they had all been sympathetic but none of them had offered to help and Amber didn't want to ask. They hadn't done much for her mother when she was alive, so she didn't think they'd be so willing now. Besides, she didn't want to listen to their paltry excuses.

The next thing she had decided to do was to go through her mother's things. She doubted whether her mother would have left a will, but she wanted to make sure. Amber needed to know the details of her mother's finances anyway. The undertaker had told her that the State would pay for the funeral as her mother was registered as unemployed but then there were all the other expenses to think of such as the wake and the running of the house.

The obvious place for Amber to start was in her mother's bedroom. It was the place where Loretta kept all her private things. She went through her mother's wardrobe and chest of drawers first. The wardrobe was a triple one and was packed tight with clothing. At first Amber was confused as she didn't recall her mother having so many clothes but, when she started searching through it, she realised that about half of the outfits were things she no longer wore.

She pulled out a red mini dress and was instantly swept back in time. She remembered her mother wearing it a few times when she went out on dates with Dale. There were also a few tops and a couple of short skirts she recalled her mother wearing years ago when she was dressed up for a date or a night on the town. Others she didn't recognise but she could tell they were old.

Rummaging through her mother's wardrobe was a bit like going through a time warp. Amber felt a sense of sadness on seeing how many of her old outfits her mother had held on to and it seemed that they probably had a special emotional significance for her.

Next, she reached up to the top shelf of her mother's wardrobe where she could see a white box. She wondered if it might contain some of her mother's paperwork and she pulled it out. Amber laid the box down on the bed. It was yellowing around the edges and she carefully lifted off the lid, nervous of it disintegrating if she pulled too hard. Inside she could see folds of white material: satin, lace and chiffon. She guessed right away what it was, but she couldn't resist taking it out of the box and holding it against herself.

The wedding dress was in an old-fashioned eighties style with puffed sleeves and a full skirt. It was cut low at the front in a sweetheart neckline and Amber couldn't resist a smile, thinking about how her mother would have pulled out all the stops to wow everybody on her wedding day. The dress was now an off-white colour, and Amber wondered how often her mother would have taken the dress out of the box to admire it.

She couldn't help but feel as though she was intruding on her mother's former happiness and, feeling remorseful, she folded the dress carefully into the box. Before she put it back inside the wardrobe, she pulled out another box that had been sitting underneath it and took the lid off that too. The breath caught in her throat when she realised it was her parents' wedding album.

Amber sat on the bed with the album beside her, feeling

a mix of excitement and sorrow. She could remember her mother showing her photographs of her father in the days before she started seeing Dale. One time she had seen tears in her mother's eyes, but Loretta had brushed it off and said it was just irritation because of the dust from the old album. But then she had stopped bringing the photos out, and Amber couldn't ever remember a time when she had shown her the wedding photos. Perhaps that had been too painful for her.

She gently opened the album. It felt surreal to see her mother staring back at her while standing beside the father Amber had never known. She could see now that Nathan bore a striking resemblance to him. Her parents seemed so happy together and her mother looked stunning in the wedding dress, back in a time when the material was still gleaming white. Amber spotted her grandparents too, looking young, and a couple of aunties and uncles she still recognised. But the rest of the people in the photographs were strangers to her.

She wiped a tear from her eye and put both boxes neatly back inside the wardrobe before venturing underneath the bed. Amber took out a large box and opened it. She was greeted by the sweet, musky smell of old paper. This seemed a likely place to find all the important documents.

Amber worked her way through birthday cards from her father and Dale, photographs of her mother and father and another picture of her mother, Dale, Nathan and herself as a child, on a day out to the seaside. She remembered the day well; it was one of her best childhood memories.

There were also some cinema tickets and a party invitation all dated around the same time. Amber realised with sadness that it would have been around the period when her mother had been seeing Dale.

But the item that upset her the most was a love letter from her father. It was folded up and worn at the corners and it struck Amber that it must have been opened and read over many times. She knew she shouldn't really intrude on her parents' private lives even though they were no longer with her, but she was overcome by curiosity, so she opened it up and read the contents.

My darling Loretta,

I just had to drop you a note to let you know that you have made me the happiest man on earth. Whenever I'm with you I feel ecstatic and when we're apart I count down the hours till we can be together again. I love to show you off when we're out and about too. You looked stunning last night, and I felt so proud.

I hope you have given some thought to the question I asked you. Sorry if it took you by surprise. It felt right at the time and I can't think of anything that would make me happier than having you as my wife. I will always love you and I'll always be there for you. Please say you will.

Till the next time we meet.

All my love,

Greg xxx

Amber's eyes felt steamy and she quickly put the letter to one side so her tears wouldn't spill onto the paper and smudge the words. It was obvious from reading the letter that her father had loved her mother very much and Amber thought it was heart-breaking that he should die so young. Thinking of all her mother had been through, it didn't surprise her that she had ended up the way she had.

The most heart-breaking sentence of all was the one that read, '*I will always love you and I'll always be there for you.*' It must have felt to her mother like a dagger through her heart every time she read and reread that sentence, knowing that he had been snatched away from her far too soon.

Amber tried to take her mind off the sad reminders of her mother's past and focus on what she was really looking for. And she thought she may have found it because inside the box, nestled amongst all the treasured mementoes, was a folder marked 'accounts'. She quickly opened it, trying to make up for the time she had spent rummaging through her mother's things.

Given that her mother was an alcoholic who could act irresponsibly at times, she was surprised to find that she had kept details of bank accounts, utility bills, et cetera. But she was in for an even bigger surprise when she began to read through them and discovered the details surrounding her mother's financial affairs.

58

It was the weekend and Nathan was having a lie-in. He had just made love to his gorgeous girlfriend before bringing her coffee and biscuits in bed. She was so special to him that he wanted to spoil her in whatever way he could. After fetching the coffees, he had jumped back in bed beside her and now, as they lay there sipping their drinks and making plans for the house, he was feeling content.

Since Amber had told him about his mother's death, he had tried not to dwell on it too much. He was sad, who wouldn't be if they had just been told their mother had died? And it would have been easy to get carried away, thinking about his terrible upbringing and the injustice of it all. But he didn't want to go there. His life had changed for the better and he saw no need to be dragged down by his unfortunate past.

They were deep in discussion about the colour scheme for the bedroom when his mobile rang. He didn't welcome the intrusion but, nevertheless, he put down his coffee and grabbed his phone.

'It's Amy,' he said. 'I'd better answer it; she's probably got a date for the funeral.'

'Alright,' said Chloe.

His sister got straight to the point. 'The funeral director just rang. It's next Wednesday.'

'OK, I'll put in a request to have the day off. Chloe will probably be coming too. What time will it be and where?'

She gave him the details and he was about to end the call, but he sensed she had something more to say. 'Is that it?'

'No, it isn't.' He heard a heavy sigh before she carried on. 'I've been going through Mum's paperwork.'

'Oh yeah?'

'Yeah. She's in shedloads of debt, Nathan. The gas, the leccy, the rent. She owes a ton on all of them.'

'OK, so why are you telling me?'

'Well, I'm in a bit of a fix, Nathan. I can't afford to pay all the arrears on my own.'

'No! Oh no,' he snapped. 'There's no way you're getting me involved in that. I don't even live there, for Christ's sake.'

'But it's not my fault she's got behind with everything, and she's your mother too.'

'*Was* my mother,' he said smugly, thinking to himself, *more's the pity*.

'But I can't manage all these bills on my own, Nathan. I'll get thrown out of the house if I don't pay the rent and they might cut off the leccy.'

'It isn't my concern so do me a favour and stop calling me. I'm not interested!'

Then he cut the call. 'Bloody cheek!' he fumed, turning to Chloe. 'She's only after bloody money off me.'

Chloe shrugged. 'I don't mind if she needs our help.'

'Well I do, Chloe. If we give in to her now, we'll never have her off our backs. I'm sad to say it but she's as big a menace as our mother was, and she needs to learn to stand on her own two feet. I want an end to that life. My future is with you and, as I've told you before, I'm not going to let anybody, or anything destroy it.'

Amber stared at her phone with her lip quivering. She couldn't believe her own brother would treat her like this. Although they'd never really got along, it was difficult to accept that even he could be this callous.

She was in despair and for a few moments she sat and cried. Never in her life had she felt so alone. Her mother had died, her brother had disowned her, her relatives kept her at arm's length and most of her friends had moved on. She didn't know who she could turn to for help.

When she'd first found out the extent of her mother's debt, she'd put off ringing Nathan. Knowing how he was towards her, she didn't want to ask him for help. But she was desperate so she'd decided to wait until she rang him about the funeral, hoping he would be more receptive in recognition of their mother's death.

But now, it was apparent that she had to find a way to get out of this mess on her own. That put her in a predicament because her money was already down from not being able to work the streets. For a moment she toyed with the idea of going back on the beat, but how could she when she ran the risk of bumping into Kev?

In the end she pulled herself together. Sitting there crying wasn't going to get her anywhere; she needed to take control. She decided to take another look at the figures, hoping she could come up with a way of sorting the arrears out. Maybe she'd be able to manage, she thought but, at the same time, she was weighed down by the burden of her own drugs habit, knowing that it took up a huge chunk of money every day.

Amber went over to the pile of bills, which she had stacked up on the coffee table. She had been ready to reel off some of the figures to Nathan but never got the chance. She grabbed the letter on top of the pile and unfolded it. But Amber wished she hadn't bothered because it emphasised her dire situation. It was an eviction notice, telling her she only had two weeks remaining before she would be thrown out of her home.

59

March 2016

Sapphire was enjoying Skinner's company. They had arranged to keep in touch ever since she had bumped into him in Piccadilly a few weeks earlier and were now sitting inside the Rose and Crown with Skinner's friend, Elena. Skinner could be witty at times and it felt good to be in his company, especially as not many of her crowd seemed to come into the pub these days.

She hadn't seen Amber since that night when things had been awkward between them, and that had been about two or three weeks ago. She hadn't seen Angie since then either. It had been the night when Angie was really ill with her chest. Sapphire couldn't help but worry about both of them, but she had no way of getting in touch; she didn't have a phone number for Amber or Angie.

Knowing there wasn't much she could do about either of them, Sapphire was trying to relax and enjoy herself with Skinner and Elena. When a stunning looking girl walked into the pub, Skinner turned to Sapphire and said, 'Well, my date's arrived so I'm dumping you two.' He made as if to leave the table and nodded at the girl, a mischievous grin lighting up his face.

Skinner had always acknowledged his lack of looks, and often joked about them in a self-deprecating way. It was one of the things Sapphire liked about him; the fact that he could make light of something that would bother most people. She laughed with him. 'You should be so bloody lucky!'

'What is happening?' asked Elena. 'Does he know this woman? And what is dumping?'

Sapphire and Skinner both giggled. Elena struggled with the subtle nuances of the English language at times and it amused them. 'He fancies her,' said Sapphire.

'Oh, you mean, he finds her attractive?'

'Yeah, that's right. He's pretending she's here to see him, so he doesn't want to stay with us anymore.'

Elena laughed but she wore a bewildered expression. Then, trying to join in the fun, she looked at the door and announced. 'This one is for me.'

Sapphire spun around on her seat and both she and Skinner followed Elena's gaze. 'Shit!' said Skinner, with a look of terror on his face.

Sapphire didn't understand his extreme reaction at first but when she looked more closely at the good-looking man who had just entered the pub, she recognised him. It was Kev Pike!

Sapphire felt her heart thud and she turned away from the door, keeping her eyes averted and hoping he wouldn't notice her. But Skinner seemed just as shocked. He let out a loud splutter and she gazed up to see him choking on his drink, his loud cough drawing attention from other tables. Elena got up from her seat and slapped him on the back several times.

'For fuck's sake!' Sapphire whispered. 'Keep a low profile, will yer? I don't want the bastard coming over here.'

But Kev Pike had already noticed them and, even though she had her back to the door, Sapphire could sense his approach as she watched Skinner's face blanch, and his shoulders tighten up towards his ears. She tensed too as she waited for Kev Pike to reach them.

'Are you a mate of Amber's?' he asked Sapphire once he had reached them and had turned to face her.

She looked up at him, feeling her adrenalin pulse as she took in his stern features. 'I know her. But I haven't seen her for a while.'

As she spoke, she watched Skinner across the table from her and noticed his lips twitching nervously; she was glad Kev Pike had his back to him.

'Does she come in here?' Kev asked.

'She used to but, like I say, I haven't seen her for a while.'

'Any idea where she might be?'

Sapphire shrugged. 'Not really, no. We're not really that close.'

Kev Pike walked away without thanking them, and Sapphire and Skinner exchanged worried looks.

'He's gone to the bar,' whispered Skinner.

'What? Who is this man?' asked Elena, picking up on their nervousness.

Skinner visibly jumped on hearing how loudly Elena had spoken. 'Shut the fuck up!' he hissed. 'We don't want him to hear us.'

Sapphire sat in silence while Skinner kept gazing over to the bar surreptitiously and giving her a quiet commentary about Kev's actions. 'He's talking to the barmaid,' he whispered. 'I think he's asking her summat.'

'Stop looking at him for fuck's sake! You don't want to give the game away, d'you?'

'What is this game?' asked Elena. 'What is happening?'

'Shush!' whispered Skinner then he switched his attention to Sapphire while quickly looking down at the drink in front of him. 'Don't look now, he's going.'

He gave it several seconds before looking across the pub again. 'Thank fuck for that! He's gone.'

'What is it? What is happening?' asked Elena, becoming exasperated.

Skinner took a deep breath. 'I can't tell you, Elena. Sorry, but I just can't.'

Elena glanced inquisitively across at Sapphire who had already decided that if Skinner wouldn't trust Elena enough to confide in her then there was no way she was going to either.

For a few seconds, Sapphire and Skinner continued to exchange worried glances until Elena eventually got up from her seat and pushed it noisily back into the table.

'OK. I know you don't want me here,' she raged. 'It seems like you no longer like me, Skinner, now you've got your new friend.' As she spoke, she scowled at Sapphire then added, 'You two are always keeping secrets. I will go now!'

'No, it's OK. Don't go, Elena,' Skinner said, but she was already on her way out of the door and Sapphire could tell his pleas were half-hearted. Like her, he needed to talk. 'Fuck, that was close!' he said once Elena had gone.

'You nearly gave the fuckin' game away,' Sapphire complained, 'especially when you started fuckin' choking. You need to play it cool with someone like him. You don't want him to suss out that you saw him killing Cora. And, for fuck's sake, don't say anything to Elena. We don't know whether you can trust her to keep it to herself.'

'Don't worry, I won't,' Skinner replied, before asking, 'Do you think he suspects anything?'

'No, he had his back to you, didn't he? How could he know? But, like I say, you need to be careful who you tell. Elena already suspects something, and we can't risk anyone else knowing. You'll have to think of something to tell her.'

'Don't worry I will. I'll tell her you were worried he was after you for protection or summat.'

Sapphire was lost in thought for a moment then she shared what was worrying her. Keeping it to herself was stressing her out and she knew she had to confide in someone. 'Skinner, y'know when I told you that one of my friends was paying protection to Kev Pike?'

'Yeah.'

'Well, what I didn't tell you was that it was my friend Amber. She wasn't just paying him protection; she was seeing him too.'

'What you mean…?'

'Yeah, she was in a relationship with him. So, I told her about Cora.' Skinner looked alarmed. 'Sorry,' she added, 'I know I said I wouldn't tell anyone, but I had to tell her. She's a mate and I needed to warn her. The trouble is, I've only seen her once since. And now I'm worried shitless that something might have happened to her.'

'But why would he come looking in here if he'd done something to her?'

'Dunno, unless he's bluffing to cover his tracks. Do you think she might have gone into hiding so he can't find her?'

Skinner shrugged. 'Dunno.'

Sapphire shuddered. 'I'm really worried now. Even if he hasn't topped her, it's obvious he's determined to get hold of her. You know what, I think we need to find Amber before he does. It's too late now – I need to get to work – but we should do it tomorrow night. She needs to know he's looking for her in case she starts taking chances. If she's still on the beat, he could easily come across her, and I'd hate anything bad to happen.'

60

March 2016

When she heard the knock on the door Amber knew exactly who it would be. She also knew that they wouldn't wait long for her to answer so she scanned the living room one last time before leaving it. There was no longer any furniture. Amber had sold what she could and for the past couple of days she'd managed by sitting on cushions while she ate her meals.

She hadn't raised much cash from selling the furniture, and certainly not enough to hold off the bailiffs. It was too old and jaded but at least it had given her a little extra money. She felt sad looking around the room. Although most of her memories here were bad ones, it was still her home and the place she had been brought up. Recollections of her first home were now buried in the distant past.

Amber walked out into the hallway where she had lined up some plastic carrier bags containing her scant belongings. There were clothes, cosmetics and toiletries as well as a few other possessions, which were precious to her. These included the photographs her mother had kept of them as a family and of her father and Dale.

The knocking became more insistent and she rushed to open the door. Two dour-looking men stared back at her. 'We're here to evict you from the property,' said the first one. 'Have you got the keys?'

Amber nodded and passed them over to him. 'Let me just get my things.'

'There's no time for that, I'm afraid,' said the man as he barged past her and into the hallway.

'I've already packed them,' said Amber, quickly gathering up her bags from the hall while the men carried on into the house.

She struggled to pick up the bags as there were six of them altogether. It had been difficult deciding which items to take with her because she had nowhere to store them. But she'd got them down to a minimum, and now, all the items inside the bags were ones she was reluctant to part with.

When Amber emerged onto the garden path, she was disheartened to see that several neighbours were out of their houses and were avidly watching the spectacle. She noticed Mrs Wiley at her gate and two women across the street were outside their houses too. One of them nudged the other and whispered something.

The rain that had threatened all morning had now arrived with callous precision and Amber could feel it penetrating her clothing and soaking her hair. It didn't seem to bother the neighbours, though, who had come prepared with rain macs and umbrellas.

Nasty-minded bitches, she thought, *taking pleasure in*

my misfortune. Despite her upset, Amber raised her chin and glared across at them, all her grief and angst of the past few weeks making her angry. *Just let any of them say anything, and I'll tell them exactly what I think!*

She made it to the gate, but her arms were already aching, and the handles of the carrier bags were becoming slippery. It was shut, but she didn't want to put the bags down on the drenched garden path while she opened it. So, instead, she shifted most of the bags into her left hand so she could manage with her right.

Unfortunately, the two bags remaining in her right hand were making it difficult. Amber reached for the latch but, as she did so, she could see the plastic handles becoming stretched. She had just about managed to grasp the trigger and was lifting it up when one of the bag handles snapped and some of her clothing slipped out onto the soggy garden path. The action made her lose her grip on the latch and it dropped away as well as the two bags she had been clutching with her right hand.

'Shit!' she yelled, staring at the drenched and soiled clothing.

She kicked the gate in temper and could hear a snigger from across the road.

For a moment she stood still, wondering what to do and fighting back tears. Then she became aware of somebody outside the gate. She looked up to see an unlikely saviour in the form of Mrs Wiley who was now holding the gate open for her.

'I can see you're struggling,' she said, stepping inside. 'You take them, and I'll sort out those.' She nodded towards the two bags, which had now spilt much of their contents onto the soggy ground. 'Take them to mine. You can have a dry-off before you go on your way.'

Amber picked up on the implicit meaning of Mrs Wiley's words. She was welcome to dry off but not to stay. Still, it was better than nothing and preferable to the ridicule on offer from the neighbours over the road. Mrs Wiley would have made a difficult housemate anyway with her overbearing, no-nonsense approach and Amber's occupation would have caused obvious difficulties. But, at the moment, Amber would have settled for anything.

She waited outside Mrs Wiley's door while her neighbour caught up with her. 'Go on, inside. Don't stand on ceremony, girl,' she ordered as she trundled up the path carrying Amber's two remaining bags.

'Pop them down in the hallway. That's right. We can sort them out later but right now I think you need to dry off, and a nice cuppa to warm you up wouldn't go amiss either. What d'you say?'

'Yes thanks, Mrs Wiley,' muttered Amber.

'Now don't go getting any ideas. You're welcome to have a cuppa and a warm but I've no room to put you up.'

'Oh, that's OK. I'm gonna sleep on a friend's sofa.' The lie flowed from Amber's mouth.

They went through to the kitchen and Mrs Wiley put the kettle on. 'Sit down,' she said, talking to Amber as she busied herself around the kitchen taking out cups, teabags and a packet of biscuits. She put the biscuits down in front of Amber. 'Help yourself. I always think they're nice with a cup of tea.'

I wouldn't know, thought Amber.

She'd had no time to think about biscuits or any other

trivialities lately but seeing them placed in front of her, she couldn't help but tuck in.

Mrs Wiley soon came over with two steaming cups of tea and plonked herself down on the seat next to Amber. 'I know you've not had it easy, love,' she said. 'And I'm not just talking about your mother passing away either.' She grabbed Amber's hand in a show of affection. Amber was shocked at her forthright attitude and for a moment she stared at her, dumbstruck. 'Oh, I know, love, I'm not daft. There's been some right goings-on in that house, hasn't there?'

Suddenly, Amber was besieged by a surge of emotions. Her current situation combined with Mrs Wiley's show of sympathy had finally got to her. To her embarrassment she burst into tears.

'I'm sorry,' she said, feeling foolish.

'That's alright, love. Don't mind me.'

It took her a while to recover and Mrs Wiley waited patiently till Amber was calm before she spoke again. 'I tell you what I'll do, Amy. Like I say, I've no room for you to stay but if you're looking for somewhere to store your things, I'll keep them for you. I mean, you can't be dragging that lot through the streets, can you?'

Amber was amazed at Mrs Wiley's perception. It was as if she knew that the tale about staying on her friend's sofa had been a fabrication. 'Yes, thanks. I appreciate that. But I'll need to take some of them with me.'

'Course you will, love. Tell you what, when you've finished your tea, go and sort out what you're taking, and I'll store the rest. And don't worry about the dirty clothes; put them to one side and I'll get them washed and dried for you.'

'Thanks,' Amber repeated.

After she had sorted through her things and piled a few essential items into one carrier bag, Mrs Wiley bid her goodbye and Amber left her cosy home. She was glad to see that the rain had now eased, and the neighbours were back indoors.

Mrs Wiley waited until Amber had reached the garden gate, then she shut the front door. Amber stepped back towards her old house, which had now been shut up. For a while she stood staring at its frontage, as if wishing it a final goodbye before she departed.

In a way she was glad to see the back of it; all that it represented for her was sorrow and unhappiness. But, at the same time, she was sad to leave. It was the only home she had ever really known and now that she had lost it, she didn't know what to do next.

61

March 2016

Sapphire had arranged to meet Skinner in the pub so they could go and search for Amber together. It seemed to her that looking for Amber was all she ever did these days but, nevertheless, she knew it was important to find her.

She had already asked Moira whether she had seen anything of Amber or whether she had a phone number for her, but Moira knew nothing. And, like Sapphire, she hadn't seen anything of Angie either, so there was no chance of checking whether Angie might have Amber's phone number.

As her meeting time with Skinner was still half an hour away, she was surprised when he turned up, panting, and looking more jittery than ever.

He came straight over and, when he reached her, it was apparent straightaway that there was something troubling him. 'For fuck's sake, Saph, I've been trying to get hold of you. What the fuck's wrong with your phone?'

Sapphire took her mobile out and examined it. 'Shit! I didn't realise the battery's flat. I need to charge it up as soon as possible. There might be clients trying to get hold of me. Anyway, what's the problem?'

Skinner sat down and stared pointedly at her. 'I've just heard some bad news, Saph.'

She could see his lips twitching in that characteristic way of his, and her heart started racing. 'What is it, Skinner?'

'There's another girl been killed, and she's been strangled the same as Cora.'

'Shit! No. Who is it? Do you know?'

'Not yet, no, but I'm worried it might be your mate, especially after he'd been looking for her.'

'Fuck! Don't say that, Skinner.'

'Have you not heard anything from her yet?'

Sapphire's face clouded over. 'No.' She took a gulp of her drink, deciding to leave the rest. 'C'mon, we need to go. We need to ask around on the beat, see if anyone's seen Amber.'

'But what if they haven't?'

Sapphire didn't want to dwell on the possible outcome of that. 'We need to know for sure whether it was Amber. Maybe someone knows.'

They left the pub and arrived at the red-light district a few minutes later after dashing through the streets of the city centre. Sapphire looked up the road, which was lined with street girls. It looked like a busy night.

'You take that side and I'll take this,' she told Skinner. 'Then we'll meet at the end and take the side streets together. If you find out anything in the meantime, let me know.'

'Yeah, sure,' said Skinner who raced across the road and made his way towards the first prostitute.

Sapphire didn't have any luck with the first three women she spoke to. They either didn't know Amber by name or hadn't seen her, and they didn't know who the dead girl was either, only that she had been strangled. But Sapphire noticed the last woman she spoke to eying her suspiciously and she had a feeling there was something she wasn't telling her, so she persevered with a fourth one.

A tall peroxide blonde, she knew Amber by name as soon as Sapphire mentioned her. 'You as well?' she asked.

'What d'you mean?' asked Sapphire.

'Well, you're not the only one who's been looking for her. Kev Pike's been looking for her too, and it's not the first time. He seems pretty keen to get his hands on her if you ask me. In fact, last time I saw Amber, I warned her he'd been looking for her.'

'Shit!' said Sapphire. 'I'm really worried about her especially after hearing about that girl who got strangled. Have you heard about it?'

'Oh yeah, but it's not her.'

'How d'you know?'

'A friend of a friend found her body and called the cops. It was in the early hours of this morning. They're saying it's a Romanian girl – Elena I think she's called.'

'Shit!' Sapphire repeated.

'What? Do you know her?'

Sapphire glanced over the road to where Skinner was deep in conversation with another girl some distance ahead. 'Yeah, a bit. But my mate over there knows her better. He'll be gutted.'

'Sorry,' said the peroxide blonde. Then she lowered her voice and asked, 'You don't think Kev Pike had anything to do with it, do you? I've heard he's got a bad reputation, but don't say I told you that.'

Sapphire could see that the girls on this beat were nervous. It wasn't surprising after the second killing in a few months. But she was more concerned about the news she had just heard. She turned and looked at Skinner again and waited for a car to pass so she could cross the road. Almost forgetting to thank the girl, she swiftly spun round. 'Thanks. Take care.'

Then she shouted Skinner's name and ran towards him. Her haste put him on his guard. 'Have you found out summat?'

Sapphire took a moment to get her breath back. 'Yeah, but it's not Amber.' She put her hand on his arm. 'I'm really sorry, Skinner, but they're saying it's a Romanian girl called Elena.'

'Fuck, no! Why?'

'I dunno. I'm sorry.'

When he burst into tears, she put her arms around him. Giving him a chance to recover from the shock of his friend's death, she held him for a few seconds before a thought occurred to her, and she pulled away.

'Shit! They found her this morning, Skinner.' Skinner stared at her dumbfounded till she elucidated. 'That means she was probably killed last night after she left us. You don't think she caught up with Kev outside the Rose and Crown, do you?'

Skinner sniffed back his tears. 'Fuck! She could have done.'

'Yeah, and if she did catch up with him, she might have wound him up. I mean, she was a bit pissed off when she left us, wasn't she?'

'Shit, yeah. What if she told him about us? Y'know, about

what we said after he left? She might have given him a clue that we suspect something.'

Sapphire tried to think back to what they had said in front of Elena and whether any of it could incriminate them. She remembered saying something about Skinner giving the game away but other than that, and the fact that they were nervous around Kev, she didn't think there was anything specific.

As Skinner was already in a state, she didn't bother sharing all that. Instead, she just said, 'Nah, we didn't say anything till she'd gone, did we?'

Skinner's taut muscles visibly slumped with relief. Sapphire was relieved too because, as concerned as she was for the death of Skinner's friend, at least it wasn't Amber. But for how long would Amber remain alive?

And there was another unanswered question: If Kev hadn't killed Amber, then what the hell had happened to her?

62

March 2016

Amber stood under the shower letting the hot spray massage her skin till it tingled. Then she grabbed the sachet of shampoo and gave her hair a good wash, twice, just to make sure, followed by conditioner. *Ooh, how nice it would be to do this every day*, she thought. She was rinsing the suds off her body when she heard a loud knock on the door.

'You alright in there? Only, I need a piss.'

Amber snapped out of her daydream and back to reality. For a moment she forgot where she was. But one look around the elegantly tiled and well-equipped bathroom reminded her she was in one of Manchester's better hotels.

'I won't be a minute,' she said, switching off the shower then grabbing for the towel.

When she walked out of the bathroom the client was sitting on the bed with his legs crossed.

He laughed. 'Bloody hell. I'm used to girls showering

after we've done the business, but I've never known one to wash her hair as well.'

Amber suddenly felt embarrassed. 'My boiler's on the blink.'

The client seemed to accept her excuse and said no more as he dashed past her to use the bathroom. While he was gone, she fished inside her handbag for the hair-styling product she had brought with her and made use of the hairdryer provided by the hotel.

Ten minutes later she was outside the hotel and back on the streets of Manchester city centre. For a moment she was indecisive about what to do next. She had nothing planned for the rest of the day and nowhere to go either. In the end, she decided to venture into the red-light area, hoping to bump into an old friend who might be able to help her out by providing a sofa for the night.

It had been a few weeks since Kev had stopped phoning and sending her texts so she hoped it would now be safe. Nevertheless, she couldn't help looking around her to make sure he wasn't lurking anywhere.

She didn't spot either Kev or his car for the first five minutes or so and was beginning to relax a little as she strode through the streets at the back of Piccadilly station. A flash silver Audi TT passed by and, knowing Kev drove a black BMW, she didn't take much notice of it until the driver stopped further up the road and turned the vehicle around.

The driver drew up on the other side of the road, facing in the opposite direction to which she was walking. At first, she thought it must have been a punter. There were no other girls nearby so she assumed the driver must have stopped for her. It was only when the driver wound down his window that she realised it was Kev.

'Get inside, Amber!' he ordered.

Knowing she would have a head start while he turned the car around, Amber started to run. As she raced up the road, she cursed the high heels she had worn for her client meeting and kept looking over her shoulder to see where Kev was. She heard the screech of tyres as he spun the car around, and then the shrill beeping of a car horn as Kev just missed the car in front of him.

It wasn't long before he was almost alongside her and she darted into a side road, which she knew had a pathway leading off it. She raced up the pathway and didn't stop till she was far away from the road and Kev's car. As she ran, she tried to ignore the crippling pain from her uncomfortable shoes, and the breathlessness that was now beginning to bite.

When she could run no longer, she slowed to a fast walk. She could see that the pathway would soon be at an end, which meant she would be back on the road. There was nothing else for it: she would have to take her chance and hope Kev didn't catch her.

She emerged onto the street and did a quick scan of the road. There was no sign of the silver Audi, so she continued along the pavement at a brisk pace. Then she turned into the next side street, trying to vary her route in the hope that it would make it more difficult for him to find her.

Amber carried on hobbling for several minutes through the maze of streets. She had turned into a one-way street when she saw a silver Audi TT pass across the top. Her heart thudded but then she realised that, even if it was him, he wouldn't be able to get to her here; he would have to go right round and approach the street from the other end.

Good, she thought, limping as fast as she could. That would give her chance to further the distance between them.

But she had underestimated Kev's blatant disregard for the law. To her amazement, she saw the Audi heading towards her from the wrong end of the street. There was a car in the way, but Kev didn't stop. Instead, he beeped his horn and carried on at speed, forcing the other motorist to mount the pavement in order to avoid him.

Amber turned and ran in the other direction. But she had no chance against a car. Kev pulled up, mounting the pavement to block her way. She turned again. Too late! Before she knew it, he was out of the car and grabbing her by the arm.

'Get in the fuckin' car!' he yelled. 'I'm sick of playing games with you.'

Amber tried to pull away from him and was about to yell for help when he hissed at her. 'Carry on like that and you'll fuckin' regret it! Even if you get away, I'll catch up with you eventually. And when I do, you'll be fuckin' sorry.'

He began dragging her towards the car but Amber still tried to resist, looking at a passer-by for help. But the man ignored her, not wanting to get involved. Feeling panicked, Amber ignored Kev's warning and started yelling as well as struggling.

But he was too strong for her. It wasn't long before he had bundled her into the car and slammed on the locks, letting out a stream of invective as he sped away. 'You're not leaving me, Amber. I won't fuckin' let you! And I'll make you sorry you even tried.'

63

Kev led her through his flat and into the lounge. But it no longer felt the same to Amber. Instead of having that comforting familiarity that it once had, his home was now a hostile environment. The lingering smell of that evening's cooking seemed stale rather than appetising, and the modern interior felt stark and cold instead of impressive.

'Sit down,' he ordered, pushing her towards the couch and releasing the tight grip he'd had on her arm since they got out of the car.

He glared at her for a moment before he began pacing the room. Twice he paused, and opened his mouth to speak, but then stopped himself. Amber sat there rigid with fear and waiting to see how this would pan out. Then he spoke:

'Why, Amber? Why did you just piss off like that without even a fuckin' word? You knew how much you meant to me!'

'Because I knew you wouldn't like it if I told you.'

'But why? Why did you want to break up anyway? We were getting on alright, weren't we?'

She heard the sorrow in his voice and realised she was getting a rare glimpse of his sensitive side. But she had to stay strong without revealing the real reason for the break-up. 'It wasn't right for me, Kev. You were always the one in charge.'

'Why didn't you fuckin' say so then?'

His anger had returned, and Amber decided to tread carefully so she just shrugged. But his next words took her by surprise.

'You're lying. I fuckin' know you are! That's a load of bollocks about me being the one in charge. You never seemed to mind that; you fuckin' loved being here, hogging the TV and helping yourself to everything in the fuckin' fridge. No, there's another reason you split with me.'

'There isn't,' she protested.

'Don't fuckin' lie! What happened on that last night when I spoke to you, Amber? One minute, you've arranged to meet me after work, and the next, you just fuckin' vanished into thin air. What happened that night? Or was it before that because you'd already been ignoring my fuckin' calls and texts? Did someone say summat to put you off me?'

Amber felt an icy chill run down her spine; she was worried he knew the truth and was just playing with her.

'No, no one said anything. I told you, it wasn't right for me, Kev. You were always ordering me around.'

'Was I fuck! We were getting along fine the last time I saw you. I know there's something else so you'd better fuckin' tell me because, if someone's been bad-mouthing me, I swear I'll...'

Amber quickly deflected. 'No one's said anything. I can make my own decisions you know. You don't own me.'

'I never fuckin' said I did! But we were a couple, Amber. You don't just fuck off on someone without telling them why. You must have known how much it would hurt me. But you still did it.'

'Look, I'm sorry if I hurt you, Kev, I really am. But this isn't going to change anything so you might as well just let me go.'

She stood up to leave but Kev pushed her down again. 'You're not fuckin' going anywhere!'

By now Amber realised she wasn't going to get away without putting up a fight. But she needed to prepare herself first. 'Sit down then, Kev. Let's talk this through.'

He sat on the sofa next to her and took her hand. 'Let me take my shoes off,' she said. 'I need to get comfortable.'

Amber was glad to be rid of the shoes, which were cutting into her feet. She also knew that they were a hindrance.

Once she was settled, he looked at her and asked, 'Why, Amber? You still haven't explained properly.'

Amber shot up off the sofa and made for the door. But she'd only taken a couple of strides before she felt him grabbing her arms again. She tried to shake him off and kept running, feeling his fingernails cutting into her flesh. When he'd gained purchase, he pulled her close then spun her around to face him, his hands briefly slipping from her.

Her arms stung and the pain angered her. Taking advantage of his loss of grip, Amber barged into Kev then tried to sidestep him. It didn't work. Kev grabbed hold of her arms once more while Amber fought to free herself. She managed to loosen one arm and smashed into him with her fist. The shock made him loosen his hold, and she pummelled his body, trying to break away.

Kev reacted angrily, thumping her, but she fought back. Amber was desperate by now, hitting him wildly and oblivious to the torture of his heavy blows. But Kev was becoming angrier too. When he couldn't beat her into submission, he gripped her throat with both hands.

Amber's oblivion now switched to panic. She struggled to breathe, taking in shallow and frantic puffs of air. Her throat was tightening, and she felt dizzy. She was going to die. *Oh God, no! Please don't let me die like this.* Amber clawed at his arms, trying to pull them away from her throat. She was getting nowhere. Kev tightened his deadly grip.

In a last desperate attempt to free herself, she lifted her knee and aimed it hard at his crotch. Yelling in agony, he grasped his genitals. She felt relieved, but light-headedness stopped her resuming her escape bid.

Struggling to get her breath back, Amber stood still for a moment, watching Kev squeal in agony. He would soon recover. She had to do something. Fighting was no good; he was too big and strong. Her body was throbbing where he had hit her. And she knew she would be no physical match for him. But he did have a weak spot.

Amber decided to use it to her advantage. 'You don't really want to kill me, do you, Kev?' she asked. 'You've already lost your mother.'

His head shot up, despite his pain. 'Don't you fuckin' dare mention my mother!' he said.

'It's only because I know how you feel, Kev. I've lost my mother too, and only recently.'

She could see a flicker of emotion in his eyes, so she persisted even though she was nervous. It felt like prodding a scab with a big stick. 'My mother wasn't like yours, Kev. She did some bad things. But your mother was good, wasn't she?'

'She was a fuckin' saint for what she had to put up with!'

The anger was still there but she sensed a softening as well. So, she persevered: 'You don't want to lose another woman who's special to you, do you, Kev?'

She could see his hesitation. His doubt about where he stood with her. Maybe she'd said the wrong thing. Amber knew she had to play him just right. It could mean the difference between life and death.

'Your father hurt her didn't he, Kev?'

'Yes!' he shouted, pulling his hands away from his genitals and examining his palms with a bewildered expression. Staring at those evil weapons! It was a vital clue. Was he thinking about Cora and what he had done? Maybe he was also thinking about them. Their relationship. His constant battle to retain control. The tremendous effort not to hurt the woman he loved despite his violent tendencies.

'You saw it, didn't you, Kev?'

His look of confusion was now suffused with pain, and the tears slid unknowingly down his face.

'You saw him kill her, didn't you? You saw him strangle her.'

Amber held her breath as she waited for him to react. He'd tightened in on himself and appeared like a simmering cauldron about to boil over. It was clear that he was going through huge internal turmoil and she dreaded how it would manifest itself. But, instead of erupting in violence, he broke down, squealing like an overwrought toddler, his torment palpable. 'I was only a fuckin' kid!' he screamed.

Kev then dropped to his knees, wailing at an excruciating pitch, his body convulsing with spasms of agonising emotion. Amber knew she'd guessed right. And she watched him crumple as the harrowing memories resurfaced. For a moment she felt sorry for him. She knew all about harrowing memories and what they could do to you.

Then she snapped to and, making the most of his moment of weakness, she ran. Out into the hallway. Through the door. Down the stairs. Out of the building. Feeling the harsh concrete rough on her feet. And scattered stones cutting her soles.

Still she kept running. No turning back. Unsure if he was close behind. Her lungs screaming for air.

She didn't stop till she could run no more. Taking just a moment to check behind her, she continued walking swiftly, trying to regain her breath. There was no one there. But she didn't know how far away Kev was or whether he'd even followed her.

Amber couldn't afford to take any chances. She had to keep moving. And, after today, she would need to get away. It was the only way she would feel safe. She had to escape to a place where he would never think of looking for her.

64

May 2016

The woman on the reception desk of the massage parlour looked Amber up and down distastefully, her nostrils twitching as though detecting a bad odour. This immediately put Amber on her guard. Did she smell? She did her best to keep clean, but it wasn't always easy when all you had were the public toilets and a packet of baby wipes.

'Yes, what can I do for you?' the woman asked.

Amber had met her type before; painstakingly preened and trying her best to sound well-spoken in a vain attempt to hide whatever misfortunes in life had led her to work in a glorified brothel. Her attempt had failed, and Amber could spot the guttural accent of the inner-city suburbs, which accompanied her anguished facial expression. Despite all this, Amber was aware that the woman's groomed appearance was a vast contrast to her own.

'I was wondering if you're taking on any new girls,' said Amber.

The woman pulled her head back as if shocked that she

should even ask such a question. Her words underlined her attitude. 'This is a high-class establishment!'

Amber wasn't in the mood for hidden insults. She'd prefer it if the silly cow just came straight to the point. 'Is that a yes or a no then?'

'I'm afraid it's a no. Like I say, we're a high-class establishment.'

Amber couldn't hide her look of resignation and her shoulders slumped as she stood back from the reception desk ready to depart. The woman seemed to regret her harsh words and quickly added, 'You could always try somewhere else. There's a place up the road that might consider you.'

'Cheers,' mumbled Amber, already on her way out.

There was no point in telling the stuck-up bitch that she'd already tried the place up the road and many more, but the answer was always the same: no! Some were more polite about it than others, but it didn't change the outcome. Amber knew she had been pushing her luck in trying this place, but she was becoming desperate.

There was probably only one place she hadn't tried and that was Ruby's parlour. She remembered Ruby from her days on the game. She had been more a friend to Crystal than her and had always been scary. Somehow, Amber couldn't pluck up the courage to visit her and ask for work.

She knew her appearance was putting them off. She hadn't had a shower in days or changed her clothing, and her hair was lank and greasy. She had also lost weight in the past few months, making her appear skinny and gaunt, the malnourishment emphasised by her pale complexion and the sores on her face.

Amber needed to earn some money soon; for food, for

a place to stay and to feed her constant craving for drugs. The client visits were drying up as they took one look at her unkempt appearance and decided not to rebook. A couple of them had been even more brutal and refused to go ahead with their arrangement.

But she still daren't work the streets; it was risky enough touring the city centre massage parlours and saunas. Her last encounter with Kev a few weeks ago was still clear in her mind. She knew how close she had been to becoming his next victim and she couldn't take the chance. The thought of it made her shiver. Despite her current poor quality of life, she wasn't ready for death yet and when it did happen, she'd prefer it to be less painful and distressing.

Thoughts of death made her cast her mind back to her mother. She was surprised how much she missed her. Although she had been bad to her in a lot of ways, she was still her mother and all that Amber had really had. The relationship with her grandparents no longer existed and Amber imagined they were so elderly now that they couldn't have coped with her anyway. And, as for her brother and her aunts and uncles, they didn't want to know.

Amber was all alone in the world and she didn't know how she could move forward with her life. She had thought about reporting Kev for attacking her and for the suspected killings of Cora and Elena. At least with him behind bars she would be able to go back on the beat.

But would the police take her seriously? She didn't have proof about any of it. And why would they believe someone so obviously down on her luck to someone who was tidy and well-groomed and had a nice flat?

She carried on plodding down the street. There was no

point trying any more massage parlours or saunas. She'd exhausted all the ones she knew of and had been rejected by them all. Instead she would focus on more immediate matters; it was getting late and she needed to find somewhere to sleep for the night.

65

Crystal was having a great time. Candice was now in her final year of secondary school. It was the end of term holidays and she had taken the Friday off especially to be with her daughter. They'd spent the morning touring all the upmarket shops: Selfridges, Harvey Nicholls and others along King Street, and when Crystal's feet were throbbing and she felt she could walk no more, they stopped for brunch in a trendy little restaurant off King Street.

Now they were walking along Deansgate and feeling replete, on their way to Crystal's Manchester store. 'Mum, after we've checked in at the store, do you think we could go to just one more shop?' asked Candice.

Crystal pretended to be exasperated. 'Oh no! Candice, you'll be the death of me. My feet are starting to hurt again already and look at the state of my hands.' She slipped all the shopping into one hand so she could show Candice the red marks on her other hand where the carrier bags had dug into her fingers.

'Aw, poor Mummy,' mocked Candice. 'I tell you what, why don't we have a rest and a cuppa at the shop? It'll help you sober up from all that wine you drank at brunch, and we can leave these bags there till later. Maybe you can grab a pair of flatties from the shop and you'll be fine.'

'Cheeky,' said Crystal. 'I'm not drunk at all; I'm just feeling merry. Anyway, I would have thought you'd have had enough of the shops by now.'

'Well, I was thinking about that dress I nearly bought. It would be perfect for my friend's party. Can we go back and get it later?'

'Go on then.' Crystal smiled but then her smile was wiped away by something she spotted at the side of the pavement.

There was a homeless woman sitting outside a shop with a battered tin in her hand containing a few coins. She sat cross-legged and as close to the shop window as possible, huddled up to protect herself from the biting cold. She had sad eyes and a red nose, and her lips were almost blue. Her appearance was dishevelled and emaciated, her hair bedraggled and her clothes shabby.

As Crystal drew up close, the woman stared upwards and shook the tin. But she didn't speak. Something about her struck pity into Crystal's heart. For a second her pace slowed almost to a crawl and she was transfixed on the homeless woman who looked so wretched with her eyes dull and heavy from lack of sleep.

Crystal couldn't take her eyes off her, but she didn't stop walking altogether. It wasn't wise to stop for these people; you never knew how intoxicated and unpredictable they could be. It was only when she heard Candice's voice that she realised she had slowed down.

'Mum, did you not hear what I said?'

'What? Oh, sorry, love, I was miles away.' Crystal sped up, trying to put the woman out of her mind. 'What was it you were saying?'

But her thoughts weren't on Candice; they were on the woman, because Crystal realised that she knew her. She'd changed a lot in the last year but the more Crystal thought about the slight frame and the blue eyes that were still full of kindness despite her dire situation, the more Crystal was certain that she had just passed her old friend Amber.

Guilt tore away at her just like on the last occasion when she'd walked past Amber without acknowledging her. It was clear from the state of her that she'd fallen on hard times and Crystal wondered if she could have prevented that by coming to her rescue a year ago.

She was shocked and upset to see her like that and she deliberated over whether to go back and at least give her some money to help her get by. But how could she? Not when she had Candice with her. What if Amber recognised her and started wanting to chat? How could she possibly explain to Candice where she knew her from?

Despite her resolve not to go back, Crystal felt besieged by guilt. It was obvious that Amber was desperately in need of help. It made her reflect on the lifestyle she herself used to lead and she knew that it could just as easily have been her who had ended up living on the streets.

They carried on to the shop, Candice still chatting away animatedly, and Crystal going through the motions. But she was no longer enjoying their day out. That reminder of the past had spoilt it, and she was experiencing an acute attack of conscience for abandoning her one-time friend.

She was glad when they had come off the street and sought refuge inside her shop. Perhaps Candice would find someone else to chat to so she could be left alone with her thoughts until she had worked through them and regained some normality. But everyone was busy, so Candice followed her through to the back office where they switched on the kettle and made themselves a brew.

Once they were seated around the large office desk, Candice turned to her mother. 'What's wrong?'

'Nothing, love. I'm just tired from our shopping trip, that's all.'

'Are you sure, Mum? Only, I noticed the way you were looking at that homeless woman. We've seen her before, about a year ago but she didn't look as bad then. She tried to talk to you and looked as though she knew you. Do you remember?'

Crystal was shocked at her daughter's perception and found herself babbling. 'No, I don't. How could she possibly know me? Probably drunk or on drugs or summat.'

'No, Mum. It isn't that. You seemed upset when you saw her and looked as though you were going to stop. I think it's because you recognised her. You know her too, don't you?'

66

October 2016

Crystal didn't know what to say but Candice did the talking for her.

'It's OK, Mum. I remember what things were like before you had the shops, when we lived in that scruffy house and you used to... well, you used to drink a lot and take drugs.'

Crystal felt her face flush with shame. 'I... I'm sorry you had to go through that, love. I didn't know you knew about the drugs.'

'Course I did, I might have only been a kid but I'm not daft.'

Candice reached out and touched her mother's hand and Crystal had to fight hard to hold back the tears. 'I'm sorry for bringing it up but I don't hold it against you. I'm proud of you, Mum, I really am. You must have been through some bad times and if you'd have carried on like that, I wouldn't have had the great life I have now.

'But you didn't carry on; you turned things around,

and that's why I'll always be proud of you no matter what you've done in the past. I know you're a good person so whatever you did was because of your circumstances.'

Crystal was touched by her daughter's speech and her eyes welled up. When had she become so grown up and astute? 'I'm proud of you too,' she said, her voice cracking.

'Where do you know that homeless woman from, Mum?'

Crystal could feel her heart thudding in her chest. Her daughter might have been level-headed and forgiving but how would she react to the fact that her mother had been a prostitute? No, she couldn't do it.

Candice picked up on her hesitation. 'It's OK, Mum. You don't have to tell me if you don't want. But I know you're a good person. You wanted to help that woman, didn't you?'

Crystal nodded, afraid to speak in case her voice broke altogether.

'Then we should do it, Mum. She needs our help.'

Crystal smiled at her. 'Candice, I'm beyond proud of you, love.'

She leaned across and hugged her daughter, each of them holding the other tightly for precious moments. Then Candice stood up and pulled away. 'Come on then. What are we waiting for?'

A few minutes later they were approaching the spot where they had seen Amber earlier. Just the thought of finding her friend like that filled Crystal with emotion but she knew she had to be strong. She was going to help Amber, not to break down and blubber like a baby.

As they drew nearer Crystal could feel her heart hammering inside her chest. Although she wanted to see her friend, she was nervous about what Amber might say. What if she revealed everything and Candice changed her mind regarding how she felt about her mother? Crystal glanced at the spot where Amber previously sat but saw that she was no longer there.

At first Crystal felt relieved; maybe she wouldn't have to face this after all. But her relief was short-lived and was soon replaced by that familiar feeling of guilt. It was bad to feel relieved when she knew how much Amber needed her help. Then she noticed the rug on which Amber had been sitting. It was still there. She realised Amber couldn't be far away at the same time as she spotted two youths with their backs to her and Amber standing on the other side of them chatting.

'Let's wait here until they've gone,' said Crystal, slowing down and taking hold of Candice's arm. 'Then we can talk to Amber on her own.'

They pretended to look in the shop window. While they waited, Crystal made eye contact with Amber and she noticed a look of recognition flash across Amber's face. Her friend seemed to cut short the conversation she was having and then she walked back towards the ragged old rug on which she had been sitting.

Crystal stepped forward. 'Amber.'

She didn't know what sort of reaction she had expected but, nevertheless, she felt disappointed when Amber stared vacantly back at her and didn't say anything. Crystal knew it was up to her to take the initiative. There was no point in asking how she was; that was obvious from her appearance. Ignoring the unclean stench that emanated from her, Crystal reached forward and took hold of her arm.

'Come on, Amber. You're coming with me.'

Amber shook her head. 'Where? Where are we going?'

'Back to mine.'

'But… why?'

'Because I want to help you, Amber.'

Amber gazed across at Candice, and Crystal picked up on her doubt. 'It's OK, Candice knows you're an old friend. She wants to help too.'

Crystal noticed Amber chewing on her bottom lip, an old habit of hers that had never gone away. She remembered how she always used to do it whenever she was under stress, nervous or uncomfortable about something.

'It'll be fine, Amber, I promise. I'm gonna get you booked into rehab. It worked for me so, hopefully, it'll work for you.

'And after that, it's up to you what you make of your life, but you'll have the chance to change things. You don't have to live like this anymore.'

67

It was later that evening and Crystal and Amber were sitting in her living room having a chat. Crystal had sorted out some clothes for Amber to wear and, after she'd showered, they had eaten. It was easy to see how ravenous Amber was by the way in which she had demolished every morsel of food that Crystal put in front of her.

Candice had gone out and Crystal was taking the opportunity to do some catching up with Amber. She glanced across at her friend who looked a lot better than when she had found her earlier. Amber had washed and styled her hair and put a bit of makeup on, but she was still painfully thin and unhealthy-looking.

'Did you recognise me the first time I walked past with Candice?' Crystal asked.

'Yes, but I knew you wouldn't want to talk to me when you were with your daughter, so I didn't say anything.'

'Thanks. I know I ignored you a year ago and I feel bad

about that now, but I was frightened of Candice finding out about my past.'

'Does she know?'

'Not all of it. You won't tell her, will you?'

'No, don't worry, I won't tell her anything you don't want her to know, Crystal.'

'How long have you been homeless?'

'A few months,' said Amber.

It wasn't long before she was confiding in Crystal about everything that had happened to her recently. Crystal was shocked to hear just how much her friend had been through. She knew the need to divulge must have been weighing heavily on Amber so she sat quietly and let her go through everything: the death of her mother, her brother abandoning her, losing the house, ending up on the street and the dodgy boyfriend who she suspected of murder.

Finally, when Amber had finished, Crystal said, 'Jesus Christ, Amber! You haven't half fuckin' been through it, haven't you? Why didn't you go to someone for help? And why didn't you report Kev to the police?'

'There was no one to ask. I hadn't seen my grandparents for years because of what my mum was like. Apparently, they're really old now and don't go out much. Most of the relatives didn't turn up at the funeral and those who did couldn't get away quickly enough. And I've lost touch with most of my friends.'

Crystal felt a pang of conscience knowing she had ignored Amber the previous time she had seen her. She also noticed that Amber hadn't answered her question about Kev, and she was determined to come back to that later.

'What about Sapphire?' she asked. 'Wouldn't she have helped you? Doesn't she still go in the Rose and Crown?'

'Yeah, but I haven't been in there for ages because of Kev looking for me, and last time I saw Sapphire we weren't on very good terms. She was the one who warned me about Kev, only I wouldn't take her seriously at first, so things got a bit awkward after that.'

'Jesus, I can't believe all this has been going on. I didn't know old Angie had died either.'

'Old Angie? You mean, you knew?'

'That she was your mother? Yeah, I guessed. Don't forget, Amber, I knew you better than any of the other girls, and I had a feeling right from the start. From the bits you'd told me about your mother, it all seemed to fit.'

'Did anybody else know?'

'No, not as I know of – just me. You might have tried to disown her, Amber, but you still cared despite how she had treated you, didn't you? She was your mother after all. But I presumed you had your reasons for not telling anyone, and it was your secret to keep, not mine.'

'Thanks,' mumbled Amber.

Crystal noticed her eyes glisten with tears, but she didn't add anything more, so Crystal decided to move on. There were other matters that had to be dealt with.

'I'm going to get you booked into rehab as soon as possible, Amber.'

'But I believe it's hell.'

'It's no walk in the park but it's the only way you're gonna move forward with your life. Don't worry, I had a worse drug problem than you and I managed alright so I'm sure you'll be able to. I had to do it cold turkey as well, but we'll make sure you have a bit longer to get the drugs out of your system.

'Once you're clean, we can talk about finding you work.'

'Thanks,' said Amber.

'That's OK. But before all that, there's something else we need to sort out. We need to report your bloody ex-boyfriend to the police. We'll go and see Sapphire and ask her to take us to her friend, Skinner. We'll need his evidence if we're going to get anywhere, and you'll need to tell the police what he did to you too.'

'Oh, I don't know, Crystal. I don't really want to get involved with Kev again. He's bad news.'

'You won't fuckin' have to! Don't worry, all you need to do is tell the cops what he did. He won't be able to find you while you're with me.'

'But I don't think Skinner will come forward anyway. He'll be too scared to tell the cops what he saw. Sapphire already said he was shitting himself.'

'Don't worry,' Crystal repeated. 'He'll squeal once we've had a word with him. I'll get Ruby involved. She'll be able to talk him into it.'

Amber went to protest but Crystal stood firm. 'We're doing it, Amber, and that's that. We owe it to all the girls still out on the streets. We need to keep them bloody safe.'

68

May 2017

Amber looked around her group of friends and smiled. Crystal, Sapphire, Skinner and Ruby; they were all here. They had been to court where they had been pleased to hear the guilty verdict in Kev Pike's trial. Once it was over, they had piled back to their favourite haunt, the Rose and Crown, where Ruby had bought them all a drink to celebrate.

'Skinner, you were really brave,' said Sapphire. 'Giving evidence like that. I know how much you were dreading it.'

'Dead right, but it was worth it. Did you see his fuckin' face when the guilty verdict came in?'

Amber smiled. 'You're my hero,' she said, giving his arm a squeeze.

'I don't know about that,' said Skinner, grinning self-consciously. 'I didn't have any fuckin' choice. It was either that or face Crystal and Ruby, and they were very persuasive, especially Ruby. She's fuckin' scary!'

Ruby laughed. 'Don't push your luck or you won't get another drink.'

Skinner soon finished his pint of lager, and Amber was just about to offer him another one when Crystal beat her to it, 'Skinner, let me buy you a drink.'

'I haven't bought him one yet,' said Amber.

Skinner held out his hands, palms upwards. 'Chill, ladies, no need to fight over me; I can handle two women at once.'

There was a jeer from the girls and Sapphire laughed as she said, 'You're not used to having all these gorgeous women fighting over you, are you, Skinner?'

'Eh, that's what you fuckin' think. Once they've had a bit of the Skinner magic, they all come running back for more. I might be skinny but I'm broad where it counts and long too.'

As he spoke, he winked, and the girls let out another jeer.

'I tell you what though,' Skinner continued, 'I could soon get used to being surrounded by fit birds buying me drinks.'

His cheeky comment made everyone laugh again including Amber. She was enjoying having the old gang back even if it was only a one-off. She loved the banter and the camaraderie; it was just like old times.

But then she felt a surge of emotion as she thought about the one person who was missing: her mother, otherwise known as old Angie. She'd been a menace in the pub most of the time with her drunkenness and waffling on about nonsense, but it still didn't seem right not seeing her here with all the girls.

Amber also reflected on everything she had been through, not only during the past couple of years but for the whole of her life. It had been hell and she didn't know how she had made it through at times. But she had done, by drawing on her own survival instincts and with help from her wonderful friend, Crystal.

She felt a tear in her eye then spotted Crystal watching her and quickly fought back her impulse to cry. The sad days were over and, as much as she was enjoying being in the Rose and Crown with her old friends, it was the last time she would do it. This life wasn't for her anymore.

It was time to be happy now. In fact, she was already getting there, and had vowed to stay clean. Crystal had given her a job in one of her high fashion shops and Amber loved it. And when she thought about all she had achieved in the past few months compared to how things had been not so long ago, Amber was extremely grateful.

As Crystal had rightly said, she'd given her a chance by getting her booked into rehab; it was now up to her what she made of her life.

Acknowledgements

This book has been the most challenging one in the series so far for reasons that I have described in my letter to readers.

In researching this novel, I received some valuable help, which gave me an insight into the social care sector, the plight of Manchester's homeless, and prostitution in Manchester. I would therefore like to give big thanks to the following people and organisations for their co-operation:

Judith Vickers from Lifeshare, Manchester for sparing me the time to answer my questions relating to the homeless in Manchester.

Janelle Hardacre of Manchester Action on Street Health (MASH) for information relating to the life of a working girl in Manchester.

Christine Schora for information relating to children in care homes during the period in which the novel is set.

Mary Johnson of the UK Crime Book Group on Facebook for information about the social care system during the years in which the novel is set.

Sarah Richards for information about the social care system during the period in which the novel is set.

I would also like to thank the staff at Aria, Head of

Zeus for all your hard work and support and, in particular, Hannah Smith who is a top-notch editor, Vicky Joss, Nikky Ward, Rhea Kurien, Helena Newton and Laura Palmer.

Thanks to my agent, Jo Bell, for all your support and good advice and to all the staff at Bell Lomax Moreton who are a great bunch to work with.

Big thanks again to all the readers who have followed the series so far, to my fellow authors for your support and to the community of book bloggers and reviewers who play a valuable role in recommending books to readers.

Last, but by no means least, I would like to thank all my family and friends who have supported me throughout my writing career. A special mention goes to Pascoe, Kerry, Baz, Phil, Andy, Tracey, Diane, Mary, Karen, Olwyn, Lisa, June, Terrie, Hazel, Christine and Jo.

About the Author

HEATHER BURNSIDE started her writing career more than twenty years ago when she began to work as a freelance writer while studying for a writing diploma. As part of her studies Heather wrote the first chapters of her debut novel, Slur. She later ran a writing services business before returning to Slur, which became the first book in The Riverhill Trilogy. Heather followed the Riverhill Trilogy with the Manchester Trilogy then her current series, The Working Girls.

You can find out more about the author by signing up to the Heather Burnside mailing list for the latest updates including details of new releases and book bargains, or by following her on social media.

Hello from Aria

We hope you enjoyed this book! If you did let us know, we'd love to hear from you.

We are Aria, a dynamic digital-first fiction imprint from award-winning independent publishers Head of Zeus. At heart, we're committed to publishing fantastic commercial fiction – from romance and sagas to crime, thrillers and historical fiction. Visit us online and discover a community of like-minded fiction fans!

We're also on the look out for tomorrow's superstar authors. So, if you're a budding writer looking for a publisher, we'd love to hear from you. You can submit your book online at ariafiction.com/we-want-read-your-book

You can find us at:
Email: aria@headofzeus.com
Website: www.ariafiction.com
Submissions: www.ariafiction.com/we-want-read-your-book

f @ariafiction
𝕏 @Aria_Fiction
📷 @ariafiction